"Madam," said I, "let me at least, alone" Page 49

54-40 or Fight

By Emerson Hough

Author of
"The Mississippi Bubble," "The Way of the Man,"
Etc.

WITH FOUR ILLUSTRATIONS
BY ARTHUR I. KELLER

A. L. BURT COMPANY
Publishers   New York

CONTENTS

CONTENTS—*Continued*

54-40 or Fight

FIFTY-FOUR FORTY
OR FIGHT

CHAPTER I

THE MAKERS OF MAPS

There is scarcely a single cause in which a woman is not engaged in some way fomenting the suit.—Juvenal.

"THEN you offer me no hope, Doctor?"

The gray mane of Doctor Samuel Ward waved like a fighting crest as he made answer: "Not the sort of hope you ask." A moment later he added: "John, I am ashamed of you."

The cynical smile of the man I called my chief still remained upon his lips, the same drawn look of suffering still remained upon his gaunt features; but in his blue eye I saw a glint which proved that the answer of his old friend had struck out some unused spark of vitality from the deep, cold flint of his heart.

"I never knew you for a coward, Calhoun," went on Doctor Ward; "nor any of your family. I give you now the benefit of my personal acquaintance

1

with this generation of the Calhouns. I ask something more of you than faint-heartedness."

The keen eyes turned upon him again with the old flame of flint which a generation had known— a generation, for the most part, of enemies. On my chief's face I saw appear again the fighting flush, proof of his hard-fibered nature, ever ready to rejoin with challenge when challenge came.

"Did not Saul fall upon his own sword?" asked John Calhoun. "Have not devoted leaders from the start of the world till now sometimes rid the scene of the responsible figures in lost fights, the men on whom blame rested for failures?"

"Cowards!" rejoined Doctor Ward. "Cowards, every one of them! Were there not other swords upon which they might have fallen—those of their enemies?"

"It is not my own hand—my own sword, Sam," said Calhoun. "Not that. You know as well as I that I am already marked and doomed, even as I sit at my table to-night. A walk of a wet night here in Washington—a turn along the Heights out there when the winter wind is keen—yes, Sam, I see my grave before me, close enough; but how can I rest easy in that grave? Man, we have not yet dreamed how great a country this may be. We *must* have Texas. We *must* have also Oregon. We must have—"

"Free?" The old doctor shrugged his shoulders and smiled at the arch pro-slavery exponent.

"Then, since you mention it, yes!" retorted Calhoun fretfully. "But I shall not go into the old argument of those who say that black is white, that South is North. It is only for my own race that I plan a wider America. But then—" Calhoun raised a long, thin hand. "Why," he went on slowly, "I have just told you that I have failed. And yet you, my old friend, whom I ought to trust, condemn me to live on!"

Doctor Samuel Ward took snuff again, but all the answer he made was to waggle his gray mane and stare hard at the face of the other.

"Yes," said he, at length, "I condemn you to fight on, John;" and he smiled grimly.

"Why, look at you, man!" he broke out fiercely, after a moment. "The type and picture of combat! Good bone, fine bone and hard; a hard head and bony; little eye, set deep; strong, wiry muscles, not too big—fighting muscles, not dough; clean limbs; strong fingers; good arms, legs, neck; wide chest—"

"Then you give me hope?" Calhoun flashed a smile at him.

"No, sir! If you do your duty, there is no hope for you to live. If you do not do your duty, there is no hope for you to die, John Calhoun, for more than two years to come—perhaps five years—six. Keep up this work—as you must, my friend—and you die as surely as though I shot you through as you sit there. Now, is this any comfort to you?"

A gray pallor overspread my master's face. That truth is welcome to no man, morbid or sane, sound or ill; but brave men meet it as this one did.

"Time to do much!" he murmured to himself. "Time to mend many broken vessels, in those two years. One more fight—yes, let us have it!"

But Calhoun the man was lost once more in Calhoun the visionary, the fanatic statesman. He summed up, as though to himself, something of the situation which then existed at Washington.

"Yes, the coast is clearer, now that Webster is out of the cabinet, but Mr. Upshur's death last month brings in new complications. Had he remained our secretary of state, much might have been done. It was only last October he proposed to Texas a treaty of annexation."

"Yes, and found Texas none so eager," frowned Doctor Ward.

"No; and why not? You and I know well enough. Sir Richard Pakenham, the English plenipotentiary here, could tell if he liked. *England* is busy with Texas. Texas owes large funds to *England*. *England* wants Texas as a colony. There is fire under this smoky talk of Texas dividing into two governments, one, at least, under England's gentle and unselfish care!

"And now, look you," Calhoun continued, rising, and pacing up and down, "look what is the evidence. Van Zandt, *chargé d'affaires* in Washington for the Republic of Texas, wrote Secretary Upshur only a month before Upshur's death, and told him to go carefully or he would drive Mexico to resume the war, *and so cost Texas the friendship of England!* Excellent Mr. Van Zandt! I at least know what the friendship of England means. So, he asks us if we will protect Texas with troops and ships in case she *does* sign that agreement of annexation. Cunning Mr. Van Zandt! He knows what that answer must be to-day, with England ready to fight us for Texas and Oregon both, and we wholly unready for war. Cunning Mr. Van Zandt, covert friend of England! And lucky Mr. Upshur, who was killed, and so never had to make that answer!"

"But, John, another will have to make it, the one way or the other," said his friend.

"Yes!" The long hand smote on the table.

"President Tyler has offered you Mr. Upshur's portfolio as secretary of state?"

"Yes!" The long hand smote again.

Doctor Ward made no comment beyond a long whistle, as he recrossed his legs. His eyes were fixed on Calhoun's frowning face. "There will be events!" said he at length, grinning.

"I have not yet accepted," said Calhoun. "If I do, it will be to bring Texas and Oregon into this Union, one slave, the other free, but both vast and of a mighty future for us. That done, I resign at once."

"Will you accept?"

Calhoun's answer was first to pick up a paper from his desk. "See, here is the despatch Mr. Pakenham brought from Lord Aberdeen of the British ministry to Mr. Upshur just two days before his death. Judge whether Aberdeen wants liberty—or territory! In effect he reasserts England's right to interfere in our affairs. We fought one war to disprove that. England has said enough on this continent. And England has meddled enough."

Calhoun and Ward looked at each other, sober in their realization of the grave problems which then beset American statesmanship and American thought. The old doctor was first to break the silence. "Then do you accept? Will you serve again, John?"

"Listen to me. If I do accept, I shall take Mr. Upshur's and Mr. Nelson's place only on one con-dition—yes, if I do, here is what *I* shall say to Eng-land regarding Texas. I shall show her what a Monroe Doctrine is; shall show her that while Texas

is small and weak, Texas *and* this republic are not.
This is what I have drafted as a possible reply. I
shall tell Mr. Pakenham that his chief's avowal of
intentions has made it our *imperious duty,* in self-
defense, to hasten the annexation of Texas, cost
what it may, mean what it may! John Calhoun does
not shilly-shally.

"*That* will be my answer," repeated my chief at
last. Again they looked gravely, each into the
other's eye, each knowing what all this might mean.

"Yes, I shall have Texas, as I shall have Oregon,
settled before I lay down my arms, Sam Ward. No,
I am *not* yet ready to die!" Calhoun's old fire now
flamed in all his mien.

"The situation is extremely difficult," said his
friend slowly. "It must be done; but how? We are
as a nation not ready for war. You as a statesman
are not adequate to the politics of all this. Where is
your political party, John? You have none. You
have outrun all parties. It will be your ruin, that
you have been honest!"

Calhoun turned on him swiftly. "You know as
well as I that mere politics will not serve. It will
take some extraordinary measure—you know men—
and, perhaps, *women.*"

"Yes," said Doctor Ward, "and a precious silly lot
they are; the two running after each other and for-
getting each other; using and wasting each other;

ruining and despoiling each other, all the years,
from Troy to Rome! But yes! For a man, set a
woman for a trap. *Vice versa,* I suppose?"

Calhoun nodded, with a thin smile. "As it
chances, I need a man. Ergo, and very plainly, I
must use a woman!"

They looked at each other for a moment. That
Calhoun planned some deep-laid stratagem was
plain, but his speech for the time remained enigmatic, even to his most intimate companion.

"There are two women in our world to-day," said
Calhoun. "As to Jackson, the old fool was a mon-
ogamist, and still is. Not so much so Jim Polk of
Tennessee. Never does he appear in public with
eyes other than for the Doña Lucrezia of the Mexican legation! Now, one against the other—Mexico
against Austria—"

Doctor Ward raised his eyebrows in perplexity.

"That is to say, England, and *not* Austria," went
on Calhoun coldly. "The ambassadress of England
to America was born in Budapest! So I say, Austria; or perhaps Hungary, or some other country,
which raised this strange representative who has
made some stir in Washington here these last few
weeks."

"Ah, *you mean the baroness!*" exclaimed Doctor
Ward. "Tut! Tut!"

Calhoun nodded, with the same cold, thin smile.

"Yes," he said, "I mean Mr. Pakenham's reputed mistress, his assured secret agent and spy, the beautiful Baroness von Ritz!"

He mentioned a name then well known in diplomatic and social life, when intrigue in Washington, if not open, was none too well hidden.

"Gay Sir Richard!" he resumed. "You know, his ancestor was a brother-in-law of the Duke of Wellington. He himself seems to have absorbed some of the great duke's fondness for the fair. Before he came to us he was with England's legation in Mexico. 'Twas there he first met the Doña Lucrezia. 'Tis said he would have remained in Mexico had it not been arranged that she and her husband, Señor Yturrio, should accompany General Almonte in the Mexican ministry here. On *these* conditions, Sir Richard agreed to accept promotion as minister plenipotentiary to Washington!"

"That was nine years ago," commented Doctor Ward.

"Yes; and it was only last fall that he was made envoy extraordinary. He is at least an extraordinary envoy! Near fifty years of age, he seems to forget public decency; he forgets even the Doña Lucrezia, leaving her to the admiration of Mr. Polk and Mr. Van Zandt, and follows off after the sprightly Baroness von Ritz. Meantime, Señor Yturrio *also* forgets the Doña Lucrezia, and proceeds *also* to follow after the baroness—although with less hope than Sir Richard, as they say! At least Pakenham has taste! The Baroness von Ritz has brains and beauty both. It is *she* who is England's real envoy. Now, I believe she knows England's real intentions as to Texas."

Doctor Ward screwed his lips for a long whistle, as he contemplated John Calhoun's thin, determined face.

"I do not care at present to say more," went on my chief; "but do you not see, granted certain motives, Polk might come into power pledged to the extension of our Southwest borders—"

"Calhoun, are you mad?" cried his friend. "Would you plunge this country into war? Would you pit two peoples, like cocks on a floor? And would you use women in our diplomacy?"

Calhoun now was no longer the friend, the humanitarian. He was the relentless machine; the idea; the single purpose, which to the world at large he had been all his life in Congress, in cabinets, on this or the other side of the throne of American power. He spoke coldly as he went on:

"In these matters it is not a question of means, but of results. If war comes, let it come; although I hope it will not come. As to the use of women—tell me, *why not women?* Why anything *else* but women? It is only playing life against life; one variant against another. That is politics, my friend. I *want* Pakenham. So, I must learn what *Pakenham* wants! Does he want Texas for England, or the Baroness von Ritz *for himself?*"

Ward still sat and looked at him. "My God!" said he at last, softly; but Calhoun went on:

"Why, who has made the maps of the world, and who has written pages in its history? Who makes and unmakes cities and empires and republics to-day? *Woman,* and not man! Are you so ignorant —and you a physician, who know them both? Gad, man, you do not understand your own profession, and yet you seek to counsel me in mine!"

"Strange words from you, John," commented his friend, shaking his head; "not seemly for a man who stands where you stand to-day."

"Strange weapons—yes. If I could always use my old weapons of tongue and brain, I would not need these, perhaps. Now you tell me my time is short. I must fight now to win. I have never fought to lose. I can not be too nice in agents and instruments."

The old doctor rose and took a turn up and down the little room, one of Calhoun's modest ménage at the nation's capital, which then was not the city it is to-day. Calhoun followed him with even steps.

"Changes of maps, my friend? Listen to me. The geography of America for the next fifty years rests under a little roof over in M Street to-night—a roof which Sir Richard secretly maintains. The map of the United States, I tell you, is covered with a down counterpane *à deux,* to-night. You ask me to go on with my fight. I answer, first I must find the woman. Now, I say, I have found her, as you know. Also, I have told you *where* I have found her. Under a counterpane! Texas, Oregon, these United States under a counterpane!"

Doctor Ward sighed, as he shook his head. "I don't pretend to know now all you mean."

Calhoun whirled on him fiercely, with a vigor which his wasted frame did not indicate as possible.

"Listen, then, and I will tell you what John Calhoun means—John Calhoun, who has loved his own state, who has hated those who hated him, who has never prayed for those who despitefully used him, who has fought and will fight, since all insist on that. It is true Tyler has offered me again to-day the portfolio of secretary of state. Shall I take it? If I do, it means that I am employed by this administration to secure the admission of Texas. Can you believe me when I tell you that my ambition is for it all—*all,* every foot of new land, west to the Pacific, that we can get, slave *or* free? Can you believe John Calhoun, pro-slavery advocate and orator all his life, when he says that he believes he is an humble instrument destined, with God's aid, and through the use of such instruments as our human society affords, to build, *not* a wider slave country, but a wider America?"

"It would be worth the fight of a few years more, Calhoun," gravely answered his old friend. "I admit I had not dreamed this of you."

"History will not write it of me, perhaps," went on my chief. "But you tell me to fight, and now I shall fight, and in my own way. I tell you, that answer shall go to Pakenham. And I tell you, Pakenham shall not *dare* take offense at me. War with Mexico we possibly, indeed certainly, shall have. War on the Northwest, too, we yet may have unless—" He paused; and Doctor Ward prompted him some moments later, as he still remained in thought.

"Unless what, John? What do you mean—still hearing the rustle of skirts?"

"Yes!—unless the celebrated Baroness Helena von Ritz says otherwise!" replied he grimly.

"How dignified a diplomacy have we here! You plan war between two embassies on the distaff side!" smiled Doctor Ward.

Calhoun continued his walk. "I do not say so," he made answer; "but, if there must be war, we may reflect that war is at its best when woman is in the field!"

CHAPTER II

In all eras and all climes a woman of great genius or beauty has done what she chose.—Ouida.

"NICHOLAS," said Calhoun, turning to me suddenly, but with his invariable kindli-' ness of tone, "oblige me to-night. I have written a message here. You will see the address—"

"I have unavoidably heard this lady's name," I hesitated.

"You will find the lady's name above the seal. Take her this message from me. Yes, your errand is to bring the least known and most talked of woman in Washington, alone, unattended save by yourself; to a gentleman's apartments, to his house, at a time past the hour of midnight! That gentleman is myself! You must not take any answer in the negative."

As I sat dumbly, holding this sealed document in my hand, he turned to Doctor Ward, with a nod toward myself.

14

"I choose my young aide, Mr. Trist here, for good reasons. He is just back from six months in the wilderness, and may be shy; but once he had a way with women, so they tell me—and you know, in approaching the question *ad feminam* we operate *per hominem.*"

Doctor Ward took snuff with violence as he regarded me critically.

"I do not doubt the young man's sincerity and faithfulness," said he. "I was only questioning one thing."

"Yes?"

"His age."

Calhoun rubbed his chin. "Nicholas," said he, "you heard me. I have no wish to encumber you with useless instructions. Your errand is before you. Very much depends upon it, as you have heard. All I can say is, keep your head, keep your feet, and keep your heart!"

The two older men both turned now, and smiled at me in a manner not wholly to my liking. Neither was this errand to my liking.

It was true, I was hardly arrived home after many months in the West; but I had certain plans of my own for that very night, and although as yet I had made no definite engagement with my fiancée, Miss Elisabeth Churchill, of Elmhurst Farm, for meeting her at the great ball this night, such certainly was

my desire and my intention. Why, I had scarce seen
Elisabeth twice in the last year.

"How now, Nick, my son?" began my chief.
"Have staff and scrip been your portion so long that
you are wholly wedded to them? Come, I think the
night might promise you something of interest. I
assure you of one thing—you will receive no willing
answer from the fair baroness. She will scoff at
you, and perhaps bid you farewell. See to it, then;
do what you like, but bring her *with* you, and bring
her *here*.

"You will realize the importance of all this when
I tell you that my answer to Mr. Tyler must be
in before noon to-morrow. That answer will depend upon the answer the Baroness von Ritz makes
to *me,* here, to-night! I can not go to her, so she
must come to me. You have often served me well,
my son. Serve me to-night. My time is short; I
have no moves to lose. It is *you* who will decide
before morning whether or not John Calhoun is the
next secretary of state. And that will decide
whether or not Texas is to be a state." I had never
seen Mr. Calhoun so intent, so absorbed.

We all three now sat silent in the little room
where the candles guttered in the great glass *cylin-
dres* on the mantel—an apartment scarce better
lighted by the further aid of lamps fed by oil.

"He might be older," said Calhoun at length,

speaking of me as though I were not present. "And
'tis a hard game to play, if once my lady Helena
takes it into her merry head to make it so for him.
But if I sent one shorter of stature and uglier of
visage and with less art in approaching a crinoline—
why, perhaps he would get no farther than her door.
No; he will serve—he *must* serve!"

He arose now, and bowed to us both, even as I
rose and turned for my cloak to shield me from the
raw drizzle which then was falling in the streets.
Doctor Ward reached down his own shaggy top hat
from the rack.

"To bed with you now, John," said he sternly.

"No, I must write."

"You heard me say, to bed with you! A stiff
toddy to make you sleep. Nicholas here may wake
you soon enough with his mysterious companion. I
think to-morrow will be time enough for you to
work, and to-morrow very likely will bring work
for you to do."

Calhoun sighed. "God!" he exclaimed, "if I but
had back my strength! If there were more than
those scant remaining years!"

"Go!" said he suddenly; and so we others passed
down his step and out into the semi-lighted streets.

So this, then, was my errand. My mind still
tingled at its unwelcome quality. Doctor Ward
guessed something of my mental dissatisfaction.

"Never mind, Nicholas," said he, as we parted at the street corner, where he climbed into the rickety carriage which his colored driver held awaiting him. "Never mind. I don't myself quite know what Calhoun wants; but he would not ask of you anything personally improper. Do his errand, then. It is part of your work. In any case—" and I thought I saw him grin in the dim light—"you may have a night which you will remember."

There proved to be truth in what he said.

CHAPTER III

The egotism of women is always for two.—Mme. De Staël.

THE thought of missing my meeting with Elisabeth still rankled in my soul. Had it been another man who asked me to carry this message, I must have refused. But this man was my master, my chief, in whose service I had engaged.

Strange enough it may seem to give John Calhoun any title showing love or respect. To-day most men call him traitor—call him the man responsible for the war between North and South—call him the arch apostle of that impossible doctrine of slavery, which we all now admit was wrong. Why, then, should I love him as I did? I can not say, except that I always loved, honored and admired courage, uprightness, integrity.

For myself, his agent, I had, as I say, left the old Trist homestead at the foot of South Mountain in Maryland, to seek my fortune in our capital city. I had had some three or four years' semi-diplomatic

19

training when I first met Calhoun and entered his service as assistant. It was under him that I finished my studies in law. Meantime, I was his messenger in very many quests, his source of information in many matters where he had no time to go into details.

Strange enough had been some of the circumstances in which I found myself thrust through this relation with a man so intimately connected for a generation with our public life. Adventures were always to my liking, and surely I had my share. I knew the frontier marches of Tennessee and Alabama, the intricacies of politics of Ohio and New York, mixed as those things were in Tyler's time. I had even been as far west as the Rockies, of which young Frémont was now beginning to write so understandingly. For six months I had been in Mississippi and Texas studying matters and men, and now, just back from Natchitoches, I felt that I had earned some little rest.

But there was the fascination of it—that big game of politics. No, I will call it by its better name of statesmanship, which sometimes it deserved in those days, as it does not to-day. That was a day of Warwicks. The nominal rulers did not hold the greatest titles. Naturally, I knew something of these things, from the nature of my work in Calhoun's office. I have had insight into documents which never be-

came public. I have seen treaties made. I have seen
the making of maps go forward. This, indeed, I
was in part to see that very night, and curiously, too.

How the Baroness von Ritz—beautiful adventuress as she was sometimes credited with being, charming woman as she was elsewhere described, fascinating and in some part dangerous to any man, as
all admitted—could care to be concerned with this
purely political question of our possible territories,
I was not shrewd enough at that moment in advance
to guess; for I had nothing more certain than the
rumor she was England's spy. I bided my time,
knowing that ere long the knowledge must come to
me in Calhoun's office even in case I did not first
learn more than Calhoun himself.

Vaguely in my conscience I felt that, after all, my
errand was justified, even though at some cost to my
own wishes and my own pride. The farther I walked
in the dark along Pennsylvania Avenue, into which
finally I swung after I had crossed Rock Bridge, the
more I realized that perhaps this big game was
worth playing in detail and without quibble as the
master mind should dictate. As he was servant of a
purpose, of an ideal of triumphant democracy, why
should not I also serve in a cause so splendid?

I was, indeed, young—Nicholas Trist, of Maryland; six feet tall, thin, lean, always hungry, perhaps a trifle freckled, a little sandy of hair, blue I

suppose of eye, although I am not sure; good rider and good marcher, I know; something of an expert with the weapons of my time and people; fond of a horse and a dog and a rifle—yes, and a glass and a girl, if truth be told. I was not yet thirty, in spite of my western travels. At that age the rustle of silk or dimity, the suspicion of adventure, tempts the worst or the best of us, I fear. Woman!—the very sound of the word made my blood leap then. I went forward rather blithely, as I now blush to confess. "If there are maps to be made to-night," said I, "the Baroness Helena shall do her share in writing on my chief's old mahogany desk, and not on her own dressing case."

That was an idle boast, though made but to myself. I had not yet met the woman.

CHAPTER IV

THE BARONESS HELENA

Woman is seldom merciful to the man who is timid.
                                        —*Edward Bulwer Lytton.*

THERE was one of our dim street lights at a central corner on old Pennsylvania Avenue, and under it, after a long walk, I paused for a glance at the inscription on my sealed document. I had not looked at it before in the confusion of my somewhat hurried mental processes. In addition to the name and street number, in Calhoun's writing, I read this memorandum: "Knock at the third door in the second block beyond M Street."

I recalled the nearest cross street; but I must confess the direction still seemed somewhat cryptic. Puzzled, I stood under the lamp, shielding the face of the note under my cloak to keep off the rain, as I studied it.

The sound of wheels behind me on the muddy pavement called my attention, and I looked about. A carriage came swinging up to the curb where I stood. It was driven rapidly, and as it approached

23

the door swung open, I heard a quick word, and the driver pulled up his horses. I saw the light shine through the door on a glimpse of white satin. I looked again. Yes, it was a beckoning hand! The negro driver looked at me inquiringly.

Ah, well, I suppose diplomacy under the stars runs much the same in all ages. I have said that I loved Elisabeth, but also said I was not yet thirty. More-over, I was a gentleman, and here might be a lady in need of help. I need not say that in a moment I was at the side of the carriage. Its occupant made no exclamation of surprise; in fact, she moved back upon the other side of the seat in the darkness, as though to make room for me!

I was absorbed in a personal puzzle. Here was I, messenger upon some important errand, as I might guess. But white satin and a midnight adventure—at least, a gentleman might bow and ask if he could be of assistance!

A dark framed face, whose outlines I could only dimly see in the faint light of the street lamp, leaned toward me. The same small hand nervously reached out, as though in request.

I now very naturally stepped closer. A pair of wide and very dark eyes was looking into mine. I could now see her face. There was no smile upon her lips. I had never seen her before, that was sure —nor did I ever think to see her like again; I could

say that even then, even in the half light. Just a
trifle foreign, the face; somewhat dark, but not too
dark; the lips full, the eyes luminous, the forehead
beautifully arched, chin and cheek beautifully
rounded, nose clean-cut and straight, thin but not
pinched. There was nothing niggard about her.
She was magnificent—a magnificent woman. I saw
that she had splendid jewels at her throat, in her
ears—a necklace of diamonds, long hoops of diamonds and emeralds used as ear-rings; a sparkling
clasp which caught at her white throat the wrap
which she had thrown about her ball gown—for
now I saw she was in full evening dress. I guessed
she had been an attendant at the great ball, that ball
which I had missed with so keen a regret myself—
the ball where I had hoped to dance with Elisabeth.
Without doubt she had lost her way and was asking
the first stranger for instructions to her driver.

My lady, whoever she was, seemed pleased with
her rapid temporary scrutiny. With a faint murmur, whether of invitation or not I scarce could tell,
she drew back again to the farther side of the seat.
Before I knew how or why, I was at her side. The
driver pushed shut the door, and whipped up his
team.

Personally I am gifted with but small imagination. In a very matter of fact way I had got into
this carriage with a strange lady. Now in a sober

and matter of fact way it appeared to me my duty to find out the reason for this singular situation.

"Madam," I remarked to my companion, "in what manner can I be of service to you this evening?"

I made no attempt to explain who I was, or to ask who or what she herself was, for I had no doubt that our interview soon would be terminated.

"I am fortunate that you are a gentleman," she said, in a low and soft voice, quite distinct, quite musical in quality, and marked with just the faintest trace of some foreign accent, although her English was perfect.

I looked again at her. Yes, her hair was dark; that was sure. It swept up in a great roll above her oval brow. Her eyes, too, must be dark, I confirmed. Yes—as a passed lamp gave me aid—there were strong dark brows above them. Her nose, too, was patrician; her chin curving just strongly enough, but not too full, and faintly cleft, a sign of power, they say.

A third gracious lamp gave me a glimpse of her figure, huddled back among her draperies, and I guessed her to be about of medium height. A fourth lamp showed me her hands, small, firm, white; also I could catch a glimpse of her arm, as it lay outstretched, her fingers clasping a fan. So I knew her arms were round and taper, hence all her limbs and figure finely molded, because nature does not do such things by halves, and makes no bungles in her symmetry of contour when she plans a noble speci-men of humanity. Here *was* a noble specimen of what woman may be.

On the whole, as I must confess, I sighed rather comfortably at the fifth street lamp; for, if my chief must intrust to me adventures of a dark night—ad-ventures leading to closed carriages and strange companions—I had far liefer it should be some such woman as this. I was not in such a hurry to ask again how I might be of service. In fact, being somewhat surprised and somewhat pleased, I re-mained silent now for a time, and let matters adjust themselves; which is not a bad course for any one similarly engaged.

She turned toward me at last, deliberately, her fan against her lips, studying me. And I did as much, taking such advantage as I could of the pass-ing street lamps. Then, all at once, without warning or apology, she smiled, showing very even and white teeth.

She smiled. There came to me from the purple-colored shadows some sort of deep perfume, strange to me. I frown at the description of such things and such emotions, but I swear that as I sat there, a stranger, not four minutes in companionship with this other stranger, I felt swim up around me some sort of amber shadow, edged with purple—the shadow, as I figured it then, being this perfume, curious and alluring!

It was wet, there in the street. Why should I rebel at this stealing charm of color or fragrance—let those name it better who can. At least I sat, smiling to myself in my purple-amber shadow, now in no very special hurry. And now again she smiled, thoughtfully, rather approving my own silence, as I guessed; perhaps because it showed no unmanly perturbation—my lack of imagination passing for aplomb.

At last I could not, in politeness, keep this up further.

"How may I serve the Baroness?" said I.

She started back on the seat as far as she could go.

"How did you know?" she asked. "And who are *you?"*

I laughed. "I did not know, and did not guess until almost as I began to speak; but if it comes to that, I might say I am simply an humble gentleman of Washington here. I might be privileged to peep in at ambassadors' balls—through the windows, at least."

"But you were not there—you did not see me? I never saw you in my life until this very moment—how, then, do you know me? Speak! At once!" Her satins rustled. I knew she was tapping a foot on the carriage floor.

"Madam," I answered, laughing at her; "by this amber purple shadow, with flecks of scarlet and pink; by this perfume which weaves webs for me here in this carriage, I know you. The light is poor, but it is good enough to show one who can be no one else but the Baroness von Ritz."

I was in the mood to spice an adventure which had gone thus far. Of course she thought me crazed, and drew back again in the shadow; but when I turned and smiled, she smiled in answer—herself somewhat puzzled.

"The Baroness von Ritz can not be disguised," I said; "not even if she wore her domino."

She looked down at the little mask which hung from the silken cord, and flung it from her.

"Oh, then, very well!" she said. "If you know who I am, who are *you,* and why do you talk in this absurd way with me, a stranger?"

"And why, Madam, do you take me up, a stranger, in this absurd way, at midnight, on the streets of Washington?—I, who am engaged on business for my chief?"

She tapped again with her foot on the carriage floor. "Tell me who you are!" she said.

"Once a young planter from Maryland yonder; sometime would-be lawyer here in Washington. It is my misfortune not to be so distinguished in fame or beauty that my name is known by all; so I need not tell you my name perhaps, only assuring you that I am at your service if I may be useful."

"Your name!" she again demanded.

I told her the first one that came to my lips—I do not remember what. It did not deceive her for a moment.

"Of course that is not your name," she said; "because it does not fit you. You have me still at disadvantage."

"And me, Madam? You are taking me miles out of my way. How can I help you? Do you perhaps wish to hunt mushrooms in the Georgetown woods when morning comes? I wish that I might join you, but I fear—"

"You mock me," she retorted. "Very good. Let me tell you it was not your personal charm which attracted me when I saw you on the pavement! 'Twas because you were the only man in sight."

I bowed my thanks. For a moment nothing was heard save the steady patter of hoofs on the ragged pavement. At length she went on.

"I am alone. I have been followed. I was followed when I called to you—by another carriage. I asked help of the first gentleman I saw, having heard that Americans all are gentlemen."

"True," said I; "I do not blame you. Neither do I blame the occupant of the other carriage for following you."

"I pray you, leave aside such chatter!" she exclaimed.

"Very well, then, Madam. Perhaps the best way is for us to be more straightforward. If I can not be of service I beg you to let me descend, for I have business which I must execute to-night."

This, of course, was but tentative. I did not care to tell her that my business was with herself. It seemed almost unbelievable to me that chance should take this turn.

She dismissed this with an impatient gesture, and continued.

"See, I am alone," she said. "Come with me. Show me my way—I will pay—I will pay anything in reason." Actually I saw her fumble at her purse, and the hot blood flew to my forehead.

"What you ask of me, Madam, is impossible," said I, with what courtesy I could summon. "You oblige me now to tell my real name. I have told you that I am an American gentleman—Mr. Nicholas Trist. We of this country do not offer our services to ladies for the sake of pay. But do not be troubled over any mistake—it is nothing. Now, you have perhaps had some little adventure in which you do not wish to be discovered. In any case, you ask me to shake off that carriage which follows us. If that is all, Madam, it very easily can be arranged."

"Hasten, then," she said. "I leave it to you. I was sure you knew the city."

I turned and gazed back through the rear window of the carriage. True, there was another vehicle following us. We were by this time nearly at the end of Washington's limited pavements. It would be simple after that. I leaned out and gave our driver some brief orders. We led our chase across the valley creeks on up the Georgetown hills, and soon as possible abandoned the last of the pavement, and took to the turf, where the sound of our wheels was dulled. Rapidly as we could we passed on up the hill, until we struck a side street where there was no paving. Into this we whipped swiftly, following the flank of the hill, our going, which was all of earth or soft turf, now well wetted by the rain. When at last we reached a point near the summit of the hill, I stopped to listen. Hearing nothing, I told the driver to pull down the hill by the side street, and to drive slowly. When we finally came into our main street again at the foot of the Georgetown hills, not far from the little creek which divided that settlement from the main city, I could hear nowhere any sound of our pursuer.

"Madam," said I, turning to her; "I think we may safely say we are alone. What, now, is your wish?"

"Home!" she said.

"And where is home?"

She looked at me keenly for a time, as though to read some thought which perhaps she saw suggested either in the tone of my voice or in some glimpse she might have caught of my features as light afforded. For the moment she made no answer.

"Is it here?" suddenly I asked her, presenting to her inspection the sealed missive which I bore.

"I can not see; it is quite dark," she said hurriedly.

"Pardon me, then—" I fumbled for my case of lucifers, and made a faint light by which she might read. The flare of the match lit up her face perfectly, bringing out the framing roll of thick dark hair, from which, as a high light in a mass of shadows, the clear and yet strong features of her face showed plainly. I saw the long lashes drooped above her dark eyes, as she bent over studiously. At first the inscription gave her no information. She pursed her lips and shook her head.

"I do not recognize the address," said she, smiling, as she turned toward me.

"Is it this door on M Street, as you go beyond this other street?" I asked her. "Come—think!"

Then I thought I saw the flush deepen on her face, even as the match flickered and failed.

I leaned out of the door and called to the negro driver. "Home, now, boy—and drive fast!"

She made no protest.

CHAPTER V

ONE OF THE WOMEN IN THE CASE

There is a woman at the beginning of all great things.
—*Lamartine.*

A QUARTER of an hour later, we slowed down on a rough brick pavement, which led toward what then was an outlying portion of the town—one not precisely shabby, but by no means fashionable. There was a single lamp stationed at the mouth of the narrow little street. As we advanced, I could see outlined upon our right, just beyond a narrow pavement of brick, a low and not more than semi-respectable house, or rather, row of houses; tenements for the middle class or poor, I might have said. The neighborhood, I knew from my acquaintance with the city, was respectable enough, yet it was remote, and occupied by none of any station. Certainly it was not to be considered fit residence for a woman such as this who sat beside me. I admit I was puzzled. The strange errand of my chief now assumed yet more mystery, in spite of his forewarnings.

34

"This will do," said she softly, at length.   The driver already had pulled up.

So, then, I thought, she had been here before. But why? Could this indeed be her residence? Was she incognita here? Was this indeed the covert embassy of England?

There was no escape from the situation as it lay before me. I had no time to ponder. Had the circumstances been otherwise, then in loyalty to Elisabeth I would have handed my lady out, bowed her farewell at her own gate, and gone away, pondering only the adventures into which the beckoning of a white hand and the rustling of a silken skirt betimes will carry a man, if he dares or cares to go.   Now, I might not leave. My duty was here. This was my message; here was she for whom it was intended; and this was the place which I was to have sought alone.   I needed only to remember that my business was not with Helena von Ritz the woman, beautiful, fascinating, perhaps dangerous as they said of her, but with the Baroness von Ritz, in the belief of my chief the ally and something more than ally of Pakenham, in charge of England's fortunes on this continent. I did remember my errand and the gravity of it.   I did not remember then, as I did later, that I was young.

I descended at the edge of the narrow pavement, and was about to hand her out at the step, but as I glanced down I saw that the rain had left a puddle of mud between the carriage and the walk.

"Pardon, Madam," I said; "allow me to make a light for you—the footing is bad."

I lighted another lucifer, just as she hesitated at the step. She made as though to put out her right foot, and withdrew it. Again she shifted, and extended her left foot. I faintly saw proof that nature had carried out her scheme of symmetry, and had not allowed wrist and arm to forswear themselves! I saw also that this foot was clad in the daintiest of white slippers, suitable enough as part of her ball costume, as I doubted not was this she wore. She took my hand without hesitation, and rested her weight upon the step—an adorable ankle now more frankly revealed. The briefness of the lucifers was merciful or merciless, as you like.

"A wide step, Madam; be careful," I suggested. But still she hesitated.

A laugh, half of annoyance, half of amusement, broke from her lips. As the light flickered down, she made as though to take the step; then, as luck would have it, a bit of her loose drapery, which was made in the wide-skirted and much-hooped fashion of the time, caught at the hinge of the carriage door. It was a chance glance, and not intent on my part, but I saw that her other foot was stockinged, but not shod!

"I beg Madam's pardon," I said gravely, looking aside, "but she has perhaps not noticed that her other slipper is lost in the carriage."

"Nonsense!" she said. "Allow me your hand across to the walk, please. It is lost, yes."

"But lost—where?" I began.

"In the other carriage!" she exclaimed, and laughed freely.

Half hopping, she was across the walk, through the narrow gate, and up at the door before I could either offer an arm or ask for an explanation. Some whim, however, seized her; some feeling that in fairness she ought to tell me now part at least of the reason for her summoning me to her aid.

"Sir," she said, even as her hand reached up to the door knocker; "I admit you have acted as a gentleman should. I do not know what your message may be, but I doubt not it is meant for me. Since you have this much claim on my hospitality, even at this hour, I think I must ask you to step within. There may be some answer needed."

"Madam," said I, "there *is* an answer needed. I am to take back that answer. I know that this message is to the Baroness von Ritz. I guess it to be important; and I know you are the Baroness von Ritz."

"Well, then," said she, pulling about her half-bared shoulders the light wrap she wore; "let me be as free with you. If I have missed one shoe, I have not lost it wholly. I lost the slipper in a way not quite planned on the program. It hurt my foot. I sought to adjust it behind a curtain. My gentleman of Mexico was in wine. I fled, leaving my escort, and he followed. I called to you. You know the rest. I am glad you are less in wine, and are more a gentleman."

"I do not yet know my answer, Madam."

"Come!" she said; and at once knocked upon the door.

I shall not soon forget the surprise which awaited me when at last the door swung open silently at the hand of a wrinkled and brown old serving-woman— not one of our colored women, but of some dark foreign race. The faintest trace of surprise showed on the old woman's face, but she stepped back and swung the door wide, standing submissively, waiting for orders.

We stood now facing what ought to have been a narrow and dingy little room in a low row of dingy buildings, each of two stories and so shallow in extent as perhaps not to offer roof space to more than a half dozen rooms. Instead of what should have been, however, there was a wide hall—wide as each building would have been from front to back, but longer than a half dozen of them would have been! I did not know then, what I learned later, that the partitions throughout this entire row had been removed, the material serving to fill up one of the houses at the farthest extremity of the row. There was thus offered a long and narrow room, or series of rooms, which now I saw beyond possibility of doubt constituted the residence of this strange woman whom chance had sent me to address; and whom still stranger chance had thrown in contact with me even before my errand was begun!

She stood looking at me, a smile flitting over her features, her stockinged foot extended, toe down, serving to balance her on her high-heeled single shoe.

"Pardon, sir," she said, hesitating, as she held the sealed epistle in her hand. "You know me—perhaps you follow me—I do not know. Tell me, are you a spy of that man Pakenham?"

Her words and her tone startled me. I had supposed her bound to Sir Richard by ties of a certain sort. Her bluntness and independence puzzled me as much as her splendid beauty enraptured me. I tried to forget both.

"Madam, I am spy of no man, unless I am such at order of my chief, John Calhoun, of the United States Senate—perhaps, if Madam pleases, soon of Mr. Tyler's cabinet."

In answer, she turned, hobbled to a tiny marquetry table, and tossed the note down upon it, unopened. I waited patiently, looking about me meantime. I discovered that the windows were barred with narrow slats of iron within, although covered with heavy draperies of amber silk. There was a double sheet of iron covering the door by which we had entered.

"Your cage, Madam?" I inquired. "I do not blame England for making it so secret and strong! If so lovely a prisoner were mine, I should double the bars."

The swift answer to my presumption came in the flush of her cheek and her bitten lip. She caught up the key from the table, and half motioned me to the door. But now I smiled in turn, and pointed to the unopened note on the table. "You will pardon me, Madam," I went on. "Surely it is no disgrace to represent either England or America. They are not at war. Why should we be?" We gazed steadily at each other.

The old servant had disappeared when at length her mistress chose to pick up my unregarded document. Deliberately she broke the seal and read. An instant later, her anger gone, she was laughing gaily.

"See," said she, bubbling over with her mirth; "I pick up a stranger, who should say good-by at my curb; my apartments are forced; and this is what this stranger asks: that I shall go with him, to-night, alone, and otherwise unattended, to see a man, perhaps high in your government, but a stranger to me, at his own rooms—alone! Oh, la! la! Surely these Americans hold me high!"

"Assuredly we do, Madam," I answered. "Will it please you to go in your own carriage, or shall I return with one for you?"

She put her hands behind her back, holding in them the opened message from my chief. "I am tired. I am bored. Your impudence amuses me; and your errand is not your fault. Come, sit down. You have been good to me. Before you go, I shall have some refreshment brought for you."

I felt a sudden call upon my resources as I found myself in this singular situation. Here, indeed, more easily reached than I had dared hope, was the woman in the case. But only half of my errand, the easier half, was done.

CHAPTER VI

THE BOUDOIR OF THE BARONESS

A woman's counsel brought us first to woe.—Dryden.

"WAIT!" she said. "We shall have candles." She clapped her hands sharply, and again there entered the silent old serving-woman, who, obedient to a gesture, proceeded to light additional candles in the prism stands and sconces. The apartment was now distinct in all its details under this additional flood of light. Decently as I might I looked about. I was forced to stifle the exclamation of surprise which rose to my lips.

We were plain folk enough in Washington at that time. The ceremonious days of our first presidents had passed for the democratic time of Jefferson and Jackson; and even under Mr. Van Buren there had been little change from the simplicity which was somewhat our boast. Washington itself was at that time scarcely more than an overgrown hamlet, not in the least to be compared to the cosmopolitan cen-

ters which made the capitals of the Old World.
Formality and stateliness of a certain sort we had,
but of luxury we knew little. There was at that time,
as I well knew, no state apartment in the city which
in sheer splendor could for a moment compare with
this secret abode of a woman practically unknown.
Here certainly was European luxury transferred to
our shores. This in simple Washington, with its
vast white unfinished capitol, its piecemeal miles of
mixed residences, boarding-houses, hotels, restau-
rants, and hovels! I fancied stern Andrew Jackson
or plain John Calhoun here!

The furniture I discovered to be exquisite in detail, of rosewood and mahogany, with many brass
chasings and carvings, after the fashion of the Empire, and here and there florid ornamentation
following that of the court of the earlier Louis. Fan-
ciful little clocks with carved scrolls stood about;
Cupid tapestries had replaced the original tawdry
coverings of these common walls, and what had once
been a dingy fireplace was now faced with embossed
tiles never made in America. There were paintings
in oil here and there, done by master hands, as one
could tell. The curtained windows spoke eloquently
of secrecy. Here and there a divan and couch
showed elaborate care in comfort. Beyond a lace-
screened grille I saw an alcove—doubtless cut
through the original partition wall between two of

these humble houses—and within this stood a high tester bed, its heavy mahogany posts beautifully carved, the couch itself piled deep with foundations of I know not what of down and spread most daintily with a coverlid of amber satin, whose edges fringed out almost to the floor. At the other extremity, screened off as in a distinct apartment, there stood a smaller couch, a Napoleon bed, with carved ends, furnished more simply but with equal richness. Everywhere was the air not only of comfort, but of ease and luxury, elegance and sensuousness contending. I needed no lesson to tell me that this was not an ordinary apartment, nor occupied by an ordinary owner.

One resented the liberties England took in establishing this manner of ménage in our simple city, and arrogantly taking for granted our ignorance regarding it; but none the less one was forced to commend the thoroughness shown. The ceilings, of course, remained low, but there was visible no trace of the original architecture, so cunningly had the interior been treated. As I have said, the dividing partitions had all been removed, so that the long interior practically was open, save as the apartments were separated by curtains or grilles. The floors were carpeted thick and deep. Silence reigned here. There remained no trace of the clumsy comfort which had sufficed the early builder. Here was no longer a series of modest homes, but a boudoir which might have been the gilded cage of some favorite of an ancient court. The breath and flavor of this suspicion floated in every drapery, swam in the faint perfume which filled the place. My first impression was that of surprise; my second, as I have said, a feeling of resentment at the presumption which installed all this in our capital of Washington.

I presume my thought may have been reflected in some manner in my face. I heard a gentle laugh, and turned about. She sat there in a great carved chair, smiling, her white arms stretched out on the rails, the fingers just gently curving. There was no apology for her situation, no trace of alarm or shame or unreadiness. It was quite obvious she was merely amused. I was in no way ready to ratify the rumors I had heard regarding her.

She had thrown back over the rail of the chair the rich cloak which covered her in the carriage, and sat now in the full light, in the splendor of satin and lace and gems, her arms bare, her throat and shoulders white and bare, her figure recognized graciously by every line of a superb gowning such as we had not yet learned on this side of the sea. Never had I seen, and never since have I seen, a more splendid instance of what beauty of woman may be.

She did not speak at first, but sat and smiled, studying, I presume, to find what stuff I was made or Seeing this, I pulled myself together and proceeded briskly to my business.

"My employer will find me late, I fear, my dear baroness," I began.

"Better late than wholly unsuccessful," she rejoined, still smiling. "Tell me, my friend, suppose you had come hither and knocked at my door?"

"Perhaps I might not have been so clumsy," I essayed.

"Confess it!" she smiled. "Had you come here and seen the exterior only, you would have felt yourself part of a great mistake. You would have gone away."

"Perhaps not," I argued. "I have much confidence in my chief's acquaintance with his own purposes and his own facts. Yet I confess I should not have sought madam the baroness in this neighborhood. If England provides us so beautiful a picture, why could she not afford a frame more suitable? Why is England so secret with us?"

She only smiled, showing two rows of exceedingly even white teeth. She was perfect mistress of herself. In years she was not my equal, yet I could see that at the time I did scarcely more than amuse her.

"Be seated, pray," she said at last. "Let us talk over this matter."

Obedient to her gesture, I dropped into a chair opposite to her, she herself not varying her posture

and still regarding me with the laugh in her
closed eyes.

"What do you think of my little place?" she asked
finally.

"Two things, Madam," said I, half sternly. "If it
belonged to a man, and to a minister plenipotentiary,
I should not approve it. If it belonged to a lady of
means and a desire to see the lands of this little
world, I should approve it very much."

She looked at me with eyes slightly narrowed, but
no trace of perturbation crossed her face. I saw it
was no ordinary woman with whom we had to do.

"But," I went on, "in any case and at all events, I
should say that the bird confined in such a cage,
where secrecy is so imperative, would at times find
weariness—would, in fact, wish escape to other employment. You, Madam"—I looked at her directly
—"are a woman of so much intellect that you could
not be content merely to live."

"No," she said, "I would not be content merely
to live."

"Precisely. Therefore, since to make life worth
the living there must be occasionally a trifle of spice,
a bit of adventure, either for man or woman, I suggest to you, as something offering amusement, this
little journey with me to-night to meet my chief.
You have his message. I am his messenger, and, believe me, quite at your service in any way you may

Let us be frank. If you are agent, so am I. See; I have come into your camp. Dare you not come into ours? Come; it is an adventure to see a tall, thin old man in a dressing-gown and a red woolen nightcap. So you will find my chief; and in apartments much different from these."

She took up the missive with its broken seal. "So your chief, as you call him, asks me to come to him, at midnight, with you, a stranger?"

"Do you not believe in charms and in luck, in evil and good fortune, Madam?" I asked her. "Now, it is well to be lucky. In ordinary circumstances, as you say, I could not have got past yonder door. Yet here I am. What does it augur, Madam?"

"But it is night!"

"Precisely. Could you go to the office of a United States senator and possible cabinet minister in broad daylight and that fact not be known? Could he come to your apartments in broad daylight and that fact not be known? What would 'that man Pakenham' suspect in either case? Believe me, my master is wise. I do not know his reason, but he knows it, and he has planned best to gain his purpose, whatever it may be. Reason must teach you, Madam, that night, this night, this hour, is the only time in which this visit could be made. Naturally, it would be impossible for him to come here. If you go to him, he will—ah, he will reverence you, as I do, Madam. Great necessity sets aside conventions, sets aside everything. Come, then!"

But still she only sat and smiled at me. I felt that purple and amber glow, the emanation of her personality, of her senses, creeping around me again as she leaned forward finally, her parted red-bowed lips again disclosing her delicate white teeth. I saw the little heave of her bosom, whether in laughter or emotion I could not tell. I was young. Resenting the spell which I felt coming upon me, all I could do was to reiterate my demand for haste. She was not in the least impressed by this.

"Come!" she said. "I am pleased with these Americans. Yes, I am not displeased with this little adventure."

I rose impatiently, and walked apart in the room. "You can not evade me, Madam, so easily as you did the Mexican gentleman who followed you. You have him in the net also? Is not the net full enough?"

"Never!" she said, her head swaying slowly from side to side, her face inscrutable. "Am I not a woman? Ah, am I not?"

"Madam," said I, whirling upon her, "let me, at least, alone. I am too small game for you. I am but a messenger. Time passes. Let us arrive at our business."

"What would you do if I refused to go with you?"

she asked, still smiling at me. She was waiting for
the spell of these surroundings, the spirit of this
place, to do their work with me, perhaps; was willing to take her time with charm of eye and arm and
hair and curved fingers, which did not openly invite
and did not covertly repel. But I saw that her attitude toward me held no more than that of bird of
prey and some little creature well within its power.
It made me angry to be so rated.

"You ask me what I should do?" I retorted sav-
agely. "I shall tell you first what I *will* do if you
continue your refusal. I will *take* you with me,
and so keep my agreement with my chief. Keep
away from the bell rope! Remain silent! Do not
move! You should go if I had to carry you there in
a sack—because that is my errand!"

"Oh, listen at him threaten!" she laughed still.
"And he despises my poor little castle here in the
side street, where half the time I am so lonely! What
would Monsieur do if Monsieur were in my place—
and if I were in Monsieur's place? But, bah! you
would not have me following *you* in the first hour we
met, boy!"

I flushed again hotly at this last word. "Madam
may discontinue the thought of my boyhood; I am
older than she. But if you ask me what I would do
with a woman if I followed her, or if she followed
me, then I shall tell you. If I owned this place and

all in it, I would tear down every picture from these walls, every silken cover from yonder couches! I would rip out these walls and put back the ones that once were here! You, Madam, should be taken out of luxury and daintiness—"

"Go on!" She clapped her hands, for the first time kindling, and dropping her annoying air of patronizing me. "Go on! I like you now. Tell me what Americans do with women that they love! I have heard they are savages."

"A house of logs far out in the countries that I know would do for you, Madam!" I went on hotly. "You should forget the touch of silk and lace. No neighbor you should know until I was willing. Any man who followed you should meet *me*. Until you loved me all you could, and said so, and proved it, I would wring your neck with my hands, if necessary, until you loved me!"

"Excellent! What then?"

"Then, Madam the Baroness, I would in turn build you a palace, one of logs, and would make you a most excellent couch of the husks of corn. You should cook at my fireplace, and for *me!*"

She smiled slowly past me, at me. "Pray be seated," she said. "You interest me."

"It is late," I reiterated. "Come! Must I do some of these things—force you into obedience—carry you away in a sack? My master can not wait."

"Don Yturrió of Mexico, on the other hand," she mused, "promised me not violence, but more jewels. Idiot!"

"Indeed!" I rejoined, in contempt. "An American savage would give you but one gown, and that of your own weave; you could make it up as you liked. But come, now; I have no more time to lose."

"Ah, also, idiot!" she murmured. "Do you not see that I must reclothe myself before I could go with you—that is to say, if I choose to go with you? Now, as I was saying, my ardent Mexican promises thus and so. My lord of England—ah, well, they may be pardoned. Suppose I might listen to such suits—might there not be some life for me—some life with events? On the other hand, what of interest could America offer?"

"I have told you what life America could give you."

"I imagined men were but men, wherever found," she went on; "but what you say interests me, I declare to you again. A woman is a woman, too, I fancy. She always wants one thing—to be all the world to one man."

"Quite true," I answered. "Better that than part of the world to one—or two? And the opposite of it is yet more true. When a woman is all the world to a man, she despises him."

"But yes, I should like that experience of being a

cook in a cabin, and being bruised and broken and
choked!" She smiled, lazily extending her flawless
arms and looking down at them, at all of her splendid figure, as though in interested examination. "I
am alone so much—so bored!" she went on. "And
Sir Richard Pakenham is so very, very fat. Ah,
God! You can not guess how fat he is. But you, you
are not fat." She looked me over critically, to my
great uneasiness.

"All the more reason for doing as I have suggested, Madam; for Mr. Calhoun is not even so fat
as I am. This little interview with my chief, I doubt
not, will prove of interest. Indeed"—I went on se-
riously and intently—"I venture to say this much
without presuming on my station: the talk which
you will have with my chief to-night will show you
things you have never known, give you an interest
in living which perhaps you have not felt. If I am
not mistaken, you will find much in common between
you and my master. I speak not to the agent of
England, but to the lady Helena von Ritz."

"He is old," she went on. "He is very old. His
face is thin and bloodless and fleshless. He is old."

"Madam," I said, "his mind is young, his purpose
young, his ambition young; and his country is
young. Is not the youth of all these things still your
own?"

She made no answer, but sat musing, drumming

lightly on the chair arm. I was reaching for her cloak. Then at once I caught a glimpse of her stockinged foot, the toe of which slightly protruded from beneath her ball gown. She saw the glance and laughed.

"Poor feet," she said. "Ah, *mes pauvres pieds la!* You would like to see them bruised by the hard going in some heathen country? See you have no carriage, and mine is gone. I have not even a pair of shoes. Go look under the bed beyond."

I obeyed her gladly enough. Under the fringe of the satin counterpane I found a box of boots, slippers, all manner of footwear, daintily and neatly arranged. Taking out a pair to my fancy, I carried them out and knelt before her.

"Then, Madam," said I, "since you insist on this, I shall choose. America is not Europe. Our feet here have rougher going and must be shod for it. Allow me!"

Without the least hesitation in the world, or the least immodesty, she half protruded the foot which still retained its slipper. As I removed this latter, through some gay impulse, whose nature I did not pause to analyze, I half mechanically thrust it into the side pocket of my coat.

"This shall be security," said I, "that what you speak with my master shall be the truth, the whole truth, and nothing but the truth."

There was a curious deeper red in her cheek.   I
saw her bosom beat the faster rhythm.

"Quite agreed!" she answered.   But she motioned
me away, taking the stout boot in her own hand and
turning aside as she fastened it.   She looked over
her shoulder at me now and again while thus engaged.

"Tell me," she said gently, "what security do *I*
have?   You come, by my invitation, it is true, but
none the less an intrusion, into my apartments.   You
demand of me something which no man has a right
to demand.   Because I am disposed to be gracious,
and because I am much disposed to be *ennuyé,* and
because Mr. Pakenham is fat, I am willing to take
into consideration what you ask.   I have never seen
a thin gentleman in a woolen nightcap, and I am
curious.   But no gentleman plays games with ladies
in which the dice are loaded for himself.   Come,
what security shall *I* have?"

I did not pretend to understand her.   Perhaps,
after all, we all had been misinformed regarding
her?   I could not tell.   But her spirit of *camaraderie,*
her good fellowship, her courage, quite aside from
her personal charm, had now begun to impress me.

"Madam," said I, feeling in my pocket; "no
heathen has much of this world's goods. All my possessions would not furnish one of these rooms. .I can
not offer gems, as does Señor Yturrio—but, would

this be of service—until to-morrow? That will leave him and me with a slipper each. It is with reluctance I pledge to return mine!"

By chance I had felt in my pocket a little object which I had placed there that very day for quite another purpose. It was only a little trinket of Indian manufacture, which I had intended to give Elisabeth that very evening; a sort of cloak clasp, originally made as an Indian blanket fastening, with two round discs ground out of shells and connected by beaded thongs. I had got it among the tribes of the far upper plains, who doubtless obtained the shells, in their strange savage barter, in some way from the tribes of Florida or Texas, who sometimes trafficked in shells which found their way as far north as the Saskatchewan. The trinket was curious, though of small value. The baroness looked at it with interest.

"How it reminds me of this heathen country!" she said. "Is this all that your art can do in jewelry? Yet it *is* beautiful. Come, will you not give it to me?"

"Until to-morrow, Madam."

"No longer?"

"I can not promise it longer. I must, unfortunately, have it back when I send a messenger—I shall hardly come myself, Madam."

"Ah!" she scoffed. "Then it belongs to another woman?"

"Yes, it is promised to another."

"Then this is to be the last time we meet?"

"I do not doubt it."

"Are you not sorry?"

"Naturally, Madam!"

She sighed, laughing as she did so. Yet I could not evade seeing the curious color on her cheek, the rise and fall of the laces over her bosom. Utterly self-possessed, satisfied with life as it had come to her, without illusion as to life, absorbed in the great game of living and adventuring—so I should have described her. Then why should her heart beat one stroke the faster now? I dismissed that question, and rebuked my eyes, which I found continually turning toward her.

She motioned to a little table near by. "Put the slipper there," she said. "Your little neck clasp, also." Again I   ~ved her.

"Stand there!" she said, motioning to the opposite side of the table; and I did so. "Now," said she, looking at me gravely, "I am going with you to see this man whom you call your chief—this old and ugly man, thin and weazened, with no blood in him, and a woolen nightcap which is perhaps red. I shall not tell you whether I go of my own wish or because you wish it. But I need soberly to tell you this: secrecy is as necessary for me as for you. The favor may mean as much on one side as on the other—I

shall not tell you why. But we shall play fair until,
as you say, perhaps to-morrow. After that—"

"After that, on guard!"

"Very well, on guard! Suppose I do not like this
other woman?"

"Madam, you could not help it. All the world
loves her."

"Do you?"

"With my life."

"How devoted! Very well, *on guard,* then!"

She took up the Indian bauble, turning to examine
it at the nearest candle sconce, even as I thrust the
dainty little slipper of white satin again into the
pocket of my coat. I was uncomfortable. I wished
this talk of Elisabeth had not come up. I liked very
little to leave Elisabeth's property in another's
hands. Dissatisfied, I turned from the table, not
noticing for more than an instant a little crumpled
roll of paper which, as I was vaguely conscious, now
appeared on its smooth marquetry top.

"But see," she said; "you are just like a man,
after all, and an unmarried man at that! I can not
go through the streets in this costume. Excuse me
for a moment."

She was off on the instant into the alcove where
the great amber-covered bed stood. She drew the
curtains. I heard her humming to herself as she
passed to and fro, saw the flare of a light as it rose

beyond.   Once or twice she thrust a laughing face
between the curtains, held tight together with her
hands, as she asked me some question, mocking me,
still amused—yet still, as I thought, more enigmatic
than before.

"Madam," I said at last, "I would I might dwell
here for ever, but—you are slow! The night passes.
Come. My master will be waiting. He is ill; I fear
he can not sleep. I know how intent he is on meeting you. I beg you to oblige an old, a dying man!"

"And you, Monsieur," she mocked at me from beyond the curtain, "are intent only on getting rid of
me. Are you not adventurer enough to forget that
other woman for one night?"

In her hands—those of a mysterious foreign
woman—I had placed this little trinket which I had
got among the western tribes for Elisabeth—a
woman of my own people—the woman to whom my
pledge had been given, not for return on any mor-
row. I made no answer, excepting to walk up and
down the floor.

At last she came out from between the curtains,
garbed more suitably for the errand which was now
before us. A long, dark cloak covered her shoulders. On her head there rested a dainty up-flared
bonnet, whose jetted edges shone in the candle light
as she moved toward me. She was exquisite in
every detail, beautiful as mind of man could wish;

that much was sure, must be admitted by any man. I dared not look at her. I called to mind the taunt of those old men, that I was young! There was in my soul vast relief that she was not delaying me here longer in this place of spells—that in this almost providential way my errand had met success.

She paused for an instant, drawing on a pair of the short gloves of the mode then correct. "Do you know why I am to go on this heathen errand?" she demanded. I shook my head.

"Mr. Calhoun wishes to know whether he shall go to the cabinet of your man Tyler over there in that barn you call your White House. I suppose Mr. Calhoun wishes to know how he can serve Mr. Tyler?"

I laughed at this. "Serve him!" I exclaimed. "Rather say *lead* him, *tell* him, *command* him!"

"Yes," she nodded. I began to see another and graver side of her nature. "Yes, it is of course Texas."

I did not see fit to make answer to this.

"If your master, as you call him, takes the portfolio with Tyler, it is to annex Texas," she repeated sharply. "Is not that true?"

Still I would not answer. "Come!" I said.

"And he asks me to come to him so that he may decide—"

This awoke me. "No man decides for John Calhoun, Madam," I said. "You may advance facts, but *he* will decide." Still she went on.

"And Texas not annexed is a menace. Without her, you heathen people would not present a solid front, would you?"

"Madam has had much to do with affairs of state," I said.

She went on as though I had not spoken:

"And if you were divided in your southern section, England would have all the greater chance. England, you know, says she wishes slavery abolished. She says that—"

"England *says* many things!" I ventured.

"The hypocrite of the nations!" flashed out this singular woman at me suddenly. "As though diplomacy need be hypocrisy! Thus, to-night Sir Richard of England forgets his place, his protestations. He does not even know that Mexico has forgotten its duty also. Sir, you were not at our little ball, so you could not see that very fat Sir Richard paying his bored *devoirs* to Doña Lucrezia! So I am left alone, and would be bored, but for you. In return—a slight jest on Sir Richard to-night!—I will teach him that no fat gentleman should pay even bored attentions to a lady who soon will be fat, when his obvious duty should call him otherwise! Bah! 'tis as though I myself were fat; which is not true."

"You go too deep for me, Madam," I said. "I

am but a simple messenger." At the same time, I
saw how admirably things were shaping for us all.
A woman's jealousy was with us, and so a woman's
whim!

"There you have the measure of England's sincerity," she went on, with contempt. "England is
selfish, that is all. Do you not suppose I have something to do besides feeding a canary? To read, to
study—that is my pleasure. I know your politics
here in America. Suppose you invade Texas, as the
threat is, with troops of the United States, before
Texas is a member of the Union? Does that not
mean you are again at war with Mexico? And does
that not mean that you are also at war with England? Come, do you not know some of those
things?"

"With my hand on my heart, Madam," I asserted
solemnly, "all I know is that you must go to see my
master. Calhoun wants you. America needs you.
I beg you to do what kindness you may to the
heathen."

"*Et moi?*"

"And you?" I answered. "You shall have such
reward as you have never dreamed in all your life."

"How do you mean?"

"I doubt not the reward for a soul which is as
keen and able as your heart is warm, Madam. Come,
I am not such a fool as you think, perhaps. Nor are

you a fool. You are a great woman, a wonderful
woman, with head and heart both, Madam, as well
as beauty such as I had never dreamed. You are a
strange woman, Madam. You are a genius, Madam,
if you please. So, I say, you are capable of a reward, and a great one. You may find it in the gratitude of a people."

"What could this country give more than Mexico
or England?" She smiled quizzically.

"Much more, Madam! Your reward shall be in
the later thought of many homes—homes built of
logs, with dingy fireplaces and couches of husks in
them—far out, all across this continent, housing
many people, many happy citizens, men who will
make their own laws, and enforce them, man and
man alike! Madam, it is the spirit of democracy
which calls on you to-night! It is not any political
party, nor the representative of one. It is not Mr.
Calhoun; it is not I. Mr. Calhoun only puts before
you the summons of—"

"Of what?"

"Of that spirit of democracy."

She stood, one hand ungloved, a finger at her
lips, her eyes glowing. "I am glad you came," she
said. "On the whole, I am also glad I came upon
my foolish errand here to America."

"Madam," said I, my hand at the fastening of the
door, "we have exchanged pledges. Now we ex-

change places. It is you who are the messenger, not myself. There is a message in your hands. I know not whether you ever served a monarchy. Come, you shall see that our republic has neither secrets nor hypocrisies."

On the instant she was not shrewd and tactful woman of the world, not student, but once more coquette and woman of impulse. She looked at me with mockery and invitation alike in her great dark eyes, even as I threw down the chain at the door and opened it wide for her to pass.

"Is that my only reward?" she asked, smiling as she fumbled at a glove.

In reply, I bent and kissed the fingers of her un-gloved hand. They were so warm and tender that I had been different than I was had I not felt the blood tingle in all my body in the impulse of the moment to do more than kiss her fingers.

Had I done so—had I not thought of Elisabeth—then, as in my heart I still believe, the flag of England to-day would rule Oregon and the Pacific; and it would float to-day along the Rio Grande; and it would menace a divided North and South, instead of respecting a strong and indivisible Union which owns one flag and dreads none in the world.

CHAPTER VII

REGARDING ELISABETH

Without woman the two extremities of this life would be destitute of succor and the middle would be devoid of pleasure.—Proverb.

IN some forgotten garret of this country, as I do not doubt, yellowed with age, stained and indistinguishable, lost among uncared-for relics of another day, there may be records of that interview between two strange personalities, John Calhoun and Helena von Ritz, in the arrangement of which I played the part above described. I was not at that time privileged to have much more than a guess at the nature of the interview. Indeed, other things now occupied my mind. I was very much in love with Elisabeth Churchill.

Of these matters I need to make some mention. My father's plantation was one of the old ones in Maryland. That of the Churchills lay across a low range of mountains and in another county from us, but our families had long been friends. I had known Elisabeth from the time she was a tall, slim girl, boon companion ever to her father, old Daniel

65

Churchill; for her mother she had lost when she was
still young. The Churchills maintained a city estab-
lishment in the environs of Washington itself,
although that was not much removed from their
plantation in the old State of Maryland. Elmhurst,
this Washington estate was called, and it was well
known there, with its straight road approaching and
its great trees and its wide-doored halls—whereby
the road itself seemed to run straight through the
house and appear beyond—and its tall white pillars
and hospitable galleries, now in the springtime
enclosed in green. I need not state that now, having
finished the business of the day, or, rather, of the
night, Elmhurst, home of Elisabeth, was my immediate Mecca.

I had clad myself as well as I could in the fashion
of my time, and flattered myself, as I looked in my
little mirror, that I made none such bad figure of a
man. I was tall enough, and straight, thin with
long hours afoot or in the saddle, bronzed to a good
color, and if health did not show on my face, at least
I felt it myself in the lightness of my step, in the
contentedness of my heart with all of life, in my
general assurance that all in the world meant well
toward me and that everything in the world would
do well by me. We shall see what license there was
for this.

As to Elisabeth Churchill, it might have been in

line with a Maryland custom had she generally been known as Betty; but Betty she never was called, although that diminutive was applied to her aunt, Jennings, twice as large as she, after whom she had been named. Betty implies a snub nose; Elisabeth's was clean-cut and straight. Betty runs for a saucy mouth and a short one; Elisabeth's was red and curved, but firm and wide enough for strength and charity as well. Betty spells round eyes, with brows arched above them as though in query and curiosity; the eyes of Elisabeth were long, her brows long and straight and delicately fine. A Betty might even have red hair; Elisabeth's was brown in most lights, and so liquid smooth that almost I was disposed to call it dense rather than thick. Betty would seem to indicate a nature impulsive, gay, and free from care; on the other hand, it was to be said of Elisabeth that she was logical beyond her kind—a trait which she got from her mother, a daughter of old Judge Henry Gooch, of our Superior Court. Yet, disposed as she always was to be logical in her conclusions, the great characteristic of Elisabeth was serenity, consideration and charity.

With all this, there appeared sometimes at the surface of Elisabeth's nature that fire and lightness and impulsiveness which she got from her father, Mr. Daniel Churchill. Whether she was wholly reserved and reasonable, or wholly warm and impulsive, I, long as I had known and loved her, never was quite sure. Something held me away, something called me forward; so that I was always baffled, and yet always eager, God wot. I suppose this is the way of women. At times I have been impatient with it, knowing my own mind well enough.

At least now, in my tight-strapped trousers and my long blue coat and my deep embroidered waistcoat and my high stock, my shining boots and my tall beaver, I made my way on my well-groomed horse up to the gates of old Elmhurst; and as I rode I pondered and I dreamed.

But Miss Elisabeth was not at home, it seemed. Her father, Mr. Daniel Churchill, rather portly and now just a trifle red of face, met me instead. It was not an encounter for which I devoutly wished, but one which I knew it was the right of both of us to expect ere long. Seeing the occasion propitious, I plunged at once *in medias res.* Part of the time explanatory, again apologetic, and yet again, I trust, assertive, although always blundering and red and awkward, I told the father of my intended of my own wishes, my prospects and my plans.

He listened to me gravely and, it seemed to me, with none of that enthusiasm which I would have welcomed. As to my family, he knew enough. As to my prospects, he questioned me. My record was not unfamiliar to him. So, gaining confidence at last under the insistence of what I knew were worthy motives, and which certainly were irresistible of themselves, so far as I was concerned, I asked him if we might not soon make an end of this, and, taking chances as they were, allow my wedding with Elisabeth to take place at no very distant date.

"Why, as to that, of course I do not know what my girl will say," went on Mr. Daniel Churchill, pursing up his lips. He looked not wholly lovable to me, as he sat in his big chair. I wondered that he should be father of so fair a human being as Elisabeth.

"Oh, of course—that," I answered; "Miss Elisabeth and I—"

"The skeesicks!" he exclaimed. "I thought she told me everything."

"I think Miss Elisabeth tells no one quite everything," I ventured. "I confess she has kept me almost as much in the dark as yourself, sir. But I only wanted to ask if, after I have seen her to-day, and if I should gain her consent to an early day, you would not waive any objections on your own part and allow the matter to go forward as soon as possible?"

In answer to this he arose from his chair and stood looking out of the window, his back turned to me. I could not call his reception of my suggestion enthusiastic; but at last he turned.

"I presume that our two families might send you young people a sack of meal or a side of bacon now and then, as far as that is concerned," he said.

I could not call this speech joyous.

"There are said to be risks in any union, sir," I ventured to say. "I admit I do not follow you in contemplating any risk whatever. If either you or your daughter doubts my loyalty or affection, then I should say certainly it were wise to end all this; but—" and I fancied I straightened perceptibly—"I think that might perhaps be left to Miss Elisabeth herself."

After all, Mr. Dan Churchill was obliged to yield, as fathers have been obliged from the beginning of the world. At last he told me I might take my fate in my own hands and go my way.

Trust the instinct of lovers to bring them to-gether! I was quite confident that at that hour I should find Elisabeth and her aunt in the big East Room at the president's reception, the former look-ing on with her uncompromising eyes at the little pageant which on reception days regularly went for-ward there.

My conclusion was correct. I found a boy to hold my horse in front of Gautier's café. Then I hastened off across the intervening blocks and through the grounds of the White House, in which presently, having edged through the throng in the ante-chambers, I found myself in that inane procession of individuals who passed by in order, each to receive the limp handshake, the mechanical bow and the perfunctory smile of President Tyler—rather a tall, slender-limbed, active man, and of very decent presence, although his thin, shrunken cheeks and his cold blue-gray eye left little quality of magnetism in his personality.

It was not new to me, of course, this pageant, although it never lacked of interest. There were in the throng representatives of all America as it was then, a strange, crude blending of refinement and vulgarity, of ease and poverty, of luxury and thrift. We had there merchants from Philadelphia and New York, politicians from canny New England and not less canny Pennsylvania. At times there came from the Old World men representative of an easier and more opulent life, who did not always trouble to suppress their smiles at us. Moving among these were ladies from every state of our Union, picturesque enough in their wide flowered skirts and their flaring bonnets and their silken mitts, each rivalling the other in the elegance of her mien, and all unconsciously outdone in charm, perhaps, by some demure Quakeress in white and dove color, herself looking askance on all this form and ceremony, yet unwilling to leave the nation's capital without shaking the hand of the nation's chief. Add to these, gaunt, black-haired frontiersmen from across the Alleghanies; politicians from the South, clean-shaven, pompous, immaculately clad; uneasy tradesmen from this or the other corner of their commonwealth. A motley throng, indeed!

A certain air of gloom at this time hung over official Washington, for the minds of all were still oppressed by the memory of that fatal accident—the explosion of the great cannon "Peacemaker" on board the war vessel *Princeton*—which had killed Mr. Upshur, our secretary of state, with others, and had, at one blow, come so near to depriving this government of its head and his official family; the number of prominent lives thus ended or endangered being appalling to contemplate. It was this accident which had called Mr. Calhoun forward at a national juncture of the most extreme delicacy and the utmost importance. In spite of the general mourning, however, the informal receptions at the White House were not wholly discontinued, and the administration, unsettled as it was, and fronted by the gravest of diplomatic problems, made such show of dignity and even cheerfulness as it might.

I considered it my duty to pass in the long procession and to shake the hand of Mr. Tyler. That done, I gazed about the great room, carefully scanning the different little groups which were accustomed to form after the ceremonial part of the visit was over. I saw many whom I knew. I forgot them; for in a far corner, where a flood of light came through the trailing vines that shielded the outer window, my anxious eyes discovered the object of my quest—Elisabeth.

It seemed to me I had never known her so fair as she was that morning in the great East Room of the White House. Elisabeth was rather taller than the average woman, and of that splendid southern figure, slender but strong, which makes perhaps the best representative of our American beauty. She was very bravely arrayed to-day in her best pink-flowered lawn, made wide and full, as was the custom of the time, but not so clumsily gathered at the waist as some, and so serving not wholly to conceal her natural comeliness of figure. Her bonnet she had removed. I could see the sunlight on the ripples of her brown hair, and the shadows which lay above her eyes as she turned to face me, and the slow pink which crept into her cheeks.

Dignified always, and reserved, was Elisabeth Churchill. But now I hope it was not wholly conceit which led me to feel that perhaps the warmth, the glow of the air, caught while riding under the open sky, the sight of the many budding roses of our city, the scent of the blossoms which even then came through the lattice—the meeting even with myself, so lately returned—something at least of this had caused an awakening in her girl's heart. Something, I say, I do not know what, gave her greeting to me more warmth than was usual with her. My own heart, eager enough to break bounds, answered in kind. We stood—blushing like children as our hands touched—forgotten in that assemblage of Washington's pomp and circumstance.

"How do you do?" was all I could find to say. And "How do you do?" was all I could catch for answer, although I saw, in a fleeting way, a glimpse of a dimple hid in Elisabeth's cheek. She never showed it save when pleased. I have never seen a dimple like that of Elisabeth's.

Absorbed, we almost forgot Aunt Betty Jennings —stout, radiant, snub-nosed, arch-browed and curious, Elisabeth's chaperon. On the whole, I was glad Aunt Betty Jennings was there. When a soldier approaches a point of danger, he does not despise the cover of natural objects. Aunt Betty appeared to me simply as a natural object at the time. I sought her shelter.

"Aunt Betty," said I, as I took her hand; "Aunt Betty, have we told you, Elisabeth and I?"

I saw Elisabeth straighten in perplexity, doubt or horror, but I went on.

"Yes, Elisabeth and I—"

"You *dear* children!" gurgled Aunt Betty.

"Congratulate us both!" I demanded, and I put

Elisabeth's hand, covered with my own, into the
short and chubby fingers of that estimable lady.
Whenever Elisabeth attempted to open her lips I
opened mine before, and I so overwhelmed dear
Aunt Betty Jennings with protestations of my regard for her, my interest in her family, her other
nieces, her chickens, her kittens, her home—I so
quieted all her questions by assertions and demands
and exclamations, and declarations that Mr. Daniel
Churchill had given his consent, that I swear for the
moment even Elisabeth believed that what I had
said was indeed true.   At least, I can testify she
made no formal denial, although the dimple was
now frightened out of sight.

Admirable Aunt Betty Jennings! She forestalled
every assertion I made, herself bubbling and blushing in sheer delight.   Nor did she lack in charity.
Tapping me with her fan lightly, she exclaimed:
"You rogue!   I know that you two want to be
alone; that is what you want.   Now I am going
away—just down the room.   You will ride home
with us after a time, I am sure?"

Adorable Aunt Betty Jennings!   Elisabeth and I
looked at her comfortable back for some moments
before I turned, laughing, to look Elisabeth in the
eyes.

"You had no right—" began she, her face growing pink.

"Every right!" said I, and managed to find a place for our two hands under cover of the wide flounces of her figured lawn as we stood, both blushing. "I have every right. I have truly just seen your father. I have just come from him."

She looked at me intently, glowingly, happily.

"I could not wait any longer," I went on. "Within a week I am going to have an office of my own. Let us wait no longer. I have waited long enough. Now—"

I babbled on, and she listened. It was strange place enough for a betrothal, but there at least I said the words which bound me; and in the look Elisabeth gave me I saw her answer. Her eyes were wide and straight and solemn. She did not smile.

As we stood, with small opportunity and perhaps less inclination for much conversation, my eyes chanced to turn toward the main entrance door of the East Room. I saw, pushing through, a certain page, a young boy of good family, who was employed by Mr. Calhoun as messenger. He knew me perfectly well, as he did almost every one else in Washington, and with precocious intelligence his gaze picked me out in all that throng.

"Is that for me?" I asked, as he extended his missive.

"Yes," he nodded. "Mr. Calhoun told me to find you and to give you this at once."

I turned to Elisabeth. "If you will pardon me?" I said. She made way for me to pass to a curtained window, and there, turning my back and using such secrecy as I could, I broke the seal.

The message was brief. To be equally brief I may say simply that it asked me to be ready to start for Canada that night on business connected with the Department of State! Of reasons or explanations it gave none.

I turned to Elisabeth and held out the message from my chief. She looked at it. Her eyes widened. "Nicholas!" she exclaimed.

I looked at her in silence for a moment. "Elisabeth," I said at last, "I have been gone on this sort of business long enough. What do you say to this? Shall I decline to go? It means my resignation at once."

I hesitated. The heart of the nation and the nation's life were about me. Our state, such as it was, lay there in that room, and with it our problems, our duties, our dangers. I knew, better than most, that there were real dangers before this nation at that very hour. I was a lover, yet none the less I was an American. At once a sudden plan came into my mind.

"Elisabeth," said I, turning to her swiftly, "I will agree to nothing which will send me away from you again. Listen, then—" I raised a hand as she would have spoken. "Go home with your Aunt Betty as soon as you can. Tell your father that to-night at six I shall be there. Be ready!"

"What do you mean?" she panted. I saw her throat flutter.

"I mean that we must be married to-night before I go. Before eight o'clock I must be on the train."

"When will you be back?" she whispered.

"How can I tell? When I go, my wife shall wait there at Elmhurst, instead of my sweetheart."

She turned away from me, contemplative. She, too, was young. Ardor appealed to her. Life stood before her, beckoning, as to me. What could the girl do or say?

I placed her hand on my arm. We started toward the door, intending to pick up Aunt Jennings on our way. As we advanced, a group before us broke apart. I stood aside to make way for a gentleman whom I did not recognize. On his arm there leaned a woman, a beautiful woman, clad in a costume of flounced and rippling velvet of a royal blue which made her the most striking figure in the great room. Hers was a personality not easily to be overlooked in any company, her face one not readily to be equalled. It was the Baroness Helena von Ritz!

We met face to face. I presume it would have been too much to ask even of her to suppress the sudden flash of recognition which she showed. At

"Wait!" she murmured. "There is to be a meeting——" Page 79

first she did not see that I was accompanied. She
bent to me, as though to adjust her gown, and, without a change in the expression of her face, spoke to
me in an undertone no one else could hear.

"Wait!" she murmured. "There is to be a meeting—" She had time for no more as she swept by.

Alas, that mere moments should spell ruin as well
as happiness! This new woman whom I had wooed
and found, this new Elisabeth whose hand lay on
my arm, saw what no one else would have seen—
that little flash of recognition on the face of Helena
von Ritz! She heard a whisper pass. Moreover,
with a woman's uncanny facility in detail, she took
in every item of the other's costume. For myself, I
could see nothing of that costume now save one object—a barbaric brooch of double shells and beaded
fastenings, which clasped the light laces at her
throat.

The baroness had perhaps slept as little as I the
night before. If I showed the ravages of loss of
sleep no more than she, I was fortunate. She was
radiant, as she passed forward with her escort for
place in the line which had not yet dwindled away.

"You seem to know that lady," said Elisabeth to
me gently.

"Did I so seem?" I answered. "It is professional
of all to smile in the East Room at a reception,"
said I.

"Then you do not know the lady?"

"Indeed, no. Why should I, my dear girl?" Ah, how hot my face was!

"I do not know," said Elisabeth. "Only, in a way she resembles a certain lady of whom we have heard rather more than enough here in Washington."

"Put aside silly gossip, Elisabeth," I said. "And, please, do not quarrel with me, now that I am so happy. To-night—"

"Nicholas," she said, leaning just a little forward and locking her hands more deeply in my arm, "don't you know you were telling me one time about the little brooch you were going to bring me—an Indian thing—you said it should be my—my wedding present? Don't you remember that? Now, I was thinking—"

I stood blushing red as though detected in the utmost villainy. And the girl at my side saw that written on my face which now, within the very moment, it had become her *right* to question! I turned to her suddenly.

"Elisabeth," said I, "you shall have your little brooch to-night, if you will promise me now to be ready and waiting for me at six. I will have the license."

It seemed to me that this new self of Elisabeth's—warmer, yielding, adorable—was slowly going away from me again, and that her old self, none the less sweet, none the less alluring, but more logical and questioning, had taken its old place again. She put both her hands on my arm now and looked me fairly in the face, where the color still proclaimed some sort of guilt on my part, although my heart was clean and innocent as hers.

"Nicholas," she said, "come to-night. Bring me my little jewel—and bring—"

"The minister! If I do that, Elisabeth, you will marry me then?"

"Yes!" she whispered softly.

Amid all the din and babble of that motley throng I heard the word, low as it was. I have never heard a voice like Elisabeth's.

An instant later, I knew not quite how, her hand was away from my arm, in that of Aunt Betty, and they were passing toward the main door, leaving me standing with joy and doubt mingled in my mind.

CHAPTER VIII

A woman's tongue is her sword, that she never lets rust.
—*Madam Necker.*

I STRUGGLED among three courses. The impulses of my heart, joined to some prescience of trouble, bade me to follow Elisabeth. My duty ordered me to hasten to Mr. Calhoun. My interest demanded that I should tarry, for I was sure that the Baroness von Ritz would make no merely idle request in these circumstances. Hesitating thus, I lost sight of her in the throng. So I concluded I would obey the mandate of duty, and turned toward the great doors. Indeed, I was well toward the steps which led out into the grounds, when all at once two elements of my problem resolved themselves into one. I saw the tall figure of Mr. Calhoun himself coming up the walk toward me.

"Ah," said he briefly, "then my message found you?"

"I was starting for you this moment, sir," I replied.

"Wait for a moment. I counted on finding you here. Matters have changed."

I turned with him and we entered again the East Room, where Mr. Tyler still prolonged the official greeting of the curious, the obsequious, or the banal persons who passed. Mr. Calhoun stood apart for a time, watching the progress of this purely American function. It was some time ere the groups thinned. This latter fact usually would have ended the reception, since it is not etiquette to suppose that the president can lack an audience; but to-day Mr. Tyler lingered. As last through the thinning throng he caught sight of the distinctive figure of Mr. Calhoun. For the first time his own face assumed a natural expression. He stopped the line for an instant, and with a raised hand beckoned to my chief.

At this we dropped in at the tail of the line, Mr. Calhoun in passing grasping almost as many hands as Mr. Tyler. When at length we reached the president's position, the latter greeted him and added a whispered word. An instant later he turned abruptly, ending the reception with a deep bow, and retired into the room from which he had earlier emerged.

Mr. Calhoun turned now to me with a request to follow him, and we passed through the door where the president had vanished. Directed by attendants, we were presently ushered into yet another room, which at that time served the president as his cabinet room, a place for meeting persons of distinction who called upon business.

As we entered I saw that it was already occupied. Mr. Tyler was grasping the hand of a portly personage, whom I knew to be none other than Mr. Pakenham. So much might have been expected. What was not to have been expected was the presence of another—none less than the Baroness von Ritz! For this latter there was no precedent, no conceivable explanation save some exigent emergency.

So we were apparently to understand that my lady was here as open friend of England! Of course, I needed no word from Mr. Calhoun to remind me that we must seem ignorant of this lady, of her character, and of her reputed relations with the British Foreign Office.

"I pray you be seated, Mr. Pakenham," said Mr. Tyler, and he gestured also to us others to take chairs near his table. Mr. Pakenham, in rather a lofty fashion, it seemed to me, obeyed the polite request, but scarcely had seated himself ere he again rose with an important clearing of his throat. He was one who never relished the democratic title of "Mr." accorded him by Mr. Tyler, whose plain and simple ways, not much different now from those of

his plantation life, were in marked contrast to the
ceremoniousness of the Van Buren administration,
which Pakenham also had known.

"Your *Excellency,*" said he, "her Majesty the
Queen of England's wish is somewhat anticipated
by my visit here to-day. I hasten only to put in the
most prompt and friendly form her Majesty's de-
sires, which I am sure formally will be expressed in
the first mails from England. We deplore this most
unhappy accident on your warship *Princeton,* which
has come so near working irremediable injury to this
country. Unofficially, I have ventured to make this
personal visit under the flag of this enlightened
Republic, and to the center of its official home, out
of a friendship for Mr. Upshur, the late secretary of
state, a friendship as sincere as is that of my own
country for this Republic."

"Sir," said Mr. Tyler, rising, with a deep bow,
"the courtesy of your personal presence is most gratifying. Allow me to express that more intimate and
warmer feeling of friendship for yourself which
comes through our long association with you. This
respect and admiration are felt by myself and my
official family for you and the great power which
you represent. It goes to you with a special sincerity
as to a gentleman of learning and distinction, whose
lofty motives and ideals are recognized by all."

Each having thus delivered himself of words which meant nothing, both now seated themselves and proceeded to look mighty grave. For myself, I stole a glance from the tail of my eye toward the Baroness von Ritz. She sat erect in her chair, a figure of easy grace and dignity, but on her face was nothing one could read to tell who she was or why she was here. So far from any external *gaucherie*, she seemed quite as much at home here, and quite as fit here, as England's plenipotentiary.

"I seize upon this opportunity, Mr. Pakenham," said Mr. Tyler presently, with a smile which he meant to set all at ease and to soften as much as possible the severity of that which was to follow, "I gladly take this opportunity to mention in an informal way my hope that this matter which was already inaugurated by Mr. Upshur before his untimely death may come to perfectly pleasant consummation. I refer to the question of Texas."

"I beg pardon, your Excellency," rejoined Mr. Pakenham, half rising. "Your meaning is not perfectly clear to me."

The same icy smile sat upon Mr. Tyler's face as he went on: "I can not believe that your government can wish to interfere in matters upon this continent to the extent of taking the position of open ally of the Republic of Mexico, a power so recently at war upon our own borders with the brave Texans who have left our flag to set up, through fair conquest, a republic of their own."

The mottled face of Mr. Pakenham assumed a yet deeper red. "As to that, your Excellency," said he, "your remark is, as you say, quite informal, of course—that is to say, as I may state—"

"Quite so," rejoined Mr. Tyler gravely. "The note of my Lord Aberdeen to us, none the less, in the point of its bearing upon the question of slavery in Texas, appears to this government as an expression which ought to be disavowed by your own government. Do I make myself quite clear?" (With John Calhoun present, Tyler could at times assume a courage though he had it not.)

Mr. Pakenham's face glowed a deeper red. "I am not at liberty to discuss my Lord Aberdeen's wishes in this matter," he said. "We met here upon a purely informal matter, and—"

"I have only ventured to hope," rejoined Mr. Tyler, "that the personal kindness of your own heart might move you in so grave a matter as that which may lead to war between two powers."

"War, sir, *war?*" Mr. Pakenham went wholly purple in his surprise, and sprang to his feet. "War!" he repeated once more. "As though there could be any hope—"

"Quite right, sir," said Mr. Tyler grimly. "As though there could be any hope for us save in our own conduct of our own affairs, without any interference from any foreign power!"

I knew it was John Calhoun speaking these words, not Mr. Tyler. I saw Mr. Calhoun's keen, cold eyes fixed closely upon the face of his president. The consternation created by the latter's words was plainly visible.

"Of course, this conversation is entirely irregular —I mean to say, wholly unofficial, your Excellency?" hesitated Pakenham. "It takes no part in our records?"

"Assuredly not," said Mr. Tyler. "I only hope the question may never come to a matter of record at all. Once our country knows that dictation has been attempted with us, even by England herself, the North will join the South in resentment. Even now, in restiveness at the fancied attitude of England toward Mexico, the West raises the demand that we shall end the joint occupancy of Oregon with Great Britain. Do you perchance know the watchword which is now on the popular tongue west of the Alleghanies? It bids fair to become an American *Marseillaise.*"

"I must confess my ignorance," rejoined Mr. Pakenham.

"Our backwoodsmen have invented a phrase which runs *Fifty-four Forty or Fight!*"

"I beg pardon, I am sure, your Excellency?"

"It means that if we conclude to terminate the very unsatisfactory muddle along the Columbia River—a stream which our mariners first explored, as we contend—and if we conclude to dispute with England as well regarding our delimitations on the Southwest, where she has even less right to speak, then we shall contend for *all* that territory, not only up to the Columbia, but north to the Russian line, the parallel of fifty-four degrees and forty minutes! We claim that we once bought Texas clear to the Rio Grande, from Napoleon, although the foolish treaty with Spain in 1819 clouded our title—in the belief of our Whig friends, who do not desire more slave territory. Even the Whigs think that we own Oregon by virtue of first navigation of the Columbia. Both Whigs and Democrats now demand Oregon north to fifty-four degrees, forty minutes. The alternative? My Lord Aberdeen surely makes no deliberate bid to hear it!"

"Or fight!" exclaimed Pakenham. "God bless my soul! Fight *us?*"

Mr. Tyler flushed. "Such things have been," said he with dignity.

"That is to say," he resumed calmly, "our rude Westerners are egotistic and ignorant. I admit that we are young. But believe me, when the American people say *fight,* it has but one meaning. As their servant, I am obliged to convey that meaning. In this democracy, the will of the people rules. In war, we have no Whigs, no Democrats, we have only *the people!"*

At this astounding speech the British minister sat dumfounded. This air of courage and confidence on the part of Mr. Tyler himself was something foreign to his record. I knew the reason for his boldness. John Calhoun sat at his right hand.

At least, the meaning of this sudden assault was too much for England's representative. Perhaps, indeed, the Berserker blood of our frontier spoke in Mr. Tyler's gaze. That we would fight indeed was true enough.

"It only occurs to us, sir," continued the president, "that the great altruism of England's heart has led her for a moment to utter sentiments in a form which might, perhaps, not be sanctioned in her colder judgment. This nation has not asked counsel. We are not yet agreed in our Congress upon the admission of Texas—although I may say to you, sir, with fairness, that such is the purpose of this administration. There being no war, we still have Whigs and Democrats!"

"At this point, your Excellency, the dignity of her Majesty's service would lead me to ask excuse," rejoined Mr. Pakenham formally, "were it not for one fact, which I should like to offer here. I have, in short, news which will appear full warrant for any communication thus far made by her Majesty's government. I can assure you that there has come into the possession of this lady, whose able services I venture to enlist here in her presence, a communication from the Republic of Texas to the government of England. That communication is done by no less a hand than that of the attaché for the Republic of Texas, Mr. Van Zandt himself."

There was, I think, no other formal invitation for the Baroness von Ritz to speak; but now she arose, swept a curtsey first to Mr. Tyler and then to Mr. Pakenham and Mr. Calhoun.

"It is not to be expected, your Excellency and gentlemen," said she, "that I can add anything of value here." Her eyes were demurely downcast.

"We do not doubt your familiarity with many of these late events," encouraged Mr. Tyler.

"True," she continued, "the note of my Lord Aberdeen is to-day the property of the streets, and of this I have some knowledge. I can see, also, difficulty in its reception among the courageous gentlemen of America. But, as to any written communication from Mr. Van Zandt, there must be some mistake!"

"I was of the impression that you would have had it last night," rejoined Pakenham, plainly confused; "in fact, that gentleman advised me to such effect."

The Baroness Helena von Ritz looked him full in

the face and only gravely shook her head. "I regret matters should be so much at fault," said she.

"Then let me explain," resumed Pakenham, almost angrily. "I will state—unofficially, of course —that the promises of Mr. Van Zandt were that her Majesty might expect an early end of the talk of the annexation of Texas to the United States. The greater power of England upon land or sea would assure that weak Republic of a great and enlightened ally—in his belief."

"An ally!" broke out Mr. Calhoun. "And a document sent to that effect by the attaché of Texas!" He smiled coldly. "Two things seem very apparent, Mr. President. First, that this gentle lady stands high in the respect of England's ministry. Second, that Mr. Van Zandt, if all this were true, ought to stand very low in ours. I would say all this and much more, even were it a state utterance, to stand upon the records of this nation!"

"Sir," interrupted Mr. Tyler, swiftly turning to Mr. Calhoun, *"may I not ask you that it be left as a state utterance?"*

Mr. Calhoun bowed with the old-time grace habitual to him, his hand upon his heart, but he made no answer. The real reason might have been read in the mottled face of Pakenham, now all the colors of the rainbow, as he looked from one to the other.

"Mr. Calhoun," continued the president, "you

know that the office of our secretary of state is vacant. There is no one living would serve in that office more wisely than yourself, no one more in accordance with my own views as to these very questions which are before us. Since it has come to that point, I offer you now that office, and do so officially. I ask your answer."

The face of England's minister now for the first time went colorless. He knew what this meant.

As for John Calhoun, he played with both of them as a cat would with a mouse, sneeringly superior. His answer was couched in terms suited to his own purposes. "This dignity, Mr. President," said he, bowing deeply again, "so unexpected, so onerous, so responsible, is one which at least needs time for proper consideration. I must crave opportunity for reflection and for pondering. In my surprise at your sudden request, I find no proper answer ready."

Here, then, seemed an opportunity for delay, which Mr. Pakenham was swift to grasp. He arose and bowed to Mr. Tyler. "I am sure that Mr. Calhoun will require some days at least for the framing of his answer to an invitation so grave as this."

"I shall require at least some moments," said Mr. Calhoun, smiling. "That *Marseillaise* of '44, Mr. President, says *Fifty-four Forty or Fight*. That means 'the Rio Grande or fight,' as well."

A short silence fell upon us all. Mr. Tyler half

rose and half frowned as he noticed Mr. Pakenham shuffling as though he would depart.

"It shall be, of course, as you suggest," said the president to Pakenham. "There is no record of any of this. But the answer of Mr. Calhoun, which I await and now demand, is one which will go upon the records of this country soon enough, I fancy. I ask you, then, to hear what Mr. Calhoun replies."

Ah, it was well arranged and handsomely staged, this little comedy, and done for the benefit of England, after all! I almost might have believed that Mr. Calhoun had rehearsed this with the president. Certainly, the latter knew perfectly well what his answer was to be. Mr. Calhoun himself made that deliberately plain, when presently he arose.

"I have had some certain moments for reflection, Mr. President," said he, "and I have from the first moment of this surprising offer on your part been humbly sensible of the honor offered so old and so unfit a man.

"Sir, my own record, thank God, is clear. I have stood for the South. I stand now for Texas. I believe in her and her future. She belongs to us, as I have steadfastly insisted at all hours and in all places. She will widen the southern vote in Congress, that is true. She will be for slavery. That also is true. I myself have stood for slavery, but I am yet more devoted to democracy and to America than I

am to the South and to slavery. So will Texas be. I
know what Texas means. She means for us also
Oregon. She means more than that. She means also
a democracy spreading across this entire continent.
My attitude in that regard has been always clear. I
have not sought to change it. Sir, if I take this office
which you offer, I do so with the avowed and expressed purpose of bringing Texas into this Union,
in full view of any and all consequences. I shall
offer her a treaty of annexation *at once!* I shall
urge annexation at every hour, in every place, in all
ways within my means, and in full view of the consequences!" He looked now gravely and keenly at
the English plenipotentiary.   ·

"That is well understood, Mr. Calhoun," began
Mr. Tyler. "Your views are in full accord with my
own."

Pakenham looked from the one to the other, from
the thin, vulpine face to the thin, leonine one. The
pity Mr. Tyler felt for the old man's visible weak-
ness showed on his face as he spoke.

"What, then, is the answer of John Calhoun to
this latest call of his country?"

That answer is one which is in our history.

"John Calhoun accepts!" said my master, loud
and clear.

CHAPTER IX

A KETTLE OF FISH

Few disputes exist which have not had their origin in women—Juvenal.

I SAW the heavy face of Mr. Pakenham go pale, saw the face of the Baroness von Ritz flash with a swift resolution, saw the eyes of Mr. Calhoun and Mr. Tyler meet in firmness. An instant later, Mr. Tyler rose and bowed our dismissal. Our little play was done. Which of us knew all the motives that had lain behind its setting?

Mr. Pakenham drew apart and engaged in earnest speech with the lady who had accompanied him; so that meantime I myself found opportunity for a word with Mr. Calhoun.

"Now," said I, "the fat certainly is all in the fire!"

"What fat, my son?" asked Calhoun serenely; "and what fire?"

"At least"—and I grinned covertly, I fear—"it seems all over between my lady and her protector there. She turned traitor just when he had most need of her! Tell me, what argument did you use with her last night?"

Mr. Calhoun took snuff.

"You don't know women, my son, and you don't know men, either." The thin white skin about his eyes wrinkled.

"Certainly, I don't know what arts may have been employed in Mr. Calhoun's office at half-past two this morning." I smiled frankly now at my chief, and he relaxed in turn.

"We had a most pleasant visit of an hour. A delightful woman, a charming woman, and one of intellect as well. I appealed to her heart, her brain, her purse, and she laughed, for the most part. Yet she argued, too, and seemed to have some interest— as you see proved now. Ah, I wish I could have had the other two great motives to add to my appeal!"

"Meaning—?"

"Love—and curiosity! With those added, I could have won her over; for believe me, she is none too firmly anchored to England. I am sure of that, though it leaves me still puzzled. If you think her personal hold on yonder gentleman will be lessened, you err," he added, in a low voice. "I consider it sure that he is bent on her as much as he is on England. See, she has him back in hand already! I would she were *our* friend!"

"Is she not?" I asked suddenly.

"We two may answer that one day," said Calhoun enigmatically.

Now I offered to Mr. Calhoun the note I had received from his page.

"This journey to-night," I began; "can I not be excused from making that? There is a very special reason."

"What can it be?" asked Calhoun, frowning.

"I am to be married to-night, sir," said I, calmly as I could.

It was Calhoun's turn now to be surprised. *"Married?* Zounds! boy, what do you mean? There is no time to waste."

"I do not hold it quite wasted, sir," said I with dignity. "Miss Elisabeth Churchill and I for a long time——"

"Miss Elisabeth! So the wind is there, eh? My daughter's friend. I know her very well, of course. Very well done, indeed, for you. But there can be no wedding to-night."

I looked at him in amazement. He was as absorbed as though he felt empowered to settle that matter for me. A moment later, seeing Mr. Pakenham taking his leave, he stepped to the side of the baroness. I saw him and that mysterious lady fall into a conversation as grave as that which had but now been ended. I guessed, rather than reasoned, that in some mysterious way I came into their talk. But presently both approached me.

"Mr. Trist," said Mr. Calhoun, "I beg you to hand

the Baroness von Ritz to her carriage, which will wait at the avenue." We were then standing near the door at the head of the steps.

"I see my friend Mr. Polk approaching," he continued, "and I would like to have a word or so with him."

We three walked in company down the steps and a short distance along the walk, until presently we faced the gentleman whose approach had been noted. We paused in a little group under the shade of an avenue tree, and the gentlemen removed their hats as Mr. Calhoun made a somewhat formal introduction.

At that time, of course, James K. Polk, of Tennessee, was not the national figure he was soon to become at the Baltimore convention. He was known best as Speaker of the House for some time, and as a man experienced in western politics, a friend of Jackson, who still controlled a large wing of the disaffected; the Democratic party then being scarce more than a league of warring cliques. Although once governor of Tennessee, it still was an honor for Mr. Polk to be sought out by Senator John Calhoun, sometime vice-president, sometime cabinet member in different capacities. He showed this as he uncovered. A rather short man, and thin, well-built enough, and of extremely serious mien, he scarce could have been as wise as he looked, any more than

Mr. Daniel Webster; yet he was good example of conventional politics, platitudes and all.

"They have adjourned at the House, then?" said Calhoun.

"Yes, and adjourned a bear pit at that," answered the gentleman from Tennessee. "Mr. Tyler has asked me to come across town to meet him. Do you happen to know where he is now?"

"He was here a few moments ago, Governor. We were but escorting this lady to her carriage, as she claims fatigue from late hours at the ball last night."

"Surely so radiant a presence," said Mr. Polk gallantly, "means that she left the ball at an early hour."

"Quite so," replied that somewhat uncertain lady demurely. "Early hours and a good conscience are advised by my physicians."

"My dear lady, Time owns his own defeat in you," Mr. Polk assured her, his eyes sufficiently admiring.

"Such pretty speeches as these gentlemen of America make!" was her gay reply. "Is it not so, Mr. Secretary?" She smiled up at Calhoun's serious face.

Polk was possessed of a political nose which rarely failed him. "Mr. *Secretary?*" he exclaimed, turning to Calhoun.

The latter bowed. "I have just accepted the place lately filled by Mr. Upshur," was his comment.

A slow color rose in the Tennesseean's face as he held out his hand. "I congratulate you, Mr. Secretary," said he. "Now at last we shall see an end of indecision and boasting pretense."

"Excellent things to end, Governor Polk!" said Calhoun gravely.

"I am but an humble adviser," rejoined the man from Tennessee; "but assuredly I must hasten to congratulate Mr. Tyler. I have no doubt that this means Texas. Of course, my dear Madam, we talk riddles in your presence?"

"Quite riddles, although I remain interested," she answered. I saw her cool eyes take in his figure, measuring him calmly for her mental tablets, as I could believe was her wont. "But I find myself indeed somewhat fatigued, " she continued, "and since these are matters of which I am ignorant—"

"Of course, Madam," said Mr. Calhoun. "We crave your pardon. Mr. Trist—"

So now I took the lady's sunshade from her hand, and we two, making adieux, passed down the shaded walk toward the avenue.

"You are a good cavalier," she said to me. "I find you not so fat as Mr. Pakenham, nor so thin as Mr. Calhoun. My faith, could you have seen that gentleman this morning in a wrapper—and in a red worsted nightcap!"

"But what did you determine?" I asked her suddenly. "What has my chief said to cause you to fail poor Mr. Pakenham as you did? I pitied the poor man, in such a grueling, and wholly without warning!"

"Monsieur is droll," she replied evasively. "As though I had changed! I will say this much: I think Sir Richard will care more for Mexico and less for Mexicans after this! But you do not tell me when you are coming to see me, to bring back my little shoe. Its mate has arrived by special messenger, but the pair remains still broken. Do you come to-night—this afternoon?"

"I wish that I might," said I.

"Why be churlish with me?" she demanded. "Did I not call at your request upon a gentleman in a red nightcap at two in the morning? And for your sake —and the sake of sport—did I not almost promise him many things? Come now, am I not to see you and explain all that; and hear you explain all this?" She made a little *moue* at me.

"It would be my delight, Madam, but there are two reasons—"

"One, then."

"I am going to Montreal to-night, for one."

She gave me a swift glance, which I could not understand.

"So?" she said. "Why so soon?"

"Orders," said I briefly. "But perhaps I may not obey orders for once. There is another reason."

"And that one?"

"I am to be married at six."

I turned to enjoy her consternation. Indeed, there was an alternate white and red passed across her face! But at once she was in hand.

"And you allowed me to become your devoted slave," she said, "even to the extent of calling upon a man in a red nightcap; and then, even upon a morning like this, when the birds sing so sweetly and the little flowers show pink and white—now you cast down my most sacred feelings!"

The mockery in her tone was perfect. I scarce had paused to note it. I was absorbed in one thought —of Elisabeth. Where one fire burns high and clear upon the altar of the heart, there is small room for any other.

"I might have told you," said I at last, "but I did not myself know it until this morning."

"My faith, this country!" she exclaimed with genuine surprise. "What extraordinary things it does! I have just seen history made between the lightings of a cigarette, as it were. Now comes this man and announces that since midnight he has met and won the lady who is to rule his heart, and that he is to marry her at six!"

"Then congratulate me!" I demanded.

"Ah," she said, suddenly absorbed; "it was that tall girl! Yes, yes, I see, I see! I understand! So then! Yes!"

"But still you have not congratulated me."

"Ah, Monsieur," she answered lightly, "one woman never congratulates a man when he has won another! What of my own heart? Fie! Fie!" Yet she had curious color in her face.

"I do not credit myself with such fatal charms," said I. "Rather say what of my little clasp there. I promised that to the tall girl, as you know."

"And might I not wear it for an hour?"

"I shall give you a dozen better some time," said I; "but to-night—"

"And my slipper? I said I must have that back, because I can not hop along with but one shoe all my life."

"That you shall have as soon as I can get to my rooms at Brown's Hotel yonder. A messenger shall bring it to you at once. Time will indeed be short for me. First, the slipper for Madam. Then the license for myself. Then the minister. Then a friend. Then a carriage. Five miles to Elmhurst, and the train for the North starts at eight. Indeed, as you say, the methods of this country are sometimes hurried. Madam, can not you use your wits in a cause so worthy as mine?"

I could not at the time understand the swift change of her features. "One woman's wits against another's!" she flashed at me. "As for that"— She made a swift motion to her throat. "Here is the trinket. Tell the tall lady it is my present to you. Tell her I may send her a wedding present—when the wedding really is to happen. Of course, you do not mean what you have said about being married in such haste?"

"Every word of it," I answered. "And at her own home. 'Tis no runaway match; I have the consent of her father."

"But you said you had her consent only an hour ago. Ah, this is better than a play!"

"It is true," said I, "there has not been time to inform Miss Churchill's family of my need for haste. I shall attend to that when I arrive. The lady has seen the note from Mr. Calhoun ordering me to Montreal."

"To Montreal? How curious!" she mused. "But what did Mr. Calhoun say to this marriage?"

"He forbade the banns."

"But Monsieur will take her before him in a sack —and he will forbid you, I am sure, to condemn that lady to a life in a cabin, to a couch of husks, to a lord who would crush her arms and command her—"

I flushed as she reminded me of my own speech, and there came no answer but the one which I imagine is the verdict of all lovers. "She is the dearest girl in the world," I declared.

"Has she fortune?"

"I do not know."

"Have you fortune?"

"God knows, no!"

"You have but love—and this country?"

"That is all."

"It is enough," said she, sighing. "Dear God, it is enough! But then"— she turned to me suddenly — "I don't think you will be married so soon, after all. Wait."

"That is what Mr. Pakenham wanted Mr. Calhoun to do," I smiled.

"But Mr. Pakenham is not a woman."

"Ah, then you also forbid our banns?"

"If you challenge me," she retorted, "I shall do my worst."

"Then do your worst!" I said. "All of you do your joint worst. You can not shake the faith of Elisabeth Churchill in me, nor mine in her. Oh, yes, by all means do your worst!"

"Very well," she said, with a catch of her breath. "At least we both said—'on guard!'"

"I wish I could ask you to attend at our wedding," I concluded, as her carriage approached the curb; "but it is safe to say that not even friends of the family will be present, and of those not all the family will be friends."

She did not seem to see her carriage as it paused, although she prepared to enter when I opened the door. Her look, absorbed, general, seemed rather to take in the sweep of the wide grounds, the green of the young springtime, the bursting of the new white blossoms, the blue of the sky, the loom of the distant capitol dome—all the crude promise of our young and tawdry capital, still in the making of a world city. Her eyes passed to me and searched my face without looking into my eyes, as though I made part of her study. What sat on her face was perplexity, wonder, amazement, and something else, I know not what. Something of her perfect poise and confidence, her quality as woman of the world, seemed to drop away. A strange and childlike quality came into her face, a pathos unlike anything I had seen there before. She took my hand mechanically.

"Of course," said she, as though she spoke to herself, "it can not be. But, dear God! would it not be enough?"

I did not understand her speech. I stood and watched her carriage as it whirled away. Thinking of my great need for haste, mechanically I looked at my watch. It was one o'clock. Then I reflected that it was at eleven of the night previous that I had first met the Baroness von Ritz. Our acquaintance had therefore lasted some fourteen hours.

CHAPTER X

MIXED DUTIES

Most women will forgive a liberty, rather than a slight.
—*Colton.*

WHEN I crossed the White House grounds and found my way to the spot where I had left my horse, I discovered my darky boy lying on his back, fast asleep under a tree, the bridle reins hooked over his upturned foot. I wakened him, took the reins and was about to mount, when at the moment I heard my name called.

Turning, I saw emerge from the door of Gautier's little café, across the street, the tall figure of an erstwhile friend of mine, Jack Dandridge, of Tennessee, credited with being the youngest member in the House of Representatives at Washington—and credited with little else.

Dandridge had been taken up by friends of Jackson and Polk and carried into Congress without much plan or objection on either side. Since his arrival at the capital he had been present at few roll-calls, and had voted on fewer measures. His life was given up in the main to one specialty, to-wit:

the compounding of a certain beverage, invented by himself, the constituent parts of which were Bourbon whiskey, absinthe, square faced gin and a dash of *eau de vie*. This concoction, over which few shared his own personal enthusiasm, he had christened the Barn-Burner's Dream; although Mr. Dandridge himself was opposed to the tenets of the political party thus entitled—which, by the way, was to get its whimsical name, possibly from Dandridge himself, at the forthcoming Democratic convention of that year.

Jack Dandridge, it may be said, was originally possessed of a splendid constitution. Nearly six feet tall, his full and somewhat protruding eye was as yet only a trifle watery, his wide lip only a trifle loose, his strong figure only a trifle portly. Socially he had been well received in our city, and during his stay east of the mountains he had found occasion to lay desperate suit to the hand of none other than Miss Elisabeth Churchill. We had been rivals, although not enemies; for Jack, finding which way the wind sat for him, withdrew like a man, and cherished no ill will. When I saw him now, a sudden idea came to me, so that I crossed the street at his invitation.

"Come in," said he. "Come in with me, and have a Dream. I have just invented a new touch for it; I have, 'pon my word."

"Jack," I exclaimed, grasping him by the shoulder, "you are the man I want. You are the friend that I need—the very one."

"Certainly, certainly," he said; "but please do not disarrange my cravat. Sir, I move you the previous question. Will you have a Dream with me? I construct them now with three additional squirts of the absinthe." He locked his arm in mine.

"You may have a Dream," said I; "but for me, I need all my head to-day. In short, I need both our heads as well."

Jack was already rapping with the head of his cane upon the table, to call an attendant, but he turned to me. "What is the matter? Lady, this time?"

"Two of them."

"Indeed? One apiece, eh?"

"None apiece, perhaps. In any case, you lose."

"Then the names—or at least one?"

I flushed a bit in spite of myself. "You know Miss Elisabeth Churchill?"

He nodded gravely. "And about the other lady?"

"I can not tell you much about her," said I; "I have but little knowledge myself. I mean the Baroness von Ritz."

"Oh, ho!" Jack opened his eyes, and gave a long whistle. "State secrets, eh?"

I nodded, and looked him square in the eye.

"Well, why should you ask me to help you, then? Calhoun is none too good a friend of Mr. Polk, of my state. Calhoun is neither Whig nor Democrat. He does not know where he stands. If you train with him, why come to our camp for help?"

"Not that sort, Jack," I answered. "The favor I ask is personal."

"Explain."

He sipped at the fiery drink, which by this time had been placed before him, his face brightening.

"I must be quick. I have in my possession—on the bureau in my little room at my quarters in Brown's Hotel—a slipper which the baroness gave me last night—a white satin slipper—"

Jack finished the remainder of his glass at a gulp. "Good God!" he remarked.

"Quite right," I retorted hotly. "Accuse me! Anything you like! But go to my headquarters, get that slipper, go to this address with it"—I scrawled on a piece of paper and thrust it at him— "then get a carriage and hasten to Elmhurst drive, where it turns in at the road. Wait for me there, just before six."

He sat looking at me with amusement and amazement both upon his face, as I went on:

"Listen to what I am to do in the meantime. First I go post haste to Mr. Calhoun's office. Then I am

to take his message, which will send me to Canada,
to-night. After I have my orders I hurry back to
Brown's and dress for my wedding."

The glass in his hand dropped to the floor in
splinters.

"Your wedding?"

"Yes, Miss Elisabeth and I concluded this very
morning not to wait. I would ask you to help me as
my best man, if I dare."

"You do dare," said he. "You're all a-fluster. Go
on; I'll get a parson—how'll Doctor Halford do?—
and I'd take care of the license for you if I could—
Gad! sorry it's not my own!"

"You are the finest fellow in the world, Jack. I
have only one thing more to ask"— I pointed to the
splintered glass upon the floor— "Don't get another."

"Of course not, of course not!" he expostulated.
His voice was just a trifle thickened. We left now together for the license clerk, and I intrusted the
proper document in my friend's hands. An instant
later I was outside, mounted, and off for Calhoun's
office at his residence in Georgetown.

At last, as for the fourth time I flung down the
narrow walk and looked down the street, I saw
his well-known form approaching. He walked slowly, somewhat stooped upon his cane. He raised a

hand as I would have begun to speak. His customary reserve and dignity held me back.

"So you made it out well with the lady," he began.

"Yes," I answered, flushing. "Not so badly for the time that offered."

"A remarkable woman," he said. "Most remarkable!" Then he went on: "Now as to your own intended, I congratulate you. But I suggest that you keep Miss Elisabeth Churchill and the Baroness von Ritz pretty well separated, if that be possible."

"Sir," I stammered; "that certainly is my personal intent. But now, may I ask——"

"You start to Canada to-night," said Calhoun sharply—all softness gone from his voice.

"I can not well do that," I began. His hand tapped with decision.

"I have no time to choose another messenger," he said. "Time will not wait. You must not fail me. You will take the railway train at eight. You will be joined by Doctor Samuel Ward, who will give you a sealed paper, which will contain your instructions, and the proper moneys. He goes as far as Baltimore."

"You would be the better agent," he added presently, "if this love silliness were out of your head. It is not myself you are serving, and not my party. It is this country you are serving."

"But, sir—" I began.

His long thin hand was imperative. "Go on, then, with your wedding, if you will, and if you can; but see that you do not miss the train at eight!"

Half in a daze, I left him; nor did I see him again that day, nor for many after.

CHAPTER XI

WHO GIVETH THIS WOMAN

Woman is a miracle of divine contradictions.—Jules Michelet.

ON my return to my quarters at Brown's I
looked at the top of my bureau. It was
empty. My friend Dandridge had proved
faithful. The slipper of the baroness was gone! So
now, hurriedly, I began my toilet for that occasion
which to any gentleman should be the one most ex-
acting, the most important of his life's events.

Elisabeth deserved better than this unseemly
haste. Her sweetness and dignity, her adherence to
the forms of life, her acquaintance with the ele-
gancies, the dignities and conventions of the best of
our society, bespoke for her ceremony more suited
to her class and mine. Nothing could excuse these
hurly burly ways save only my love, our uncertainty
regarding my future presence, and the imperious
quality of my duties.

I told none about my quarters anything of my
plans, but arranged for my portmanteaus to be sent
to the railway station for that evening's train north.
We had not many outgoing and incoming trains in

those days in Washington.   I hurried to Bond's jewelry place and secured a ring—two rings, indeed;
for, in our haste, betrothal and wedding ring needed
their first use at the same day and hour.   I found a
waiting carriage which served my purpose, and into
it I flung, urging the driver to carry me at top speed
into Elmhurst road.   Having now time for breath, I
sat back and consulted my watch.   There were a few
moments left for me to compose myself.   If all went
well, I should be in time.

As we swung down the road I leaned forward,
studying with interest the dust cloud of an approaching carriage.   As it came near, I called to
my driver.   The two vehicles paused almost wheel
to wheel.   It was my friend Jack Dandridge who
sprawled on the rear seat of the carriage!   That is to
say, the fleshly portion of Jack Dandridge.   His
mind, his memory, and all else, were gone.

I sprang into his carriage and caught him roughly
by the arm.   I felt in all his pockets, looked on the
carriage floor, on the seat, and pulled up the dust
rug.   At last I found the license.

"Did you see the baroness?" I asked, then.

At this he beamed upon me with a wide smile.

"Did I?" said he, with gravity pulling down his
buff waistcoat.   "Did I? Mos' admi'ble woman
the worl'! Of course, Miss 'Lis'beth Churchill
mos' admi'ble woman in the worl'," he added

politely, "but I didn't see *her*. Many, many congrash'lations. Mos' admi'ble girl in worl'—whichever girl she is! I want do what's right!"

The sudden sweat broke out upon my forehead. "Tell me, what have you done with the slipper!"

He shook his head sadly. "Mishtaken, my friend! I gave mos' admi'ble slipper in the worl', just ash you said, just as baroness said, to Mish Elisabeth Churchill—mos' admi'ble woman in the worl'! Proud congrash'late you both, m' friend!"

"Did you see her?" I gasped. "Did you see her father—any of her family?"

"God blesh me, no!" rejoined this young statesman. "Feelings delicacy prevented. Realized having had three—four—five—Barn Burners; washn't in fit condition to approach family mansion. Alwaysh mos' delicate. Felt m'self no condition shtan' up bes' man to mosh admi'ble man and mosh admi'ble girl in worl'. Sent packazh in by servant, from gate—turned round—drove off—found you. Lo, th' bridegroom cometh! Li'l late!"

My only answer was to spring from his carriage into my own and to order my driver to go on at a run. At last I reached the driveway of Elmhurst, my carriage wheels cutting the gravel as we galloped up to the front door. My approach was noted. Even as I hurried up the steps the tall form of none other than Mr. Daniel Churchill appeared to greet me. I extended my hand. He did not notice it. I began to speak. He bade me pause.

"To what may I attribute this visit, Mr. Trist?" he asked me, with dignity.

"Since you ask me, and seem not to know," I replied, "I may say that I am here to marry your daughter, Miss Elisabeth! I presume that the minister of the gospel is already here?"

"The minister is here," he answered. "There lacks one thing—the bride."

"What do you mean?"

He put out his arm across the door.

"I regret that I must bar my door to you. But you must take my word, as coming from my daughter, that you are not to come here to-night."

I looked at him, my eyes staring wide. I could not believe what he said.

"Why," I began; "how utterly monstrous!"

A step sounded in the hall behind him, and he turned back. We were joined by the tall clerical figure of the Reverend Doctor Halford, who had, it seemed, been at least one to keep his appointment as made. He raised his hand as if to silence me, and held out to me a certain object. It was the slipper of the Baroness Helena von Ritz—white, delicate, dainty, beribboned.

"Miss Elisabeth does not pretend to understand why your gift should take this form; but as the slipper evidently has been worn by some one, she suggests you may perhaps be in error in sending it at all." He spoke in even, icy tones.

"Let me into this house!" I demanded. "I must see her!"

There were two tall figures now, who stood side by side in the wide front door.

"But don't you see, there has been a mistake, a horrible mistake?" I demanded.

Doctor Halford, in his grave and quiet way, assisted himself to snuff. "Sir," he said, "knowing both families, I agreed to this haste and unceremoniousness, much against my will. Had there been no objection upon either side, I would have undertaken to go forward with the wedding ceremony. But never in my life have I, and never shall I, join two in wedlock when either is not in that state of mind and soul consonant with that holy hour. This ceremony can not go on. I must carry to you this young lady's wish that you depart. She can not see you."

There arose in my heart a sort of feeling of horror, as though something was wrong, I could not tell what. All at once I felt a swift revulsion. There came over me the reaction, an icy calm. I felt all ardor leave me. I was cold as stone.

"Gentlemen," said I slowly, "what you tell me is absolutely impossible and absurd. But if Miss Elisabeth really doubts me on evidence such as this, I would be the last man in the world to ask her hand. Some time you and she may explain to me about this. It is my right. I shall exact it from you later. I have no time to argue now. Good-by!"

They looked at me with grave faces, but made no reply. I descended the steps, the dainty, beribboned slipper still in my hand, got into my carriage and started back to the city.

CHAPTER XII

THE MARATHON

As if two gods should play some heavenly match, and on this wager lay two earthly women.—Shakespeare.

A N automaton, scarcely thinking, I gained the platform of the station. There was a sound of hissing steam, a rolling cloud of sulphurous smoke, a shouting of railway captains, a creaking of the wheels. Without volition of my own, I was on my northward journey. Presently I looked around and found seated at my side the man whom I then recollected I was to meet—Doctor Samuel Ward. I presume he took the train after I did.

"What's wrong, Nicholas?" he asked. "Trouble of any kind?"

I presume that the harsh quality of my answer surprised him. He looked at me keenly.

"Tell me what's up, my son," said he.

"You know Miss Elisabeth Churchill—" I hesitated.

He nodded. "Yes," he rejoined; "and damn you, sir! if you give that girl a heartache, you'll have to settle with me!"

"Some one will have to settle with me!" I returned hotly.

"Tell me, then."

So, briefly, I did tell him what little I knew of the events of the last hour. I told him of the shame and humiliation of it all. He pondered for a minute and asked me at length if I believed Miss Elisabeth suspected anything of my errand of the night before.

"How could she?" I answered. "So far as I can recollect I never mentioned the name of the Baroness von Ritz."

Then, all at once, I did recollect! I did remember that I had mentioned the name of the baroness that very morning to Elisabeth, when the baroness passed us in the East Room! I had not told the truth—I had gone with a lie on my lips that very day, and asked her to take vows with me in which no greater truth ought to be heard than the simple truth from me to her, in any hour of the day, in any time of our two lives!

Doctor Ward was keen enough to see the sudden confusion on my face, but he made no comment beyond saying that he doubted not time would clear it all up; that he had known many such affairs.

"But mind you one thing," he added; "keep those two women apart."

"Then why do you two doddering old idiots, you and John Calhoun, with life outworn and the blood dried in your veins, send me, since you doubt me so much, on an errand of this kind? You see what it has done for me. I am done with John Calhoun. He may get some other fool for his service."

"Where do you propose going, then, my friend?"

"West," I answered. "West to the Rockies—"

Doctor Ward calmly produced a tortoise shell snuffbox from his left-hand waistcoat pocket, and deliberately took snuff. "You are going to do nothing of the kind," said he calmly. "You are going to keep your promise to John Calhoun and to me. Believe me, the business in hand is vital. You go to Canada now in the most important capacity you have ever had."

"I care nothing for that," I answered bitterly.

"But you are the agent of your country. You are called to do your country's urgent work. Here is your trouble over one girl. Would you make trouble for a million American girls—would you unsettle thousands and thousands of American homes because, for a time, you have known trouble? All life is only trouble vanquished. I ask you now to be a man; I not only expect it, but demand it of you!"

His words carried weight in spite of myself. I began to listen. I took from his hand the package, looked at it, examined it. Finally, as he sat silently regarding me, I broke the seal.

"Now, Nicholas Trist," resumed Doctor Ward

presently, "there is to be at Montreal at the date named in these papers a meeting of the directors of the Hudson Bay Company of England. There will be big men there—the biggest their country can produce; leaders of the Hudson Bay Company, many public men even of England. It is rumored that a brother of Lord Aberdeen, of the British Ministry, will attend. Do you begin to understand?".

Ah, did I not? Here, then, was further weaving of those complex plots which at that time hedged in all our history as a republic. Now I guessed the virtue of our knowing somewhat of England's secret plans, as she surely did of ours. I began to feel behind me the impulse of John Calhoun's swift energy.

"It is Oregon!" I exclaimed at last.

Doctor Ward nodded. "Very possibly. It has seemed to Mr. Calhoun very likely that we may hear something of great importance regarding the far Northwest. A missed cog now may cost this country a thousand miles of territory, a hundred years of history."

Doctor Ward continued: "England, as you know," said he, "is the enemy of this country as much to-day as ever. She claims she wishes Texas to remain free. She forgets her own record—forgets the burning cities of Rohilkhand, the imprisoned princesses of Oudh! Might is her right. She wants

Texas as a focus of contention, a rallying point of sectionalism. If she divides us, she conquers us. That is all. She wants the chance for the extension of her own hold on this continent, which she will push as far and fast as she dare. She must have cotton. She would like land as well."

"That means also Oregon?"

He nodded. "Always with the Texas question comes the Oregon question. Mr. Calhoun is none too friendly to Mr. Polk, and yet he knows that through Jackson's influence with the Southern democracy Polk has an excellent chance for the next nomination for the presidency. God knows what folly will come then. But sometime, one way or another, the joint occupancy of England and the United States in the Oregon country must end. It has been a waiting game thus far, as you know; but never think that England has been idle. This meeting in Montreal will prove that to you."

In spite of myself, I began to feel the stimulus of a thought like this. It was my salvation as a man. I began to set aside myself and my own troubles.

"You are therefore," he concluded, "to go to Montreal, and find your own way into that meeting of the directors of the Hudson Bay Company. There is a bare chance that in this intrigue Mexico will have an emissary on the ground as well. There is reason to suspect her hostility to all our plans of extension, southwest and northwest. Naturally, it is the card of Mexico to bring on war, or accept it if we urge; but only in case she has England as her ally. England will get her pay by taking Texas, and what is more, by taking California, which Mexico does not value. She owes England large sums now. That would leave England owner of the Pacific coast; for, once she gets California, she will fight us then for *all* of Oregon. It is your duty to learn all of these matters—who is there, what is done; and to do this without making known your own identity."

I sat for a moment in thought. "It is an honor," said I finally; "an honor so large that under it I feel small."

"Now," said Doctor Ward, placing a gnarled hand on my shoulder, "you begin to talk like a Marylander. It's a race, my boy, a race across this continent. There are two trails—one north and one mid-continent. On these paths two nations contend in the greatest Marathon of all the world. England or the United States—monarchy or republic— aristocracy or humanity? These are some of the things which hang on the issue of this contest. Take then your duty and your honor, humbly and faithfully."

"Good-by," he said, as we steamed into Baltimore station. I turned, and he was gone.

CHAPTER XIII

ON SECRET SERVICE

If the world was lost through woman, she alone can save it.—Louis de Beaufort.

IN the days of which I write, our civilization was, as I may say, so embryonic, that it is difficult for us now to realize the conditions which then obtained. We had great men in those days, and great deeds were done; but to-day, as one reflects upon life as it then was, it seems almost impossible that they and their deeds could have existed in a time so crude and immature.

The means of travel in its best form was at that time at least curious. We had several broken railway systems north and south, but there were not then more than five thousand miles of railway built in America. All things considered, I felt lucky when we reached New York less than twenty-four hours out from Washington.

From New York northward to Montreal one's journey involved a choice of routes. One might go up the Hudson River by steamer to Albany, and thence work up the Champlain Lake system, above which one might employ a short stretch of rails between St. John and La Prairie, on the banks of the St. Lawrence opposite Montreal. Or, one might go from Albany west by rail as far as Syracuse, up the Mohawk Valley, and so to Oswego, where on Lake Ontario one might find steam or sailing craft.

Up the Hudson I took the crack steamer *Swallow,* the same which just one year later was sunk while trying to beat her own record of nine hours and two minutes from New York to Albany. She required eleven hours on our trip. Under conditions then obtaining, it took me a day and a half more to reach Lake Ontario. Here, happily, I picked up a frail steam craft, owned by an adventurous soul who was not unwilling to risk his life and that of others on the uncertain and ice-filled waters of Ontario. With him I negotiated to carry me with others down the St. Lawrence. At that time, of course, the Lachine Canal was not completed, and the Victoria Bridge was not even conceived as a possibility. One delay after another with broken machinery, lack of fuel, running ice and what not, required five days more of my time ere I reached Montreal.

I could not be called either officer or spy, yet none the less I did not care to be recognized here in the capacity of one over-curious. I made up my costume as that of an innocent free trader from the Western fur country of the states, and was able, from my earlier experiences, to answer any questions as to beaver at Fort Hall or buffalo on the Yellowstone or the Red. Thus I passed freely in and about all the public places of the town, and inspected with a certain personal interest all its points of interest, from the Gray Nunneries to the new cathedrals, the Place d'Armes, the Champ de Mars, the barracks, the vaunted brewery, the historic mountain, and the village lying between the arms of the two rivers—a point where history for a great country had been made, and where history for our own now was planning.

As I moved about from day to day, making such acquaintance as I could, I found in the air a feeling of excitement and expectation. The hotels, bad as they were, were packed. The public places were noisy, the private houses crowded. Gradually the town became half-military and half-savage. Persons of importance arrived by steamers up the river, on whose expanse lay boats which might be bound for England—or for some of England's colonies. The Government—not yet removed to Ottawa, later capital of Ontario—was then housed in the old Château Ramezay, built so long before for the French governor, Vaudreuil.

Here, I had reason to believe, was now established no less a personage than Sir George Simpson, Governor of the Hudson Bay Company. Rumor had

it at the time that Lord Aberdeen of England himself was at Montreal. That was not true, but I established without doubt that his brother really was
there, as well as Lieutenant William Peel of the
Navy, son of Sir Robert Peel, England's prime
minister. The latter, with his companion, Captain
Parke, was one time pointed out to me proudly by
my inn-keeper—two young gentlemen, clad in the
ultra fashion of their country, with very wide and
tall bell beavers, narrow trousers, and strange long
sack-coats unknown to us in the States—of little
shape or elegance, it seemed to me.

There was expectancy in the air, that was sure.
It was open secret enough in England, as well as in
Montreal and in Washington, that a small army of
American settlers had set out the foregoing summer
for the valley of the Columbia, some said under
leadership of the missionary Whitman. Britain was
this year awakening to the truth that these men had
gone thither for a purpose. Here now was a congress
of Great Britain's statesmen, leaders of Great Britain's greatest monopoly, the Hudson Bay Company, to weigh this act of the audacious American
Republic. I was not a week in Montreal before I
learned that my master's guess, or his information,
had been correct. The race was on for Oregon!

All these things, I say, I saw go on about me. Yet
in truth as to the inner workings of this I could gain

but little actual information. I saw England's ships, but it was not for me to know whether they were to turn Cape Hope or the Horn. I saw Canada's *voyageurs,* but they might be only on their annual journey, and might go no farther than their accustomed posts in the West. In French town and English town, among common soldiers, *voyageurs,* inn-keepers and merchants, I wandered for more than one day and felt myself still helpless.

That is to say, such was the case until there came to my aid that greatest of all allies, Chance.

CHAPTER XIV

THE OTHER WOMAN

The world is the book of women.—*Rousseau.*

I NEEDED not to be advised that presently there would be a meeting of some of the leading men of the Hudson Bay Company at the little gray stone, dormer-windowed building on Notre Dame Street. In this old building—in whose vaults at one time of emergency was stored the entire currency of the Canadian treasury—there still remained some government records, and now under the steep-pitched roof affairs were to be transacted somewhat larger than the dimensions of the building might have suggested. The keeper of my inn freely made me a list of those who would be present—a list embracing so many scores of prominent men whom he then swore to be in the city of Montreal that, had the old Château Ramezay afforded twice its room, they could not all have been accommodated. For myself, it was out of the question to gain admittance.

In those days all Montreal was iron-shuttered after nightfall, resembling a series of jails; and to-night it seemed doubly screened and guarded. None

the less, late in the evening, I allowed seeming accident to lead me in a certain direction. Passing as
often as I might up and down Notre Dame Street
without attracting attention, I saw more than one
figure in the semi-darkness enter the low château
door. Occasionally a tiny gleam showed at the
edge of a shutter or at the top of some little window
not fully screened. As to what went on within I
could only guess.

I passed the château, up and down, at different
times from nine o'clock until midnight. The streets
of Montreal at that time made brave pretense of
lighting by virtue of the new gas works; at certain
intervals flickering and wholly incompetent lights
serving to make the gloom more visible. None the
less, as I passed for the last time, I plainly saw a
shaft of light fall upon the half darkness from a
little side door. There emerged upon the street the
figure of a woman. I do not know what led me to
cast a second glance, for certainly my business was
not with ladies, any more than I would have supposed ladies had business there; but, victim of some
impulse of curiosity, I walked a step or two in the
same direction as that taken by the cloaked figure.

Careless as I endeavored to make my movements,
the veiled lady seemed to take suspicion or fright.
She quickened her steps. Accident favored me.
Even as she fled, she caught her skirt on some object

which lay hidden in the shadows and fell almost at full length. This I conceived to be opportunity warranting my approach. I raised my hat and assured her that her flight was needless.

She made no direct reply to me, but as she rose gave utterance to an expression of annoyance. *"Mon Dieu!"* I heard her say.

I stood for a moment trying to recall where I had heard this same voice! She turned her face in such a way that the light illuminated it. Then indeed surprise smote me.

"Madam Baroness," said I, laughing, "it is wholly impossible for you to be here, yet you are here! Never again will I say there is no such thing as chance, no such thing as fate, no such thing as a miracle!"

She looked at me one brief moment; then her courage returned.

"Ah, then, my idiot," she said, "since it is to be our fortune always to meet of dark nights and in impossible ways, give me your arm."

I laughed. "We may as well make treaty. If you run again, I shall only follow you."

"Then I am again your prisoner?"

"Madam, I again am yours!"

"At least, you improve!" said she. "Then come."

"Shall I not call a *calèche?*—the night is dark."

"No, no!" hurriedly.

We began a midnight course that took us quite across the old French quarter of Montreal. At last she turned into a small, dark street of modest one-story residences, iron-shuttered, dark and cheerless. Here she paused in front of a narrow iron gate.

"Madam," I said, "you represent to me one of the problems of my life. Why does your taste run to such quarters as these? This might be that same back street in Washington!"

She chuckled to herself, at length laughed aloud. "But wait! If you entered my abode once," she said, "why not again? Come."

Her hand was at the heavy knocker as she spoke. In a moment the door slowly opened, just as it had done that night before in Washington. My companion passed before me swiftly. As she entered I saw standing at the opening the same brown and wrinkled old dame who had served that night before in Washington!

For an instant the light dazzled my eyes, but, determined now to see this adventure through, I stepped within. Then, indeed, I found it difficult to stifle the exclamation of surprise which came to my lips. Believe it or not, as you like, we *were* again in Washington!

I say that I was confronted by the identical arrangement, the identical objects of furnishing, which had marked the luxurious boudoir of Helena von

Ritz in Washington! The tables were the same, the chairs, the mirrors, the consoles. On the mantel stood the same girandoles with glittering crystals. The pictures upon the walls, so far as I could remember their themes, did not deviate in any particular of detail or arrangement. The oval-backed chairs were duplicates of those I had seen that other night at midnight. Beyond these same amber satin curtains stood the tall bed with its canopy, as I could see; and here at the right was the same low Napoleon bed with its rolled ends. The figures of the carpets were the same, their deep-piled richness, soft under foot, the same. The flowered cups of the sconces were identical with those I had seen before. To my eye, even as it grew more studious, there appeared no divergence, no difference, between these apartments and those I had so singularly visited— and yet under circumstances so strangely akin to these—in the capital of my own country!

"You are good enough to admire my modest place," said a laughing voice at my shoulder. Then indeed I waked and looked about me, and saw that this, stranger than any mirage of the brain, was but a fact and must later be explained by the laborious processes of the feeble reason.

I turned to her then, pulling myself together as best I could. Yes, she too was the same, although in this case costumed somewhat differently. The wide ball gown of satin was gone, and in its place was a less pretentious robing of some darker silk. I remembered distinctly that the flowers upon the white satin gown I first had seen were pink roses. Here were flowers of the crocus, cunningly woven into the web of the gown itself. The slippers which I now saw peeping out as she passed were not of white satin, but better foot covering for the street. She cast over the back of a chair, as she had done that other evening, her light shoulder covering, a dark mantle, not of lace now, but of some thin cloth. Her jewels were gone, and the splendor of her dark hair was free of decoration. No pale blue fires shone at her white throat, and her hands were ringless. But the light, firm poise of her figure could not be changed; the mockery of her glance remained the same, half laughing and half wistful. The strong curve of her lips remained, and I recalled this arch of brow, the curve of neck and chin, the droop of the dark locks above her even forehead. Yes, it was she. It could be no one else.

She clapped her hands and laughed like a child as she turned to me. "Bravo!" she said. "My judgment, then, was quite correct."

"In regard to what?"

"Yourself!"

"Pardon me?"

"You do not show curiosity! You do not ask me

questions! Good! I think I shall ask you to wait.
I say to you frankly that I am alone here. It pleases
me to live—as pleases me! You are alone in Montreal. Why should we not please ourselves?"

In some way which I did not pause to analyze, I
felt perfectly sure that this strange woman could, if
she cared to do so, tell me some of the things I ought
to know. She might be here on some errand identical with my own. Calhoun had sent for her once
before. Whose agent was she now? I found chairs
for us both.

An instant later, summoned in what way I do not
know, the old serving-woman again reappeared.
"Wine, Threlka," said the baroness; "service for
two—you may use this little table. Monsieur," she
added, turning to me, "I am most happy to make
even some slight return for the very gracious en-
tertainment offered me that morning by Mr. Calhoun at his residence. Such a droll man! Oh,
la! la!"

"Are you his friend, Madam?" I asked bluntly.

"Why should I not be?"

I could frame neither offensive nor defensive art
with her. She mocked me.

In a few moments the weazened old woman was
back with cold fowl, wine, napery, silver.

"Will Monsieur carve?" At her nod the old
woman filled my glass, after my hostess had tasted

of her own. We had seated ourselves at the table as she spoke.

"Not so bad for a black midnight, eh?" she went on, "—in a strange town—and on a strange errand? And again let me express my approbation of your conduct."

"If it pleases you, 'tis more than I can say of it for myself," I began. "But why?"

"Because you ask no questions. You take things as they come. I did not expect you would come to Montreal."

"Then you know—but of course, I told you."

"Have you then no question?" she went on at last. Her glass stood half full; her wrists rested gently on the table edge, as she leaned back, looking at me with that on her face which he had needed to be wiser than myself, who could have read.

"May I, then?"

"Yes, now you may go on."

"I thank you. First, of course, for what reason do you carry the secrets of my government into the stronghold of another government? Are you the friend of America, or are you a spy upon America? ¡Are you my friend, or are we to be enemies to-night?"

She flung back her head and laughed delightedly. "That is a good beginning," she commented.

"You must, at a guess, have come up by way of

the lakes, and by batteau from La Prairie?" I ventured.

She nodded again. "Of course. I have been here six days."

"Indeed?—you have badly beaten me in our little race."

She flashed on me a sudden glance. "Why do you not ask me outright *why* I am here?"

"Well, then, I do! I do ask you that. I ask you how you got access to that meeting to-night—for I doubt not you were there?"

She gazed at me deliberately again, parting her red lips, again smiling at me. "What would you have given to have been there yourself?"

"All the treasures those vaults ever held."

"So much? What will you give me, then, to tell you what I know?"

"More than all that treasure, Madam. A place—"

"Ah! a 'place in the heart of a people!' I prefer a locality more restricted."

"In my own heart, then; yes, of course!"

She helped herself daintily to a portion of the white meat of the fowl. "Yes," she went on, as though speaking to herself, "on the whole, I rather like him. Yet what a fool! Ah, such a droll idiot!"

"How so, Madam?" I expostulated. "I thought I was doing very well."

"Yet you can not guess how to persuade me?"

"No; how could that be?"

"Always one gains by offering some equivalent, value for value—especially with women, Monsieur."

She went on as though to herself. "Come, now, I fancy him! He is handsome, he is discreet, he has courage, he is not usual, he is not curious; but ah, *mon Dieu,* what a fool!"

"Admit me to be a fool, Madam, since it is true; but tell me in my folly what equivalent I can offer one who has everything in the world—wealth, taste, culture, education, wit, learning, beauty?"

"Go on! Excellent!"

"Who has everything as against my nothing! *What* value, Madam?"

"Why, gentle idiot, to get an answer ask a question, always."

"I have asked it."

"But you can not guess that *I* might ask one? So, then, one answer for another, we might do—what you Americans call some business—eh? Will you answer *my* question?"

"Ask it, then."

"*Were you married*—that other night?"

So, then, she was woman after all, and curious! Her sudden speech came like a stab; but fortunately my dull nerves had not had time to change my face before a thought flashed into my mind. Could I not make merchandise of my sorrow? I pulled myself into control and looked her fair in the face.

"Madam," I said, "look at my face and read your own answer."

She looked, searching me, while every nerve of me tingled; but at last she shook her head. "No," she sighed. "I can not yet say." She did not see the sweat starting on my forehead.

I raised my kerchief over my head. "A truce, then, Madam! Let us leave the one question against the other for a time."

"Excellent! I shall get my answer first, in that case, and for nothing."

"How so?"

"I shall only watch you. As we are here now, I were a fool, worse than you, if I could not tell whether or not you are married. None the less, I commend you, I admire you, because you do not tell me. If you are *not,* you are disappointed. If you *are,* you are eager!"

"I am in any case delighted that I can interest Madam."

"Ah, but you do! I have not been interested, for so long! Ah, the great heavens, how fat was Mr. Pakenham, how thin was Mr. Calhoun! But you— come, Monsieur, the night is long. Tell me of yourself. I have never before known a savage."

"Value for value only, Madam! Will you tell me in turn of yourself?"

"All?" She looked at me curiously.

"Only so much as Madam wishes."

I saw her dark eyes study me once more. At last she spoke again. "At least," she said, "it would be rather vulgar if I did not explain some of the things which become your right to know when I ask you to come into this home, as into my other home in Washington."

"In Heaven's name, how many of these homes have you, then? Are they all alike?"

"Five only, now," she replied, in the most matter-of-fact manner in the world, "and, of course, all quite alike."

"Where else?"

"In Paris, in Vienna, in London," she answered. "You see this one, you see them all. 'Tis far cooler in Montreal than in Washington in the summer time. Do you not approve?"

"The arrangement could not be surpassed."

"Thank you. So I have thought. The mere charm of difference does not appeal to me. Certain things my judgment approves. They serve, they suffice. This little scheme it has pleased me to reproduce in some of the capitals of the world. It is at least as well chosen as the taste of the Prince of Orleans, son of Louis Philippe, could advise."

This with no change of expression. I drew a long breath.

She went on as though I had spoken. "My friend," she said, "do not despise me too early. There is abundant time. Before you judge, let the testimony be heard. I love men who can keep their own tongues and their own hands to themselves."

"I am not your judge, Madam, but it will be long before I shall think a harsh thought of you. Tell me what a woman may. Do not tell me what a secret agent may *not*. I ask no promises and make none. You are very beautiful. You have wealth. I call you 'Madam.' You are married?"

"I was married at fifteen."

"At fifteen! And your husband died?"

"He disappeared."

"Your own country was Austria?"

"Call me anything but Austrian! I left my country because I saw there only oppression and lack of hope. No, I am Hungarian."

"That I could have guessed. They say the most beautiful women of the world come from that country."

"Thank you. Is that all?"

"I should guess then perhaps you went to Paris?"

"Of course," she said, "of course! of course! In time reasons existed why I should not return to my home. I had some little fortune, some singular ex-

periences, some ambitions of my own. What I did,
I did. At least, I saw the best and worst of Europe."

She raised a hand as though to brush something
from before her face. "Allow me to give you wine.
Well, then, Monsieur knows that when I left Paris I
felt that part of my studies were complete. I had
seen a little more of government, a little more of
humanity, a little more of life, a little more of men.
It was not men but mankind that I studied most. I
had seen much of injustice and hopelessness and despair. These made the fate of mankind—in that
world."

"I have heard vaguely of some such things,
Madam," I said. "I know that in Europe they have
still the fight which we sought to settle when we left
that country for this one."

She nodded. "So then, at last," she went on,
"still young, having learned something and having
now those means of carrying on my studies which I
required, I came to this last of the countries, America, where, if anywhere, hope for mankind remains.
Washington has impressed me more than any capital
of the world."

"How long have you been in Washington?" I
asked.

"Now you begin to question—now you show at
last curiosity! Well, then, I shall answer. For

THE OTHER WOMAN 147

more than one year, perhaps more than two, perhaps more than three!"

"Impossible!" I shook my head. "A woman like you could not be concealed—not if she owned a hundred hidden places such as this."

"Oh, I was known," she said. "You have heard of me, you knew of me?"

I still shook my head. "No," said I, "I have been far in the West for several years, and have come to Washington but rarely. Bear me out, I had not been there my third day before I found you!"

We sat silent for some moments, fixedly regarding each other. I have said that a more beautiful face than hers I had never seen. There sat upon it now many things—youth, eagerness, ambition, a certain defiance; but, above all, a pleading pathos! I could not find it in my heart, eager as I was, to question her further. Apparently she valued this reticence.

"You condemn me?" she asked at length. "Because I live alone, because quiet rumor wags a tongue, you will judge me by your own creed and not by mine?"

I hesitated before I answered, and deliberated. "Madam, I have already told you that I would not. I say once more that I accredit you with living up to your own creed. whatever that may have been."

She drew a long breath in turn. "Monsieur, you have done yourself no ill turn in that."

"It was rumored in diplomatic circles, of course, that you were in touch with the ministry of England," I ventured. "I myself saw that much."

"Naturally. Of Mexico also! At least, as you saw in our little carriage race, Mexico was desirous enough to establish some sort of communication with my humble self!"

"Calhoun was right!" I exclaimed. "He was entirely right, Madam, in insisting that I should bring you to him that morning, whether or not you wished to go."

"Whim fits with whim sometimes. 'Twas his whim to see me, mine to go."

"I wonder what the Queen of Sheba would have said had Solomon met her thus!"

She chuckled at the memory. "You see, when you left me at Mr. Calhoun's door in care of the Grand Vizier James, I wondered somewhat at this strange country of America. The *entresol* was dim and the Grand Vizier was slow with candles. I half fell into the room on the right. There was Mr. Calhoun bolt upright in his chair, both hands spread out on the arms. As you promised, he wore a red nightcap and long gown of wool. He was asleep, and ah! how weary he seemed. Never have I seen a face so sad as his, asleep. He was gray and thin, his hair was gray and thin, his eyes were sunken, the veins were corded at his temples, his hands were transparent. He was, as you promised me, old. Yet when I saw him I did not smile. He heard me stir as I would have withdrawn, and when he arose to his feet he was wide-awake. Monsieur, he is a great man; because, even so clad he made no more apology than you do, showed no more curiosity; and he welcomed me quite as a gentleman unashamed—as a king, if you please."

"How did he receive you, Madam?" I asked. "I never knew."

"Why, took my hand in both his, and bowed as though I indeed were queen, he a king."

"Then you got on well?"

"Truly; for he was wiser than his agent, Monsieur. He found answers by asking questions."

"Ah, you were kinder to him than to me?"

"Naturally."

"For instance, he asked—"

"What had been my ball gown that night—who was there—how I enjoyed myself! In a moment we were talking as though we had been friends for years. The Grand Vizier brought in two mugs of cider, in each a toasted apple. Monsieur, I have not seen diplomacy such as this. Naturally, I was help-less."

"Did he perhaps ask how you were induced to

come at so impossible a time? My own vanity, naturally, leads me to ask so much as that."

"No, Mr. Calhoun confined himself to the essentials! Even had he asked me I could not have replied, because I do not know, save that it was to me a whim. But at least we talked, over our cider and toasted apples."

"You told him somewhat of yourself?"

"He did not allow me to do that, Monsieur."

"But he told you somewhat of this country?"

"Ah, yes, yes! So then I saw what held him up in his work, what kept him alive. I saw something I have not often seen—a purpose, a principle, in a public man. His love for his own land touched even me, how or why I scarcely know. Yes, we spoke of the poor, the oppressed, of the weary and the heavy laden."

"Did he ask you what you knew of Mexico and England?"

"Rather what I knew of the poor in Europe. I told him some things I knew of that hopeless land, that priest-ridden, king-ridden country—my own land. Then he went on to tell me of America and its hope of a free democracy of the people. Believe me, I listened to Mr. Calhoun. Never mind what we said of Mr. Van Zandt and Sir Richard Pakenham. At least, as you know, I paid off a little score with Sir Richard that next morning. What was strangest to me was the fact that I forgot Mr. Calhoun's attire, forgot the strangeness of my errand thither. It was as though only our minds talked, one with the other. I was sorry when at last came the Grand Vizier James to take Mr. Calhoun's order for his own carriage, that brought me home—my second and more peaceful arrival there that night. The last I saw of Mr. Calhoun was with the Grand Vizier James putting a cloak about him and leading him by force from his study to his bed, as I presume. As for me, I slept no more that night. Monsieur, I admit that I saw the purpose of a great man. Yes; and of a great country."

"Then I did not fail as messenger, after all! You told Mr. Calhoun what he desired to know?"

"In part at least. But come now, was I not bound in some sort of honor to my great and good friend, Sir Richard? Was it not treachery enough to rebuke him for his attentions to the Doña Lucrezia?"

"But you promised to tell Mr. Calhoun more at a later time?"

"On certain conditions I did," she assented.

"I do not know that I may ask those?"

"You would be surprised if I told you the truth? What I required of Mr. Calhoun was permission and aid still further to study his extraordinary country, its extraordinary ways, its extraordinary ignorance of itself. I have told you that I needed to travel, to study, to observe mankind—and those governments invented or tolerated by mankind."

"Since then, Madam," I concluded, stepping to assist her with her chair, as she signified her completion of our repast, "since you do not feel now inclined to be specific, I feel that I ought to make my adieux, for the time at least. It grows late. I shall remember this little evening all my life. I own my defeat. I do not know why you are here, or for whom."

"At what hotel do you stop?"

"The little place of Jacques Bertillon, a square or so beyond the Place d'Armes."

"In that case," said she, "believe me, it would be more discreet for you to remain unseen in Montreal. No matter which flag is mine, I may say that much for a friend and comrade in the service."

"But what else?"

She looked about her. "Be my guest to-night!" she said suddenly. "There is danger—"

"For me?" I laughed. "At my hotel? On the streets?"

"No, for me."

"Where?"

"Here."

"And of what, Madam?"

"Of a man; for the first time I am afraid, in spite of all."

I looked at her straight. "Are you not afraid of *me?*" I asked.

She looked at me fairly, her color coming. "With the fear which draws a woman to a man," she said.

"Whereas, mine is the fear which causes a man to flee from himself!"

"But you will remain for my protection? I should feel safer. Besides, in that case I should know the answer."

"How do you mean?"

"I should know whether or not you were married!"

CHAPTER XV

WITH MADAM THE BARONESS

It is not for good women that men have fought battles, given their lives and staked their souls.—Mrs. W. K. Clifford.

"BUT, Madam—" I began.

She answered me in her own way. "Monsieur hesitates—he is lost!" she said. "But see, I am weary. I have been much engaged to-day. I have made it my plan never to fatigue myself. It is my hour now for my bath, my exercise, my bed, if you please. I fear I must bid you good night, one way or the other. You will be welcome here none the less, if you care to remain. I trust you did not find our little repast to-night unpleasing? Believe me, our breakfast shall be as good. Threlka is expert in omelets, and our coffee is such as perhaps you may not find general in these provinces."

Was there the slightest mocking sneer in her words? Did she despise me as a faint-heart? I could not tell, but did not like the thought.

"Believe me, Madam," I answered hotly, "you have courage, at least. Let me match it. Nor do I

154

deny that this asks courage on my part too. If you please, in these circumstances, *I shall remain.*"

"You are armed?" she asked simply.

I inserted a finger in each waistcoat pocket and showed her the butts of two derringers; and at the back of my neck—to her smiling amusement at our heathen fashion—I displayed just the tip of the haft of a short bowie-knife, which went into a leather case under the collar of my coat. And again I drew around the belt which I wore so that she could see the barrel of a good pistol, which had been suspended under cover of the bell skirt of my coat.

She laughed. I saw that she was not unused to weapons. I should have guessed her the daughter of a soldier or acquainted with arms in some way. "Of course," she said, "there might be need of these, although I think not. And in any case, if trouble can be deferred until to-morrow, why concern oneself over it? You interest me. I begin yet more to approve of you."

"Then, as to that breakfast *à la fourchette* with Madam; if I remain, will you agree to tell me what is your business here?"

She laughed at me gaily. "I might,'" she said, "provided that meantime I had learned whether or not you were married that night."

I do not profess that I read all that was in her face as she stepped back toward the satin curtains and swept me the most graceful curtsey I had ever seen in all my life. I felt like reaching out a hand to restrain her. I felt like following her. She was assuredly bewildering, assuredly as puzzling as she was fascinating. I only felt that she was mocking me. Ah, she was a woman!

I felt something swiftly flame within me. There arose about me that net of amber-hued perfume, soft, enthralling, difficult of evasion. . . . Then I recalled my mission; and I remembered what Mr. Calhoun and Doctor Ward had said. I was not a man; I was a government agent. She was not a woman; she was my opponent. Yes, but then—

Slowly I turned to the opposite side of this long central room. There were curtains here also. I drew them, but as I did so I glanced back. Again, as on that earlier night, I saw her face framed in the amber folds—a face laughing, mocking. With an exclamation of discontent, I threw down my heavy pistol on the floor, cast my coat across the foot of the bed to prevent the delicate covering from being soiled by my boots, and so rested without further disrobing.

In the opposite apartment I could hear her moving about, humming to herself some air as unconcernedly as though no such being as myself existed in the world. I heard her presently accost her servant, who entered through some passage not visible

from the central apartments. Then without concealment there seemed to go forward the ordinary rou-
tine of madam's toilet for the evening.

"No, I think the pink one," I heard her say, "and
please—the bath, Threlka, just a trifle more warm."
She spoke in French, her ancient serving-woman, as
I took it, not understanding the English language.
They both spoke also in a tongue I did not know. I
heard the rattling of toilet articles, certain sighs of
content, faint splashings beyond. I could not escape
from all this. Then I imagined that perhaps madam
was having her heavy locks combed by the serving-
woman. In spite of myself, I pictured her thus, even
more beautiful than before.

For a long time I concluded that my presence was
to be dismissed as a thing which was of no importance, or which was to be regarded as not having
happened. At length, however, after what seemed
at least half an hour of these mysterious ceremonies,
I heard certain sighings, long breaths, as though
madam were taking calisthenic movements, some
gymnastic training—I knew not what. She paused
for breath, apparently very well content with herself.

Shame on me! I fancied perhaps she stood before a mirror. Shame on me again! I fancied she
sat, glowing, beautiful, at the edge of the amber
couch.

At last she called out to me: "Monsieur!"

I was at my own curtains at once, but hers remained tight folded, although I heard her voice close behind them. *"Eh bien?"* I answered.

"It is nothing, except I would say that if Monsieur feels especially grave and reverent, he will find a very comfortable *prie-dieu* at the foot of the bed."

"I thank you," I replied, gravely as I could.

"And there is a very excellent rosary and crucifix on the table just beyond!"

"I thank you," I replied, steadily as I could.

"And there is an English Book of Common Prayer upon the stand not far from the head of the bed, upon this side!"

"A thousand thanks, my very good friend."

I heard a smothered laugh beyond the amber curtains. Presently she spoke again, yawning, as I fancied, rather contentedly.

"A la bonne heure, Monsieur!"

"A la bonne heure, Madame!"

CHAPTER XVI

DÉJEÛNER À LA FOURCHETTE

Woman is a creature between man and the angels.
—*Honoré de Balzac.*

A GOVERNMENT agent, it seems, may also in part be little more than a man, after all. In these singular surroundings I found myself not wholly tranquil. . . . At last toward morning, I must have slept. It was some time after daybreak when I felt a hand upon my shoulder as I lay still partly clad. Awakened suddenly, I arose and almost overthrew old Threlka, who stood regarding me with no expression whatever upon her brown and wrinkled countenance. She did no more than point the way to a door, where presently I found a bath-room, and so refreshed myself and made the best toilet possible under the circumstances.

My hostess I found awaiting me in the central room of the apartments. She was clad now in a girdled peignoir of rich rose-color, the sleeves, wide and full, falling back from her round arms. Her dark hair was coiled and piled high on her head this morning, regardless of current mode, and confined in a heavy twist by a tall golden comb; so that her white neck was left uncovered. She wore no jewelry, and as she stood, simple and free from any trickery of the coquette, I thought that few women ever were more fair. That infinite witchery not given to many women was hers, yet dignity as well. She was, I swear, *grande dame,* though young and beautiful as a goddess. Her brow was thoughtful now, her air more demure. Faint blue shadows lay beneath her eyes. A certain hauteur, it seemed to me, was visible in her mien, yet she was the soul of graciousness, and, I must admit, as charming a hostess as ever invited one to usual or unusual repast.

The little table in the center of the room was already spread. Madam filled my cup from the steaming urn with not the slightest awkwardness, as she nodded for me to be seated. We looked at each other, and, as I may swear, we both broke into saving laughter.

So we sat, easier now, as I admit, and, with small concern for the affairs of the world outside at the time, discussed the very excellent omelet, which certainly did not allow the reputation of Threlka to suffer; the delicately grilled bones, the crisp toasted rye bread, the firm yellow butter, the pungent early cress, which made up a meal sufficiently dainty even for her who presided over it.

Even that pitiless light of early morning, the merciless cross-light of opposing windows, was gentle with her. Yes, she was young! Moreover, she ate as a person of breeding, and seemed thoroughbred in all ways, if one might use a term so hackneyed. Rank and breeding had been hers; she needed not to claim them, for they told their own story. I wondered what extraordinary history of hers remained untold —what history of hers and mine and of others she might yet assist in making!

"I was saying," she remarked presently, "that I would not have you think that I do not appreciate the suffering in which you were plunged by the haste you found necessary in the wedding of your *jeune fille.*"

But I was on my guard. "At least, I may thank you for your sympathy, Madam!" I replied.

"Yet in time," she went on, gone reflective the next instant, "you will see how very unimportant is all this turmoil of love and marriage."

"Indeed, there is, as you say, something of a turmoil regarding them in our institutions as they are at present formed."

"Because the average of humanity thinks so little. Most of us judge life from its emotions. We do not search the depths."

"If I could oblige Madam by abolishing society

and home and humanity, I should be very glad— because, of course, that is what Madam means!"

"At any cost," she mused, "that torture of life must be passed on to coming generations for their unhappiness, their grief, their misery. I presume it was necessary that there should be this plan of the general blindness and intensity of passion."

"Yes, if, indeed, it be not the most important thing in the world for us to marry, at least it is important that we should think so. Madam is philosopher this morning," I said, smiling.

She hardly heard me. "To continue the crucifixion of the soul, to continue the misapprehensions, the debasings of contact with human life—yes, I suppose one must pay all that for the sake of the gaining of a purpose. Yet there are those who would endure much for the sake of principle, Monsieur. Some such souls are born, do you not think?"

"Yes, Sphinx souls, extraordinary, impossible for the average of us to understand."

"That torch of *life!*" she mused. "See! It was only *that* which you were so eager to pass on to another generation! That was why you were so mad to hasten to the side of that woman. Whereas," she mused still, "it were so much grander and so much nobler to pass on the torch of a *principle* as well!"

"I do not understand."

"The general business of offspring goes on unceasingly in all the nations," she resumed frankly. "There will be children, whether or not you and I ever find some one wherewith to mate in the compromise which folk call wedlock. But *principles*— ah! my friend, who is to give those to others who follow us? What rare and splendid wedlock brings forth *that* manner of offspring?"

"Madam, in the circumstances," said I, "I should be happy to serve you more omelet."

She shook her head as though endeavoring to dismiss something from her mind.

"Do not philosophize with me," I said. "I am already distracted by the puzzle you offer to me. You are so young and beautiful, so fair in your judgment, so kind—"

"In turn, I ask you not to follow that," she remarked coldly. "Let us talk of what you call, I think, business."

"Nothing could please me more. I have slept little, pondering on this that I do call business. To begin with, then, you were there at the Château Ramezay last night. I would have given all I had to have been there for an hour."

"There are certain advantages a woman may have."

"But you were there? You know what went forward?"

"Certainly."

"Did they know you were present?"

"Monsieur is somewhat importunate!"

She looked me now directly in the eye, studying me mercilessly, with a scrutiny whose like I should not care often to undergo.

"I should be glad if it were possible to answer you," she said at last enigmatically; "but I have faith to keep with—others—with you—with—myself."

Now my own eagerness ran away with me; I became almost rude. "Madam," I exclaimed, "why beat about the bush? I do not care to deceive you, and you must not deceive me. Why should we not be friends in every way, and fair ones?"

"You do not know what you are saying," she said simply.

"Are you then an enemy of my country?" I demanded. "If I thought you were here to prove traitress to my country, you should never leave this room except with me. You shall not leave it now until you have told me what you are, why you are here, what you plan to do!"

She showed no fear. She only made a pretty little gesture at the dishes between us. "At my own table!" she pouted.

Again our eyes met directly and again hers did not lower. She looked at me calmly. I was no match for her.

"My dear lady," I began again, "my relation to the affairs of the American Republic is a very humble one. I am no minister of state, and I know you deal with ministers direct. How, then, shall I gain your friendship for my country? You are dangerous to have for an enemy. Are you too high-priced to have for a friend—for a friend to our Union—a friend of the principle of democracy? Come now, you enjoy large questions. Tell me, what does this council mean regarding Oregon? Is it true that England plans now to concentrate all her traders, all her troops, and force them west up the Saskatchewan and into Oregon this coming season? Come, now, Madam, is it to be war?"

Her curved lips broke into a smile that showed again her small white teeth.

"Were you, then, married?" she said.

I only went on, impatient. "Any moment may mean everything to us. I should not ask these questions if I did not know that you were close to Mr. Calhoun."

She looked me square in the eye and nodded her head slowly. "I may say this much, Monsieur, that it has pleased me to gain a little further information."

"You will give my government that information?'"

"Why should I?"

"Yet you spoke of others who might come here. What others? Who are they? The representatives of Mexico? Some attaché of the British Embassy at Washington? Some minister from England itself, sent here direct?"

She smiled at me again. "I told you not to go back to your hotel, did I not?"

I got no further with her, it seemed.

"You interest me sometimes," she went on slowly, at last, "yet you seem to have so little brain! Now, in your employment, I should think that brain would be somewhat useful at times."

"I do not deny that suggestion, Madam."

"But you are unable to analyze. Thus, in the matter of yourself. I suppose if you were told of it, you would only say that you forgot to look in the toe of the slipper you had."

"Thus far, Baroness," I said soberly, "I have asked no special privilege, at least. Now, if it affords you any pleasure, I *beg* you, I *implore* you, to tell me what you mean!"

"Did you credit the attaché of Mexico with being nothing more than a drunken rowdy, to follow me across town with a little shoe in his carriage?"

"But you said he was in wine."

"True. But would that be a reason? Continually you show your lack of brain in accepting as conclusive results which could not possibly have occurred.

Granted he was in wine, *granted* he followed me, *granted* he had my shoe in his possession—what then? Does it follow that at the ball at the White House he could have removed that shoe? Does Monsieur think that I, too, was in wine?"

"I agree that I have no brain! I can not guess what you mean. I can only beg once more that you explain."

"Now listen. In your most youthful and charming innocence I presume you do not know much of the capabilities for concealment offered by a lady's apparel! Now, suppose I had a message—where do you think I could hide it; granted, of course, the conditions obtaining at a ball in the White House?"

"Then you did have a message? It came to you there, at that time?"

She nodded. "Certainly. Mr. Van Zandt had almost no other opportunity to meet me or get word to me."

"*Van Zandt!* Madam, are you indeed in the camp of *all* these different interests? So, what Pakenham said was true! Van Zandt is the attaché of Texas. Van Zandt is pleading with Mr. Calhoun that he shall take up the secretaryship. Van Zandt promises us the friendship of Texas if we will stand out for the annexation of Texas. Van Zandt promises us every effort in his power against England. Van Zandt promises us the sternest of fronts against treacherous Mexico. Van Zandt is known to be interested in this fair Doña Lucrezia, just as Polk is. Now, then, comes Van Zandt with his secret message slipped into the hand of Madam at the Ambassador's ball—Madam, *the friend of England!* The attaché of Mexico is curious—furious—to know what Texas is saying to England! And that message must be concealed! And Madam conceals it in—"

She smiled at me brilliantly. "You come on," she said. "Should your head be opened and analyzed, yes, I think a trace of brain might be discovered by good chemistry."

I resumed impatiently. "You put his message in your slipper?"

She nodded. "Yes," she said, "in the toe of it. There was barely chance to do that. You see, our skirts are full and wide; there are curtains in the East Room; there was wine by this time; there was music; so I effected that much. But when you took the slipper, you took Van Zandt's note! You had it. It was true, what I told Pakenham before the president—I did *not* then have that note! *You* had it. At least, I *thought* you had it, till I found it crumpled on the table the next day! It must have fallen there from the shoe when we made our little exchange that night Ah, you hurried me. I scarce knew whether I was clad or shod, until the next afternoon—after I left you at the White House grounds. So you hastily departed—to your wedding?"

"So small a shoe could not have held an extended epistle, Madam," I said, ignoring her question.

"No, but the little roll of paper caused me anguish. After I had danced I was on the point of fainting. I hastened to the cover of the nearest curtain, where I might not be noticed. Señor Yturrio of Mexico was somewhat vigilant. He wished to know what Texas planned with England. He has long made love to me—by threats, and jewels. As I stood behind the curtain I saw his face, I fled; but one shoe—the empty one—was not well fastened, and it fell. I could not walk. I reached down, removed the other shoe with its note, hid it in my handkerchief—thank Providence for the fashion of so much lace—and so, not in wine, Monsieur, as you may believe, and somewhat anxious, as you may also believe, expecting to hear at once of an encounter between Van Zandt and the Mexican minister, Señor Almonte, or his attaché Yturrio, or between one of them and some one else, I made my adieux—I will warrant the only woman in her stocking feet who bowed for Mr. Tyler at the ball that night!"

"Yes, so far as I know, Madam, you are the only lady who ever left the East Room precisely so clad. And so you got into your own carriage—alone—after a while? And so, when you were there you put

on the shoe which was left? And so Yturrio of
Mexico got the other one—and found nothing in it!
And so, he wanted this one!"

"You come on," she said. "You have something
more than a trace of brain."

"And that other shoe, which *I* got that night?"

Without a word she smoothed out a bit of paper
which she removed from a near-by desk, and handed
it to me. *"This* was in yours! As I said, in my confusion I supposed you had it. You said I should go
in a sack. I suppose I did! I suppose I lost my
head, somewhere! But certainly I thought you had
found the note and given it to Mr. Calhoun; else I
should have driven harder terms with him! I would
drive harder terms with you, now, were I not in such
haste to learn the answer to my question! Tell me,
were you married?"

"Is that answer worth more than Van Zandt?" I
smiled.

"Yes," she answered, also smiling.

I spread the page upon the cloth before me; my
eyes raced down the lines. I did not make further
reply to her.

"Madam," went on the communication, "say to
your august friend Sir Richard that we have
reached the end of our endurance of these late de-
lays. The promises of the United States mean nothing. We can trust neither Whig nor Democrat any

longer. There is no one party in power, nor will there be. There are two sections in America and there is no nation, and Texas knows not where to go. We have offered to Mr. Tyler to join the Union if the Union will allow us to join. We intend to reserve our own lands and reserve the right to organize later into four or more states, if our people shall so desire. But as a great state we will join the Union if the Union will accept us. That must be seen.

"England now beseeches us not to enter the Union, but to stand apart, either for independence or for alliance with Mexico and England. The proposition has been made to us to divide into two governments, one free and one slave. England has proposed to us to advance us moneys to pay all our debts if we will agree to this. Settled by bold men from our mother country, the republic, Texas has been averse to this. But now our own mother repudiates us, not once but many times. We get no decision. This then, dear Madam, is from Texas to England by your hand, and we know you will carry it safe and secret. We shall accept this proposal of England, and avail ourselves of the richness of her generosity.

"If within thirty days action is not taken in Washington for the annexation of Texas, Texas will never in the history of the world be one of the United States. Moreover, if the United States shall lose

Texas, also they lose Oregon, and all of Oregon. Carry this news—I am persuaded that it will be welcome—to that gentleman whose ear I know you have; and believe me always, my dear Madam, with respect and admiration, yours, for the State of Texas, Van Zandt."

I drew a deep breath as I saw this proof of double play on the part of this representative of the republic of the Southwest. "They are traitors!" I exclaimed. "But there must be action—something must be done at once. I must not wait; I must go! I must take this, at least, to Mr. Calhoun."

She laughed now, joyously clapping her white hands together. "Good!" she said. "You are a man, after all. You may yet grow brain."

"Have I been fair with you thus far?" she asked at length.

"More than fair. I could not have asked this of you. In an hour I have learned the news of years. But will you not also tell me what is the news from Château Ramezay? Then, indeed, I could go home feeling I had done very much for my chief."

"Monsieur, I can not do so. You will not tell me that other news."

"Of what?"

"Of your nuptials!"

"Madam, I can not do so. But for you, much as I owe you, I would like to wring your neck. I would like to take your arms in my hands and crush them, until—"

"Until what?" Her face was strange. I saw a hand raised to her throat.

"Until you told me about Oregon!" said I.

I saw her arms move—just one instant—her body incline. She gazed at me steadily, somberly. Then her hands fell.

"Ah, God! how I hate you both!' she said; "you and her. You *were* married, after all! Yes, it can be, it can be! A woman may love one man—even though he could give her only a bed of husks! And a man may love a woman, too—one woman! I had not known."

I could only gaze at her, now more in perplexity than ever. Alike her character and her moods were beyond me. What she was or had been I could not guess; only, whatever she was, she was not ordinary, that was sure, and was to be classified under no ordinary rule. Woman or secret agent she was, and in one or other identity she could be my friend or my powerful enemy, could aid my country powerfully if she had the whim; or damage it irreparably if she had the desire. But—yes—as I studied her that keen, tense, vital moment, she was woman!

A deep fire burned in her eyes, that was true; but on her face was—what? It was not rage, it was not passion, it was not chagrin. No, in truth and justice

I swear that what I then saw on her face was that same look I had noted once before, an expression of almost childish pathos, of longing, of appeal for something missed or gone, though much desired. No vanity could contemplate with pleasure a look like that on the face of a woman such as Helena von Ritz.

I fancied her unstrung by excitement, by the strain of her trying labor, by the loneliness of her life, uncertain, misunderstood, perhaps, as it was. I wondered if she could be more unhappy than I myself, if life could offer her less than it did to me. But I dared not prolong our masking, lest all should be unmasked.

"It is nothing!" she said at last, and laughed gaily as ever.

"Yes, Madam, it is nothing. I admit my defeat. I shall ask no more favors, expect no further information from you, for I have not earned it, and I can not pay. I will make no promise that I could not keep."

"Then we part even!"

"As enemies or friends?"

"I do not yet know. I can not think—for a long time. But I, too, am defeated."

"I do not understand how Madam can be defeated in anything."

"Ah, I am defeated only because I have won. I have your secret; you do not have mine. But I laid also another wager, with myself. I have lost it. Ceremony or not—and what does the ceremony value?—you *are* married. I had not known marriage to be possible, I had not known you—you savages. No—so much—I had not known."

"Monsieur, adieu!" she added swiftly.

I bent and kissed her hand. "Madam, *au revoir!*"

"No, *adieu!* Go!"

CHAPTER XVII

A HUNTER OF BUTTERFLIES

I love men, not because they are men, but because they are not women.—Queen Christina.

THERE was at that time in Montreal a sort of news room and public exchange, which made a place of general meeting. It was supplied with newspapers and the like, and kept up by subscriptions of the town merchants—a spacious room made out of the old Methodist chapel on St. Joseph Street. I knew this for a place of town gossip, and hoped I might hit upon something to aid me in my errand, which was no more than begun, it seemed. Entering the place shortly before noon, I made pretense of reading, all the while with an eye and an ear out for anything that might happen.

As I stared in pretense at the page before me, I fumbled idly in a pocket, with unthinking hand, and brought out to place before me on the table, an object of which at first I was unconscious—the little Indian blanket clasp. As it lay before me I felt seized of a sudden hatred for it, and let fall on it a heavy hand. As I did so, I heard a voice at my ear.

"*Mein Gott,* man, do not! You break it, surely."

I started at this. I had not heard any one approach. I discovered now that the speaker had taken a seat near me at the table, and could not fail to see this object which lay before me.

"I beg pardon," he said, in a broken speech which showed his foreign birth; "but it iss so beautiful; to break it iss wrong."

Something in his appearance and speech fixed my attention. He was a tall, bent man, perhaps sixty years of age, of gray hair and beard, with the glasses and the unmistakable air of the student. His stooped shoulders, his weakened eye, his thin, blue-veined hand, the iron-gray hair standing like a ruff above his forehead, marked him not as one acquainted with a wild life, but better fitted for other days and scenes.

I pushed the trinket along the table towards him.

" 'Tis of little value," I said, "and is always in the way when I would find anything in my pocket."

"But once some one hass made it; once it hass had value. Tell me where you get it?"

"North of the Platte, in our western territories," I said. "I once traded in that country."

"You are American?"

"Yes."

"So," he said thoughtfully. "So. A great country, a very great country. Me, I also live in it."

"Indeed?" I said. "In what part?"

"It iss five years since I cross the Rockies."

"You have crossed the Rockies? I envy you."

"You meesunderstand me. I live west of them for five years. I am now come east."

"All the more, then, I envy you! You have perhaps seen the Oregon country? That has always been my dream."

My eye must have kindled at that, for he smiled at me.

"You are like all Americans. They leave their own homes and make new governments, yess? Those men in Oregon haf made a new government for themselfs, and they tax those English traders to pay for a government which iss American!"

I studied him now closely. If he had indeed lived so long in the Oregon settlements, he knew far more about certain things than I did.

"News travels slowly over so great a distance," said I. "Of course I know nothing of these matters except that last year and the year before the missionaries have come east to ask us for more settlers to come out to Oregon. I presume they want their churches filled."

"But most their *farms!*" said the old man.

"You have been at Fort Vancouver?"

He nodded. "Also to Fort Colville, far north; also to what they call California, far south; and

again to what they may yet call Fort Victoria. I haf
seen many posts of the Hudson Bay Company."

I was afraid my eyes showed my interest; but he
went on.

"I haf been in the Columbia country, and in the
Willamette country, where most of your Americans
are settled. I know somewhat of California. Mr.
Howard, of the Hudson Bay Company, knows also
of this country of California. He said to those English gentlemans at our meeting last night that England should haf someting to offset California on the
west coast; because, though Mexico claims California, the Yankees really rule there, and will rule
there yet more. He iss right; but they laughed at
him."

"Oh, I think little will come of all this talk," I
said carelessly. "It is very far, out to Oregon." Yet
all the time my heart was leaping. So he had been
there, at that very meeting of which I could learn
nothing!

"You know not what you say. A thousand men
came into Oregon last year. It iss like one of the
great migrations of the peoples of Asia, of Europe.
I say to you, it iss a great epoch. There iss a folk-
movement such as we haf not seen since the days of
the Huns, the Goths, the Vandals, since the Cimri
movement. It iss an epoch, my friend! It iss fate
that iss in it."

"So, then, it is a great country?" I asked.

"It iss so great, these traders do not wish it known. They wish only that it may be savage; also that their posts and their harems may be undisturbed. That iss what they wish. These Scots go wild again, in the wilderness. They trade and they travel, but it iss not homes they build. Sir George Simpson wants steel traps and not ploughs west of the Rockies. That iss all!"

"They do not speak so of Doctor McLaughlin," I began tentatively.

"My friend, a great man, McLaughlin, believe me! But he iss not McKay; he iss not Simpson; he iss not Behrens; he iss not Colville; he iss not Douglas. And I say to you, as I learned last night—you see, they asked me also to tell what I knew of Oregon—I say to you that last night McLaughlin was deposed. He iss in charge no more—so soon as they can get word to him, he loses his place at Vancouver."

"After a lifetime in the service!" I commented.

"Yess, after a lifetime; and McLaughlin had brain and heart, too. If England would listen to him, she would learn sometings. He plants, he plows, he hass gardens and mills and houses and herds. Yess, if they let McLaughlin alone, they would haf a civilization on the Columbia, and not a fur-trading post. Then they could oppose your civilization there.

That iss what he preaches. Simpson preaches otherwise. Simpson loses Oregon to England, it may be."

"You know much about affairs out in Oregon," I
ventured again. "Now, I did not happen to be present at the little meeting last night."

"I heard it all," he remarked carelessly, "until I
went to sleep. I wass bored. I care not to hear of
the splendor of England!"

"Then you think there is a chance of trouble between our country and England, out there?"

He smiled. "It iss not a chance, but a certainty,"
he said. "Those settlers will not gif up. And England is planning to push them out!"

"We had not heard that!" I ventured.

"It wass only agreed last night. England will
march this summer seven hundred men up the Peace
River. In the fall they will be across the Rockies.
So! They can take boats easily down the streams to
Oregon. You ask if there will be troubles. I tell
you, yess."

"And which wins, my friend?" I feared he would
hear my heart thumping at this news.

"If you stop where you are, England wins. If
you keep on going over the mountains England shall
lose."

"What time can England make with her brigades,
west-bound, my friend?" I asked him casually. He
answered with gratifying scientific precision.

"From Edmonton to Fort Colville, west of the Rockies, it hass been done in six weeks and five days, by Sir George himself. From Fort Colville down it iss easy by boats. It takes the *voyageur* three months to cross, or four months. It would take troops twice that long, or more. For you in the States, you can go faster. And, ah! my friend, it iss worth the race, that Oregon. Believe me, it iss full of bugs—of new bugs; twelve new species I haf discovered and named. It iss sometings of honor, iss it not?"

"What you say interests me very much, sir," I said. "I am only an American trader, knocking around to see the world a little bit. You seem to have been engaged in some scientific pursuit in that country."

"Yess," he said. "Mein own government and mein own university, they send me to this country to do what hass not been done. I am insectologer. Shall I show you my bugs of Oregon? You shall see them, yess? Come with me to my hotel. You shall see many bugs, such as science hass not yet known."

I was willing enough to go with him; and true to his word he did show me such quantities of carefully prepared and classified insects as I had not dreamed our own country offered.

"Twelve new species!" he said, with pride. "Mein

own country will gif me honor for this. Five years
I spend. Now I go back home.

"I shall not tell you what nickname they gif me
in Oregon," he added, smiling; "but my real name
iss Wolfram von Rittenhofen. Berlin, it wass last
my home. Tell me, you go soon to Oregon?"

"That is very possible," I answered; and this time
at least I spoke the truth. "We are bound in opposite directions, but if you are sailing for Europe this
spring, you would save time and gain comfort by
starting from New York. It would give us great
pleasure if we could welcome so distinguished a scientist in Washington."

"No, I am not yet distinguished. Only shall I be
distinguished when I have shown my twelve new
species to mein own university."

"But it would give me pleasure also to show you
Washington. You should see also the government
of those backwoodsmen who are crowding out to
Oregon. Would you not like to travel with me in
America so far as that?"

He shook his head doubtfully. "Perhaps I make
mistake to come by the St. Lawrence? It would be
shorter to go by New York? Well, I haf no hurry. I
think it over, yess."

"But tell me, where did you get that leetle thing?"
he asked me again presently, taking up in his hand
the Indian clasp.

"I traded for it among the Crow Indians."

"You know what it iss, eh?"

"No, except that it is Indian made."

He scanned the round disks carefully. "Wait!" he exclaimed. "I show you sometings."

He reached for my pencil, drew toward him a piece of paper, taking from his pocket meantime a bit of string. Using the latter for a radius, he drew a circle on the piece of paper.

"Now look what I do!" he said, as I bent over curiously. "See, I draw a straight line through the circle. I divide it in half, so. I divide it in half once more, and make a point. Now I shorten my string, one-half. On each side of my long line I make me a half circle—only half way round on the opposite sides. So, now, what I got, eh? You understand him?"

I shook my head. He pointed in turn to the rude ornamentation in the shell clasp. I declare that then I could see a resemblance between the two designs!

"It is curious," I said.

"*Mein Gott!* it iss more than curious. It iss vonderful! I haf two *Amazonias* collected by my own hands, and twelve species of my own discovery, yess, in butterflies alone. That iss much? Listen. It iss notings! *Here* iss the *discovery!*"

He took a pace or two excitedly, and came back to thump with his forefinger on the little desk.

"What you see before you iss the sign of the Great Monad! It iss known in China, in Burmah, in all Asia, in all Japan. It iss sign of the great One, of the great Two. In your hand iss the Tah Gook—the Oriental symbol for life, for sex. Myself, I haf seen that in Sitka on Chinese brasses; I haf seen it on Japanese signs, in one land and in another land. But here you show it to me made by the hand of some ignorant aborigine of *this* continent! On *this* continent, where it did not originate and does not belong! It iss a discovery! Science shall hear of it. It iss the link of Asia to America. It brings me fame!"

He put his hand into a pocket, and drew it out half filled with gold pieces and with raw gold in the form of nuggets, as though he would offer exchange. I waved him back. "No," said I; "you are welcome to one of these disks, if you please. If you wish, I will take one little bit of these. But tell me, where did you find these pieces of raw gold?"

"Those? They are notings. I recollect me I found these one day up on the Rogue River, not far from my cabin. I am pursuing a most beautiful moth, such as I haf not in all my collection. So, I fall on a log; I skin me my leg. In the moss I find some bits of rock. I recollect me not where, but believe it wass somewhere there. But what I find now, here, by a stranger—it iss worth more than gold! My friend, I thank you, I embrace you! I am favored by fate to meet you.   Go with you to Washington?   Yess, yess, I go!"

CHAPTER XVIII

THE MISSING SLIPPER

There will always remain something to be said of woman as long as there is one on earth.—Bauflers.

MY NEW friend, I was glad to note, seemed not anxious to terminate our acquaintance, although in his amiable and childlike fashion he babbled of matters which to me seemed unimportant. He was eager to propound his views on the connection of the American tribes with the peoples of the Orient, whereas I was all for talking of the connection of England and the United States with Oregon. Thus we passed the luncheon hour at the hostelry of my friend Jacques Bertillon; after which I suggested a stroll about the town for a time, there being that upon my mind which left me ill disposed to remain idle. He agreed to my suggestion, a fact for which I soon was to feel thankful for more reasons than one.

Before we started upon our stroll, I asked him to step to my own room, where I had left my pipe. As we paused here for a moment, he noticed on the little commode a pair of pistols of American make, and, with a word of apology, took them up to examine them.

"You also are acquainted with these?" he asked politely.

"It is said that I am," I answered.

"Sometimes you need to be?" he said, smiling. There smote upon me, even as he spoke, the feeling that his remark was strangely true. My eye fell on the commode's top, casually. I saw that it now was bare. I recalled the strange warning of the baroness the evening previous. I was watched! My apartment had been entered in my absence. Property of ·mine had been taken.

My perturbation must have been discoverable in my face. "What iss it?" asked the old man. "You forget someting?"

"No," said I, stammering. "It is nothing."

He looked at me dubiously. "Well, then," I admitted; "I miss something from my commode here. Some one has taken it."

"It iss of value, perhaps?" he inquired politely.

"Well, no; not of intrinsic value. 'Twas only a ' slipper—of white satin, made by Braun, of Paris."

"*One* slipper? Of what use?—"

"It belonged to a lady—I was about to return it," I said; but I fear my face showed me none too calm. He broke out in a gentle laugh.

"So, then, we had here the stage setting," said he; "the pistols, the cause for pistols, sometimes, eh?"

"It is nothing—I could easily explain—"

"There iss not need, my young friend. Wass I not also young once? Yess, once wass I young." He laid down the pistols, and I placed them with my already considerable personal armament, which seemed to give him no concern.

"Each man studies for himself his own specialty," mused the old man. "You haf perhaps studied the species of woman. Once, also I."

I laughed, and shook my head.

"Many species are there," he went on; "many with wings of gold and blue and green, of unknown colors; creatures of air and sky. Haf I not seen them? But always that one species which we pursue, we do not find. Once in my life, in Oregon, I follow through the forest a smell of sweet fields of flowers coming to me. At last I find it—a wide field of flowers. It wass in summer time. Over the flowers were many, many butterflies. Some of them I knew; some of them I had. One great new one, such as I haf not seen, it wass there. It rested. 'I shall now make it mine,' I said. It iss fame to gif name first to this so noble a species. I would inclose it with mein little net. Like this, you see, I creep up to it. As I am about to put it gently in my net—not to harm it, or break it, or brush away the color of its wings—lo! like a puff of down, it rises and goes above my head. I reach for it; I miss. It rises still more; it flies; it disappears! So! I see it no more. It iss gone. *Stella Terræ* I name it—my Star of the Earth, that which I crave but do not always haf, eh? Believe me, my friend, yess, the study of the species hass interest. Once I wass young. Should I see that little shoe I think myself of the time when I wass young, and made studies—*Ach, Mein Gott!*—also of the species of woman! I, too, saw it fly from me, my *Stella Terræ!*"

We walked, my friend still musing and babbling, myself still anxious and uneasy. We turned out of narrow Notre Dame Street, and into St. Lawrence Main Street. As we strolled I noted without much interest the motley life about me, picturesque now with the activities of the advancing spring. Presently, however, my idle gaze was drawn to two young Englishmen whose bearing in some way gave me the impression that they belonged in official or military life, although they were in civilian garb.

Presently the two halted, and separated. The taller kept on to the east, to the old French town. At length I saw him joined, as though by appointment, by another gentleman, one whose appearance at once gave me reason for a second look. The severe air of the Canadian spring seemed not pleasing to him, and he wore his coat hunched up about his neck, as though he were better used to milder climes. He accosted my young Englishman, and without hesitation the two started off together. As they did so I gave an involuntary exclamation. The taller man I had seen once before, the shorter, very many times—in Washington!

"Yess," commented my old scientist calmly; "so strange! They go together."

"Ah, you know them!" I almost fell upon him.

"Yess—last night. The tall one iss Mr. Peel, a young Englishman; the other is Mexican, they said —Señor Yturrio, of Mexico. He spoke much. Me, I wass sleepy then. But also that other tall one we saw go back—that wass Captain Parke, also of the British Navy. His ship iss the war boat *Modesté*—a fine one. I see her often when I walk on the riffer front, there."

I turned to him and made some excuse, saying that presently I would join him again at the hotel. Dreamily as ever, he smiled and took his leave. For myself, I walked on rapidly after the two figures, then a block or so ahead of me.

I saw them turn into a street which was familiar to myself. They passed on, turning from time to time among the old houses of the French quarter. Presently they entered the short side street which I myself had seen for the first time the previous night. I pretended to busy myself with my pipe, as they turned in at the very gate which I knew, and knocked at the door which I had entered with my mysterious companion!

The door opened without delay; they both entered.

So, then, Helena von Ritz had other visitors! England and Mexico were indeed conferring here in Montreal. There were matters going forward here in which my government was concerned. That was evident. I was almost in touch with them. That also was evident. How, then, might I gain yet closer touch?

At the moment nothing better occurred to me than to return to my room and wait for a time. It would serve no purpose for me to disclose myself, either in or out of the apartments of the baroness, and it would not aid me to be seen idling about the neighborhood in a city where there was so much reason to suppose strangers were watched. I resolved to wait until the next morning, and to take my friend Von Rittenhofen with me. He need not know all that I knew, yet in case of any accident to myself or any sudden contretemps, he would serve both as a witness and as an excuse for disarming any suspicion which might be entertained regarding myself.

The next day he readily enough fell in with my suggestion of a morning stroll, and again we sallied forth, at about nine o'clock, having by that time finished a *déjeûner à la fourchette* with Jacques Bertil-

lon, which to my mind compared unfavorably with
one certain other I had shared.

A sense of uneasiness began to oppress me, I knew
not why, before I had gone half way down the little
street from the corner where we turned. It was
gloomy and dismal enough at the best, and on this
morning an unusual apathy seemed to sit upon it,
for few of the shutters were down, although the hour
was now mid-morning. Here and there a homely
habitant appeared, and bade us good morning; and
once in a while we saw the face of a good wife peer-
ing from the window. Thus we passed some dozen
houses or so, in a row, and paused opposite the little
gate. I saw that the shutters were closed, or at
least all but one or two, which were partly ajar.
Something said to me that it would be as well for me
to turn back.

I might as well have done so. We passed up the
little walk, and I raised the knocker at the door; but
even as it sounded I knew what would happen.
There came to me that curious feeling which one experiences when one knocks at the door of a house
which lacks human occupancy. Even more strongly
I had that strange feeling now, because this sound
was not merely that of unoccupied rooms—it came
from rooms empty and echoing!

I tried the door. It was not locked. I flung it
wide, and stepped within. At first I could not ad-

just my eyes to the dimness. Absolute silence reigned. I pushed open a shutter and looked about me. The rooms were not only unoccupied, but unfurnished! The walls and floors were utterly bare! Not a sign of human occupancy existed. I hastened out to the little walk, and looked up and down the street, to satisfy myself that I had made no mistake. No, this was the number—this was the place. Yesterday these rooms were fitted sumptuously as for a princess; now they were naked. Not a stick of the furniture existed, nor was there any trace either of haste or deliberation in this removal. What had been, simply was not; that was all.

Followed by my wondering companion, I made such inquiry as I could in the little neighborhood. I could learn nothing. No one knew anything of the occupant of these rooms. No one had heard any carts approach, nor had distinguished any sounds during the night.

"Sir," said I to my friend, at last; "I do not understand it. I have pursued, but it seems the butterfly has flown." So, both silent, myself morosely so, we turned and made our way back across the town.

Half an hour later we were on the docks at the river front, where we could look out over the varied shipping which lay there. My scientific friend

counted one vessel after another, and at last pointed
to a gap in the line.

"Yesterday I wass here," he said, "and I counted
all the ships and their names. The steamer *Modesté*
she lay there. Now she iss gone."

I pulled up suddenly. This was the ship which
carried Captain Parke and his friend Lieutenant
Peel, of the British Navy. The secret council at
Montreal was, therefore, apparently ended! There
would be an English land expedition, across Canada
to Oregon. Would there be also an expedition by
sea? At least my errand in Montreal, now finished,
had not been in vain, even though it ended in a mystery and a query. But ah! had I but been less
clumsy in that war of wits with a woman, what
might I have learned! Had she not been free to
mock me, what might I not have learned! She was
free to mock me, why? Because of Elisabeth. Was
it then true that faith and loyalty could purchase
alike faithlessness and—failure?

CHAPTER XIX

THE GENTLEMAN FROM TENNESSEE

Women distrust men too much in general, and not enough in particular.—Philibert Commerson.

NOW all the more was it necessary for me and my friend from Oregon to hasten on to Washington. I say nothing further of the arguments I employed with him, and nothing of our journey to Washington, save that we made it hastily as possible. It was now well toward the middle of April, and, brief as had been my absence, I knew there had been time for many things to happen in Washington as well as in Montreal.

Rumors abounded, I found as soon as I struck the first cities below the Canadian line. It was in the air now that under Calhoun there would be put before Congress a distinct and definite attempt at the annexation of Texas. Stories of all sorts were on the streets; rumors of the wrath of Mr. Clay; yet other rumors of interesting possibilities at the coming Whig and Democratic conventions. Everywhere was that strange, ominous, indescribable tension of the atmosphere which exists when a great people is moved deeply. The stern figure of Calhoun, furnishing courage for a people, even as he had for a president, loomed large in the public prints.

Late as it was when I reached Washington, I did not hesitate to repair at once to the residence of Mr. Calhoun; and I took with me as my best adjutant my strange friend Von Rittenhofen, who, I fancied, might add detailed information which Mr. Calhoun would find of value. We were admitted to Mr. Calhoun, and after the first greetings he signified that he would hear my report. He sat, his long, thin hands on his chair arm, as I went on with my story, his keen eyes scanning also my old companion as I spoke. I explained what the latter knew regarding Oregon. I saw Mr. Calhoun's eyes kindle. As usual, he did not lack decision.

"Sir," said he to Von Rittenhofen presently, "we ourselves are young, yet I trust not lacking in a great nation's interest in the arts and sciences. It occurs to me now that in yourself we have opportunity to add to our store of knowledge in respect to certain biological features."

The old gentleman rose and bowed. "I thank you for the honor of your flattery, sir," he began; but Calhoun raised a gentle hand.

"If it would please you, sir, to defer your visit to your own country for a time, I can secure for you a situation in our department in biology, where your services would be of extreme worth to us. The salary would also allow you to continue your private researches into the life of our native tribes."

Von Rittenhofen positively glowed at this. "Ach, what an honor!" he began again.

"Meantime," resumed Calhoun, "not to mention the value which that research would have for us, we could also find use, at proper remuneration, for your private aid in making up a set of maps of that western country which you know so well, and of which even I myself am so ignorant. I want to know the distances, the topography, the means of travel. I want to know the peculiarities of that country of Oregon. It would take me a year to send a messenger, for at best it requires six months to make the outbound passage, and in the winter the mountains are impassable. If you could, then, take service with us now, we should be proud to make you such return as your scientific attainments deserve."

Few could resist the persuasiveness of Mr. Calhoun's speech, certainly not Von Rittenhofen, who thus found offered him precisely what he would have desired. I was pleased to see him so happily situated and so soon. Presently we despatched him down to my hotel, where I promised later to make him more at home. In his elation over the prospect he now saw before him, the old man fairly babbled. Germany seemed farthest from his mind. After his departure, Calhoun again turned to me.

"I want you to remain, Nicholas," said he, "because I have an appointment with a gentleman who will soon be present."

"Rather a late hour, sir," I ventured. "Are you keeping faith with Doctor Ward?"

"I have no time for hobbies," he exclaimed, half petulantly. "What I must do is this work. The man we are to meet to-night is Mr. Polk. It is important."

"You would not call Mr. Polk important?" I smiled frankly, and Calhoun replied in icy kind.

"You can not tell how large a trouble may be started by a small politician," said he. "At least, we will hear what he has to say. 'Twas he that sought the meeting, not myself."

Perhaps half an hour later, Mr. Calhoun's old negro man ushered in this awaited guest, and we three found ourselves alone in one of those midnight conclaves which went on in Washington even then as they do to-day. Mr. Polk was serious as usual; his indecisive features wearing the mask of solemnity, which with so many passed as wisdom.

"I have come, Mr. Calhoun," said he—when the latter had assured him that my presence would entail no risk to him—"to talk over this Texas situation."

"Very well," said my chief. "My own intentions regarding Texas are now of record."

"Precisely," said Mr. Polk. "Now, is it wise to make a definite answer in that matter yet? Would it not be better to defer action until later—until after, I may say—"

"Until after you know what your own chances will be, Jim?" asked Mr. Calhoun, smiling grimly.

"Why, that is it, John, precisely, that is it exactly! Now, I don't know what you think of my chances in the convention, but I may say that a very large branch of the western Democracy is favoring me for the nomination." Mr. Polk pursed a short upper lip and looked monstrous grave. His extreme morality and his extreme dignity made his chief stock in trade. Different from his master, Old Hickory, he was really at heart the most aristocratic of Democrats, and like many another so-called leader, most of his love for the people really was love of himself.

"Yes, I know that some very strange things happen in politics," commented Calhoun, smiling.

"But, God bless me! you don't call it out of the way for me to seek the nomination? *Some* one must be president! Why not myself? Now, I ask your support."

"My support is worth little, Jim," said my chief. "But have you earned it? You have never consulted my welfare, nor has Jackson. I had no majority behind me in the Senate. I doubt even the House now. Of what use could I be to you?"

"At least, you could decline to do anything definite in this Texas matter."

"Why should a man ever do anything *indefinite*, Jim Polk?" asked Calhoun, bending on him his frosty eyes.

"But you may set a fire going which you can not stop. The people may get out of hand *before the convention!*"

"Why should they not? They have interests as well as we. Do they not elect us to subserve those interests?"

"I yield to no man in my disinterested desire for the welfare of the American people," began Polk pompously, throwing back the hair from his forehead.

"Of course not," said Calhoun grimly. "My own idea is that it is well to give the people what is already theirs. They feel that Texas belongs to them."

"True," said the Tennesseean, hesitating; "a good strong blast about our martial spirit and the men of the Revolution—that is always good before an election or a convention. Very true. But now in my own case—"

"Your own case is not under discussion, Jim. It is the case of the United States! I hold a brief for them, not for you or any other man!"

"How do you stand in case war should be declared against Mexico?" asked Mr. Polk. "That ought to be a popular measure. The Texans have captured the popular imagination. The Alamo rankles in our nation's memory. What would you say to a stiff demand there, with a strong show of military force behind it?"

"I should say nothing as to a strong *showing* in any case. I should only say that if war came legitimately—not otherwise—I should back it with all my might. I feel the same in regard to war with England."

"With England? What chance would we have with so powerful a nation as that?"

"There is a God of Battles," said John Calhoun.

The chin of James K. Polk of Tennessee sank down into his stock. His staring eyes went half shut. He was studying something in his own mind. At last he spoke, tentatively, as was always his way until he got the drift of things.

"Well, now, perhaps in the case of England that is good politics," he began. "It is very possible that the people hate England as much as they do Mexico. Do you not think so?"

"I think they fear her more."

"But I was only thinking of the popular imagination!"

"You are always thinking of the popular imagina-

"Fifty-four Forty or Fight!" exclaimed Polk. Page 203

tion, Jim. You have been thinking of that for some time in Tennessee. All that outcry about the whole of Oregon is ill-timed to-day."

"*Fifty-four Forty or Fight;* that sounds well!" exclaimed Polk; "eh?"

"Trippingly on the tongue, yes!" said John Calhoun. "But how would it sound to the tune of cannon fire? How would it look written in the smoke of musketry?"

"It might not come to that," said Polk, shifting in his seat. "I was thinking of it only as a rallying cry for the campaign. Dash me—I beg pardon—" he looked around to see if there were any Methodists present—"but I believe I could go into the convention with that war cry behind me and sweep the boards of all opposition!"

"And afterwards?"

"But England may back down," argued Mr. Polk. "A strong showing in the Southwest and Northwest might do wonders for us."

"But what would be behind that strong showing, Mr. Polk?" demanded John Calhoun. "We would win the combat with Mexico, of course, if that iniquitous measure should take the form of war. But not Oregon—we might as well or better fight in Africa than Oregon. It is not yet time. In God's name, Jim Polk, be careful of what you do! Cease this cry of taking all of Oregon. You will plunge this country not into one war, but two. Wait! Only wait, and we will own all this continent to the Saskatchewan—or even farther north."

"Well," said the other, "have you not said there is a God of Battles?"

"The Lord God of Hosts, yes!" half screamed old John Calhoun; "yes, the God of Battles for *nations,* for *principles*—but *not* for *parties!* For the *principle* of democracy, Jim Polk, yes, yes; but for the Democratic *party,* or the Whig *party,* or for any demagogue who tries to lead either, no, no!"

The florid face of Polk went livid. "Sir," said he, reaching for his hat, "at least I have learned what I came to learn. I know how you will appear on the floor of the convention. Sir, you will divide this party hopelessly. You are a traitor to the Democratic party! I charge it to your face, here and now. I came to ask of you your support, and find you only talking of principles! Sir, tell me, what have *principles* to do with *elections?*"

John Calhoun looked at him for one long instant. He looked down then at his own thin, bloodless hands, his wasted limbs. Then he turned slowly and rested his arms on the table, his face resting in his hands. "My God!" I heard him groan.

To see my chief abused was a thing not in my nature to endure. I forgot myself. I committed an act whose results pursued me for many a year.

"Mr. Polk, sir," said I, rising and facing him,
"damn you, sir, you are not fit to untie Mr. Ca
houn's shoe! I will not see you offer him one word
of insult. Quarrel with me if you like! You will
gain no votes here now in any case, that is sure!"

Utterly horrified at this, Mr. Polk fumbled with
his hat and cane, and, very red in the face, bowed
himself out, still mumbling, Mr. Calhoun rising and
bowing his adieux.

My chief dropped into his chair again. For a
moment he looked at me directly. "Nick," said he
at length slowly, "you have divided the Democratic
party. You split that party, right then and there."

"Never!" I protested; "but if I did, 'twas ready
enough for the division. Let it split, then, or any
party like it, if that is what must hold it together!
I will not stay in this work, Mr. Calhoun, and hear
you vilified. Platforms!"

"Platforms!" echoed my chief. His white hand
dropped on the table as he still sat looking at me.
"But he will get you some time, Nicholas!" he
smiled. "Jim Polk will not forget."

"Let him come at me as he likes!" I fumed.

At last, seeing me so wrought up, Mr. Calhoun
rose, and, smiling, shook me heartily by the hand.

"Of course, this had to come one time or another,"
said he. "The split was in the wood of their proposed platform of bluff and insincerity. 'What do

the people say?' asks Jim Polk. 'What do they *think?'* asks John Calhoun. And being now, in God's providence, chosen to do some thinking for them, I have thought."

He turned to the table and took up a long, folded document, which I saw was done in his cramped . hand and with many interlineations. "Copy this out fair for me to-night, Nicholas," said he. "This is our answer to the Aberdeen note. You have already learned its tenor, the time we met Mr. Pakenham with Mr. Tyler at the White House."

I grinned. "Shall we not take it across direct to Mr. Blair for publication in his *Globe?*"

Mr. Calhoun smiled rather bitterly at this jest. The hostility of Blair to the Tyler administration was a fact rather more than well known.

" 'Twill all get into Mr. Polk's newspaper fast enough," commented he at last. "He gets all the news of the Mexican ministry!"

"Ah, you think he cultivates the Doña Lucrezia, rather than adores her!"

"I know it! One-third of Jim Polk may be human, but the other two-thirds is politician. He will flatter that lady into confidences. She is well nigh distracted at best, these days, what with the fickleness of her husband and the yet harder abandonment by her old admirer Pakenham; so Polk will cajole her into disclosures, never fear. In return, when the time comes, he will send an army of occupation into her country! And all the while, on the one side and the other, he will appear to the public as a moral and lofty-minded man."

"On whom neither man nor woman could depend!"

"Neither the one nor the other."

The exasperation of his tone amused me, as did this chance importance of what seemed to me at the time merely a petticoat situation.

"Silk! Mr. Calhoun," I grinned. "Still silk and dimity, my faith! And you!"

He seemed a trifle nettled at this. "I must take men and women and circumstances as I find them," he rejoined; "and must use such agencies as are left me."

"If we temporarily lack the Baroness von Ritz to add zest to our game," I hazarded, "we still have the Doña Lucrezia and her little jealousies."

Calhoun turned quickly upon me with a sharp glance, as though seized by some sudden thought. "By the Lord Harry! boy, you give me an idea. Wait, now, for a moment. Do you go on with your copying there, and excuse me for a time."

An instant later he passed from the room, his tall figure bent, his hands clasped behind his back, and his face wrinkled in a frown, as was his wont when occupied with some problem.

CHAPTER XX

THE LADY FROM MEXICO

As soon as women are ours, we are no longer theirs.
—Montaigne.

AFTER a time my chief reëntered the office room and bent over me at my table. I put before him the draft of the document which he had given me for clerical care.

"So," he said, "'tis ready—our declaration. I wonder what may come of that little paper!"

"Much will come of it with a strong people back of it. The trouble is only that what Democrat does, Whig condemns. And not even all our party is with Mr. Tyler and yourself in this, Mr. Calhoun. Look, for instance, at Mr. Polk and his plans." To this venture on my part he made no present answer.

"I have no party, that is true," said he at last—"none but you and Sam Ward!" He smiled with one of his rare, illuminating smiles, different from the cold mirth which often marked him.

"At least, Mr. Calhoun, you do not take on your work for the personal glory of it," said I hotly; "and one day the world will know it!"

208

" 'Twill matter very little to me then," said he bitterly. "But come, now, I want more news about your trip to Montreal. What have you done?"

So now, till far towards dawn of the next day, we sat and talked. I put before him full details of my doings across the border. He sat silent, his eye betimes wandering, as though absorbed, again fixed on me, keen and glittering.

"So! So!" he mused at length, when I had finished, "England has started a land party for Oregon! Can they get across next fall, think you?"

"Hardly possible, sir," said I. "They could not go so swiftly as the special fur packets. Winter would catch them this side of the Rockies. It will be a year before they can reach Oregon."

"Time for a new president and a new policy," mused he.

"The grass is just beginning to sprout on the plains, Mr. Calhoun," I began eagerly.

"Yes," he nodded. "God! if I were only young!"

"I am young, Mr. Calhoun," said I. "Send *me!*"

"Would you go?" he asked suddenly.

"I was going in any case."

"Why, how do you mean?" he demanded.

I felt the blood come to my face. " 'Tis all over between Miss Elisabeth Churchill and myself," said I, as calmly as I might.

"Tut! tut! a child's quarrel," he went on, "a child's quarrel! 'Twill all mend in time."

"Not by act of mine, then," said I hotly.

Again abstracted, he seemed not wholly to hear me.

"First," he mused, "the more important things"— riding over my personal affairs as of little consequence.

"I will tell you, Nicholas," said he at last, wheeling swiftly upon me. "Start next week! An army of settlers waits now for a leader along the Missouri. Organize them; lead them out! Give them enthusiasm! Tell them what Oregon is! You may serve alike our party and our nation. You can not measure the consequences of prompt action sometimes, done by a man who is resolved upon the right. A thousand things may hinge on this. A great future may hinge upon it."

It was only later that I was to know the extreme closeness of his prophecy.

Calhoun began to pace up and down. "Besides her land forces," he resumed, "England is despatching a fleet to the Columbia! I doubt not that the *Modesté* has cleared for the Horn. There may be news waiting for you, my son, when you get across!

"While you have been busy, I have not been idle," he continued. "I have here another little paper which I have roughly drafted." He handed me the document as he spoke.

"A treaty—with Texas!" I exclaimed.

"The first draft, yes. We have signed the memorandum. We await only one other signature."

"Of Van Zandt!"

"Yes. Now comes Mr. Nicholas Trist, with word of a certain woman to the effect that Mr. Van Zandt is playing also with England."

"And that woman also is playing with England."

Calhoun smiled enigmatically.

"But she has gone," said I, "who knows where? She, too, may have sailed for Oregon, for all we know."

He looked at me as though with a flash of inspiration. "That may be," said he; "it may very well be! That would cost us our hold over Pakenham. Neither would we have any chance left with her."

"How do you mean, Mr. Calhoun?" said I. "I do not understand you."

"Nicholas," said Mr. Calhoun, "that lady was much impressed with you." He regarded me calmly, contemplatively, appraisingly.

"I do not understand you," I reiterated.

"I am glad that you do not and did not. In that case, all would have been over at once. You would never have seen her a second time. Your constancy was our salvation, and perhaps your own!"

He smiled in a way I liked none too well, but now I began myself to engage in certain reflections. Was it then true that faith could purchase faith—and win not failure, but success?

"At least she has flown," went on Calhoun. "But why? What made her go? 'Tis all over now, unless, unless—unless—" he added to himself a third time.

"But unless what?"

"Unless that chance word may have had some weight. You say that you and she talked of *principles?*"

"Yes, we went so far into abstractions."

"So did I with her! I told her about this country; explained to her as I could the beauties of the idea of a popular government. 'Twas as a revelation to her. She had never known a republican government before, student as she is. Nicholas, your long legs and my long head may have done some work after all! How did she seem to part with you?"

"As though she hated me; as though she hated herself and all the world. Yet not quite that, either. As though she would have wept—that is the truth. I do not pretend to understand her. She is a puzzle such as I have never known."

"Nor are you apt to know another her like. Look, here she is, the paid spy, the secret agent, of England. Additionally, she is intimately concerned with the private life of Mr. Pakenham. For the love of adventure, she is engaged in intrigue also with Mexico. Not content with that, born adventuress, eager devourer of any hazardous and interesting intellectual offering, any puzzle, any study, any intrigue—she comes at midnight to talk with me, whom she knows to be the representative of yet a third power!"

"And finds you in your red nightcap!" I laughed.

"Did she speak of that?" asked Mr. Calhoun in consternation, raising a hand to his head. "It may be that I forgot—but none the less, she came!

"Yes, as I said, she came, by virtue of your long legs and your ready way, as I must admit; and you were saved from her only, as I believe— Why, God bless Elisabeth Churchill, my boy, that is all! But my faith, how nicely it all begins to work out!"

"I do not share your enthusiasm, Mr. Calhoun," said I bitterly. "On the contrary, it seems to me to work out in as bad a fashion as could possibly be contrived."

"In due time you will see many things more plainly. Meantime, be sure England will be careful. She will make no overt movement, I should say, until she has heard from Oregon; which will not be before my lady baroness shall have returned and reported to Mr. Pakenham here. All of which means more time for us."

I began to see something of the structure of bold enterprise which this man deliberately was planning; but no comment offered itself; so that presently he went on, as though in soliloquy.

"The Hudson Bay Company have deceived England splendidly enough. Doctor McLaughlin, good man that he is, has not suited the Hudson Bay Company. His removal means less courtesy to our settlers in Oregon. Granted a less tactful leader than himself, there will be friction with our high-strung frontiersmen in that country. No man can tell when the thing will come to an issue. For my own part, I would agree with Polk that we ought to own that country to fifty-four forty—but what we *ought* to do and what we *can* do are two separate matters. Should we force the issue now and lose, we would lose for a hundred years. Should we advance firmly and hold firmly what we gain, in perhaps less than one hundred years we may win *all* of that country, as I just said to Mr. Polk, to the River Saskatchewan—I know not where! In my own soul, I believe no man may set a limit to the growth of the idea of an honest government by the people. *And this continent is meant for that honest government!*"

"We have already a Monroe Doctrine, Mr. Calhoun," said I. "What you enunciate now is yet more startling. Shall we call it the Calhoun Doctrine?"

He made no answer, but arose and paced up and down, stroking the thin fringe of beard under his chin. Still he seemed to talk with himself.

"We are not rich," he went on. "Our canals and railways are young. The trail across our country is of monstrous difficulty. Give us but a few years more and Oregon, ripe as a plum, would drop in our lap. To hinder that is a crime. What Polk proposes is insincerity, and all insincerity must fail. There is but one result when pretense is pitted against preparedness. Ah, if ever we needed wisdom and self-restraint, we need them now! Yet look at what we face! Look at what we may lose! And that through party—through platform—through *politics!*"

He sighed as he paused in his walk and turned to me. "But now, as I said, we have at least time for Texas. And in regard to Texas we need another woman."

I stared at him.

"You come now to me with proof that my lady baroness traffics with Mexico as well as England," he resumed. "That is to say, Yturrio meets my lady baroness. What is the inference? At least, jealousy on the part of Yturrio's wife, whether or not she cares for him! Now, jealousy between the sexes is a deadly weapon if well handled. Repugnant as it is, we must handle it."

I experienced no great enthusiasm at the trend of events, and Mr. Calhoun smiled at me cynically as he went on. "I see you don't care for this sort of commission. At least, this is no midnight interview. You shall call in broad daylight on the Señora Yturrio. If you and my daughter will take my coach and four to-morrow, I think she will gladly receive your cards. Perhaps also she will consent to take the air of Washington with you. In that case, she might drop in here for an ice. In such case, to conclude, I may perhaps be favored with an interview with that lady. I *must* have Van Zandt's signature to this treaty which you see here!"

"But these are Mexicans, and Van Zandt is leader of the Texans, their most bitter enemies!"

"Precisely. All the less reason why Señora Yturrio should be suspected."

"I am not sure that I grasp all this, Mr. Calhoun."

"Perhaps not. You presently will know more. What seems to me plain is that, since we seem to lose a valuable ally in the Baroness von Ritz, we must make some offset to that loss. If England has one woman on the Columbia, we must have another on the Rio Grande!"

CHAPTER XXI

POLITICS UNDER COVER

To a woman, the romances she makes are more amusing than those she reads.—Théophile Gautier.

IT was curious how cleverly this austere old man, unskilled in the arts of gallantry, now handled the problem to which he had addressed himself, even though that meant forecasting the whim of yet another woman. It all came easily about, precisely as he had planned.

It seemed quite correct for the daughter of our secretary of state to call to inquire for the health of the fair Señora Yturrio, and to present the compliments of Madam Calhoun, at that time not in the city of Washington. Matters went so smoothly that I felt justified in suggesting a little drive, and Señora Yturrio had no hesitation in accepting. Quite naturally, our stately progress finally brought us close to the residence of Miss Calhoun. That lady suggested that, since the day was warm, it might be well to descend and see if we might not find a sherbet; all of which also seemed quite to the wish of the lady from Mexico. The ease and warmth of Mr.

217

Calhoun's greeting to her were such that she soon was well at home and chatting very amiably. She spoke English with but little hesitancy.

Lucrezia Yturrio, at that time not ill known in Washington's foreign colony, was beautiful, in a sensuous, ripe way. Her hair was dark, heavily coiled, and packed in masses above an oval forehead. Her brows were straight, dark and delicate; her teeth white and strong; her lips red and full; her chin well curved and deep. A round arm and taper hand controlled a most artful fan. She was garbed now, somewhat splendidly, in a corded cherry-colored silk, wore gems enough to start a shop, and made on the whole a pleasing picture of luxury and opulence. She spoke in a most musical voice, with eyes sometimes cast modestly down. He had been a poor student of her species who had not ascribed to her a wit of her own; but as I watched her, somewhat apart, I almost smiled as I reflected that her grave and courteous host had also a wit to match it. Then I almost frowned as I recalled my own defeat in a somewhat similar contest.

Mr. Calhoun expressed great surprise and gratification that mere chance had enabled him to meet the wife of a gentleman so distinguished in the diplomatic service as Señor Yturrio. The Señora was equally gratified. She hoped she did not make intrusion in thus coming. Mr. Calhoun assured her that he and his were simple in their family life, and always delighted to meet their friends.

"We are especially glad always to hear of our friends from the Southwest," said he, at last, with a slight addition of formality in tone and attitude.

At these words I saw my lady's eyes flicker. "It is fate, Señor," said she, again casting down her eyes, and spreading out her hands as in resignation, "fate which left Texas and Mexico not always one."

"That may be," said Mr. Calhoun. "Perhaps fate, also, that those of kin should cling together."

"How can a mere woman know?" My lady shrugged her very graceful and beautiful shoulders —somewhat mature shoulders now, but still beautiful.

"Dear Señora," said Mr. Calhoun, "there are so many things a woman may not know. For instance, how could she know if her husband should perchance leave the legation to which he was attached and pay a visit to another nation?"

Again the slight flickering of her eyes, but again her hands were outspread in protest.

"How indeed, Señor?"

"What if my young aide here, Mr. Trist, should tell you that he has seen your husband some hundreds of miles away and in conference with a lady supposed to be somewhat friendly towards—"

"Ah, you mean that baroness—!"

So soon had the shaft gone home! Her woman's jealousy had offered a point unexpectedly weak. Calhoun bowed, without a smile upon his face.

"Mr. Pakenham, the British minister, is disposed to be friendly to this same lady. Your husband and a certain officer of the British Navy called upon this same lady last week in Montreal—informally. It is sometimes unfortunate that plans are divulged. To me it seemed only wise and fit that you should not let any of these little personal matters make for us greater complications in these perilous times. I think you understand me, perhaps, Señora Yturrio?"

She gurgled low in her throat at this, any sort of sound, meaning to remain ambiguous. But Calhoun was merciless.

"It is not within dignity, Señora, for me to make trouble between a lady and her husband. But we must have friends with us under our flag, or know that they are not our friends. You are welcome in my house. Your husband is welcome in the house of our republic. There are certain duties, even thus."

Only now and again she turned upon him the light of her splendid eyes, searching him.

"If I should recall again, gently, my dear Señora, the fact that your husband was with that particular woman—if I should say that Mexico has been found under the flag of England, while supposed to be under *our* flag—if I should add that one of the representatives of the Mexican legation had been discovered in handing over to England certain secrets of this country and of the Republic of Texas— why, then, what answer, think you, Señora, Mexico would make to me?"

"But Señor Calhoun does not mean—does not dare to say—"

"I do dare it; I do mean it! I can tell you all that Mexico plans, and all that Texas plans. All the secrets are out; and since we know them, we purpose immediate annexation of the Republic of Texas! Though it means war, Texas shall be ours! This has been forced upon us by the perfidy of other nations."

He looked her full in the eye, his own blue orbs alight with resolution. She returned his gaze, fierce as a tigress. But at last she spread out her deprecating hands.

"Señor," she said, "I am but a woman. I am in the Señor Secretary's hands. I am even in his *hand*. What can he wish?"

"In no unfair way, Señora, I beg you to understand, in no improper way are you in our hands. But now let us endeavor to discover some way in which some of these matters may be composed. In such affairs, a small incident is sometimes magnified and taken in connection with its possible consequences. You readily may see, Señora, that did I personally seek the dismissal of your husband, possibly even the recall of General Almonte, his chief, that might be effected without difficulty."

"You seek war, Señor Secretary! My people say that your armies are in Texas now, or will be."

"They are but very slightly in advance of the truth, Señora," said Calhoun grimly. "For me, I do not believe in war when war can be averted. But suppose it *could* be averted? Suppose the Señora Yturrio herself *could* avert it? Suppose the Señora could remain here still, in this city which she so much admires? A lady of so distinguished beauty and charm is valuable in our society here."

He bowed to her with stately grace. If there was mockery in his tone, she could not catch it; nor did her searching eyes read his meaning.

"See," he resumed, "alone, I am helpless in this situation. If my government is offended, I can not stop the course of events. I am not the Senate; I am simply an officer in our administration—a very humble officer of his Excellency our president, Mr. Tyler."

My lady broke out in a peal of low, rippling laughter, her white teeth gleaming. It was, after all, somewhat difficult to trifle with one who had been trained in intrigue all her life.

Calhoun laughed now in his own quiet way. "We shall do better if we deal entirely frankly, Señora," said he. "Let us then waste no time. Frankly, then, it would seem that, now the Baroness von Ritz is off the scene, the Señora Yturrio would have all the 'better title and opportunity in the affections of— well, let us say, her own husband!"

She bent toward him now, her lips open in a slow smile, all her subtle and dangerous beauty unmasking its batteries. The impression she conveyed was that of warmth and of spotted shadows such as play upon the leopard's back, such as mark the wing of the butterfly, the petal of some flower born in a land of heat and passion. But Calhoun regarded her calmly, his finger tips together, and spoke as deliberately as though communing with himself. "It is but one thing, one very little thing."

"And what is that, Señor?" she asked at length.

"The signature of Señor Van Zandt, attaché for Texas, on this memorandum of treaty between the United States and Texas."

Bowing, he presented to her the document to which he had earlier directed my own attention. "We are well advised that Señor Van Zandt is trafficking this very hour with England as against us," he explained. "We ask the gracious assistance of Señora Yturrio. In return we promise her— silence!"

"I can not—it is impossible!" she exclaimed, as she glanced at the pages. "It is our ruin—!"

"No, Señora," said Calhoun sternly; "it means annexation of Texas to the United States. But that is not your ruin. It is your salvation. Your country well may doubt England, even England bearing gifts!"

"I have no control over Señor Van Zandt—he is the enemy of my country!" she began.

Calhoun now fixed upon her the full cold blue blaze of his singularly penetrating eyes. "No, Señora," he said sternly; "but you have access to my friend Mr. Polk, and Mr. Polk is the friend of Mr. Jackson, and they two are friends of Mr. Van Zandt; and Texas supposes that these two, although they do not represent precisely my own beliefs in politics, are for the annexation of Texas, not to England, but to America. There is good chance Mr. Polk may be president. If you do not use your personal influence with him, he may consult politics and not you, and so declare war against Mexico. That war would cost you Texas, and much more as well. Now, to avert that war, do you not think that perhaps you can ask Mr. Polk to say to Mr. Van Zandt that his signature on this little treaty would end all such questions simply, immediately, and to the best benefit of Mexico, Texas and the United States? Treason? Why, Señora, 'twould be preventing treason!"

Her face was half hidden by her fan, and her

eyes, covered by their deep lids, gave no sign of her thoughts. The same cold voice went on :

"You might, for instance, tell Mr. Polk, which is to say Mr. Van Zandt, that if his name goes on this little treaty for Texas, nothing will be said to Texas regarding his proposal to give Texas over to England. It might not be safe for that little fact generally to be known in Texas as it is known to me. We will keep it secret. You might ask Mr. Van Zandt if he would value a seat in the Senate of these United States, rather than a lynching rope! So much do I value your honorable acquaintance with Mr. Polk and with Mr. Van Zandt, my dear lady, that I do not go to the latter and *demand* his signature in the name of his republic—no, I merely suggest to you that did *you* take this little treaty for a day, and presently return it to me with his signature attached, I should feel so deeply gratified that I should not ask you by what means you had attained this most desirable result! And I should hope that if you could not win back the affections of a certain gentleman, at least you might win your own evening of the scales with him."

Her face colored darkly. In a flash she saw the covert allusion to the faithless Pakenham. Here was the chance to cut him to the soul. *She could cost England Texas!* Revenge made its swift appeal to her savage heart. Revenge and jealousy, handled coolly, mercilessly as weapons—those cost England Texas!

She sat, her fan tight at her white teeth. "It would be death to me if it were known," she said. But still she pondered, her eye alight with somber fire, her dark cheek red in a woman's anger.

"But it never will be known, my dear lady. These things, however, must be concluded swiftly. We have not time to wait. Let us not argue over the unhappy business. Let me think of Mexico as our sister republic and our friend!"

"And suppose I shall not do this that you ask, Señor?"

"That, my dear lady, *I do not suppose!*"

"You threaten, Señor Secretary?"

"On the contrary, I implore! I ask you not to be treasonable to any, but to be our ally, our friend, in what in my soul I believe a great good for the peoples of the world. Without us, Texas will be the prey of England. With us, she will be working out her destiny. In our graveyard of state there are many secrets of which the public never knows. Here shall be one, though your heart shall exult in its possession. Dear lady, may we not conspire together—for the ultimate good of three republics, making of them two noble ones, later to dwell in amity? Shall we not hope to see all this continent swept free of monarchy, held *free,* for the peoples of the world?"

For an instant, no more, she sat and pondered. Suddenly she bestowed upon him a smile whose brilliance might have turned the head of another man. Rising, she swept him a curtsey whose grace I have not seen surpassed.

In return, Mr. Calhoun bowed to her with dignity and ease, and, lifting her hand, pressed it to his lips. Then, offering her an arm, he led her to his carriage. I could scarce believe my eyes and ears that so much, and of so much importance, had thus so easily been accomplished, where all had seemed so near to the impossible.

When last I saw my chief that day he was sunk in his chair, white to the lips, his long hands trembling, fatigue written all over his face and form; but a smile still was on his grim mouth. "Nicholas," said he, "had I fewer politicians and more women behind me, we should have Texas to the Rio Grande, and Oregon up to Russia, and all without a war!"

CHAPTER XXII

BUT YET A WOMAN

Woman turns every man the wrong side out,
And never gives to truth and virtue that
Which simpleness and merit purchaseth.

—Shakespeare.

MY chief played his game of chess coldly, methodically, and with skill; yet a game of chess is not always of interest to the spectator who does not know every move. Least of all does it interest one who feels himself but a pawn piece on the board and part of a plan in whose direction he has nothing to say. In truth, I was weary. Not even the contemplation of the hazardous journey to Oregon served to stir me. I traveled wearily again and again my circle of personal despair.

On the day following my last interview with Mr. Calhoun, I had agreed to take my old friend Doctor von Rittenhofen upon a short journey among the points of interest of our city, in order to acquaint him somewhat with our governmental machinery and to put him in touch with some of the sources of information to which he would need to refer in the work upon which he was now engaged. We had

228

spent a couple of hours together, and were passing across to the capitol, with the intent of looking in upon the deliberations of the houses of Congress, when all at once, as we crossed the corridor, I felt him touch my arm.

"Did you see that young lady?" he asked of me. "She looked at you, yess?"

I was in the act of turning, even as he spoke. Certainly had I been alone I would have seen Elisabeth, would have known that she was there.

It was Elisabeth, alone, and hurrying away! Already she was approaching the first stair. In a moment she would be gone. I sprang after her by instinct, without plan, clear in my mind only that she was going, and with her all the light of the world; that she was going, and that she was beautiful, adorable; that she was going, and that she was Elisabeth!

As I took a few rapid steps toward her, I had full opportunity to see that no grief had preyed upon her comeliness, nor had concealment fed upon her damask cheek. Almost with some resentment I saw that she had never seemed more beautiful than on this morning. The costume of those days was trying to any but a beautiful woman; yet Elisabeth had a way of avoiding extremes which did not appeal to her individual taste. Her frock now was all in pink, as became the gentle spring, and the bunch of silvery ribbons which fluttered at her belt had quite the agreeing shade to finish in perfection the cool, sweet picture that she made. Her sleeves were puffed widely, and for the lower arm were opened just sufficiently. She carried a small white parasol, with pinked edges, and her silken mitts, light and dainty, matched the clear whiteness of her arms. Her face, turned away from me, was shaded by a wide round bonnet, not quite so painfully plain as the scooplike affair of the time, but with a drooping brim from which depended a slight frilling of sheer lace. Her smooth brown hair was drawn primly down across her ears, as was the fashion of the day, and from the masses piled under the bonnet brim there fell down a curl, round as though made that moment, and not yet limp from the damp heat of Washington. Fresh and dainty and restful as a picture done on Dresden, yet strong, fresh, fully competent, Elisabeth walked as having full right in the world and accepting as her due such admiration as might be offered. If she had ever known a care, she did not show it; and, I say, this made me feel resentment. It was her proper business to appear miserable.

If she indeed resembled a rare piece of flawless Dresden on this morning, she was as cold, her features were as unmarked by any human pity. Ah! so different an Elisabeth, this, from the one I had last seen at the East Room, with throat fluttering

and cheeks far warmer than this cool rose pink.
But, changed or not, the full sight of her came as
the sudden influence of some powerful drug, blot-
ting out consciousness of other things. I could no
more have refrained from approaching her than I
could have cast away my own natural self and form.
Just as she reached the top of the broad marble
stairs, I spoke.

"Elisabeth!"

Seeing that there was no escape, she paused now
and turned toward me. I have never seen a glance
like hers. Say not there is no language of the eyes,
no speech in the composure of the features. Yet
such is the Sphinx power given to woman, that now
I saw, as though it were a thing tangible, a veil
drawn across her eyes, across her face, between her
soul and mine.

Elisabeth drew herself up straight, her chin high,
her eyes level, her lips just parted for a faint salutation in the conventions of the morning.

"How do you do?" she remarked. Her voice was
all cool white enamel. Then that veil dropped down
between us.

She was there somewhere, but I could not see her
clearly now. It was not her voice. I took her hand,
yes; but it had now none of answering clasp. The
flush was on her cheek no more. Cool, pale, sweet,
all white now, armed cap-a-pie with indifference,

she looked at me as formally as though I were a remote acquaintance. Then she would have passed.

"Elisabeth," I began; "I am just back. I have not
had time—I have had no leave from you to come to
see you—to ask you—to explain—"

"Explain?" she said evenly.

"But surely you can not believe that I—"

"I only believe what seems credible, Mr. Trist."

"But you promised—that very morning you
agreed— Were you out of your mind, that—"

"I was out of my mind that morning—but not that
evening."

Now she was *grande demoiselle,* patrician, superior. Suddenly I became conscious of the dullness
of my own garb. I cast a quick glance over my
figure, to see whether it had not shrunken.

"But that is not it, Elisabeth—a girl may not allow a man so much as you promised me, and then
forget that promise in a day. It *was* a promise between us. *You* agreed that I should come; I did
come. You had given your word. I say, was that the
way to treat me, coming as I did?"

"I found it possible," said she. "But, if you
please, I must go. I beg your pardon, but my Aunt
Betty is waiting with the carriage."

"Why, damn Aunt Betty!" I exclaimed. "You
shall not go! See, look here!"

I pulled from my pocket the little ring which I

had had with me that night when I drove out to Elmhurst in my carriage, the one with the single gem which I had obtained hurriedly that afternoon, having never before that day had the right to do so. In another pocket I found the plain gold one which should have gone with the gem ring that same evening. My hand trembled as I held these out to her.

"I prove to you what I meant. Here! I had no time! Why, Elisabeth, I was hurrying—I was mad! —I had a right to offer you these things. I have still the right to ask you why you did not take them? Will you not take them now?"

She put my hand away from her gently. "Keep them," she said, "for the owner of that other wedding gift—the one which I received."

Now I broke out. "Good God! How can I be held to blame for the act of a drunken friend? You know Jack Dandridge as well as I do myself. I cautioned him—I was not responsible for his condition."

"It was not that decided me."

"You could not believe it was *I* who sent you that accursed shoe which belonged to another woman."

"He said it came from you. Where did *you* get it, then?"

Now, as readily may be seen, I was obliged again to hesitate. There were good reasons to keep my lips sealed. I flushed. The red of confusion which came to my cheek was matched by that of indignation in her own. I could not tell her, and she could not understand, that my work for Mr. Calhoun with that other woman was work for America, and so as sacred and as secret as my own love for her. Innocent, I still seemed guilty.

"So, then, you do not say? I do not ask you."

"I do not deny it."

"You do not care to tell me where you got it."

"No," said I; "I will not tell you where I got it."

"Why?"

"Because that would involve another woman."

"*Involve another woman?* Do you think, then, that on this one day of her life, a girl likes to think of her—her lover—as involved with any other woman? Ah, you made me begin to think. I could not help the chill that came on my heart. Marry you?—I could not! I never could, now."

"Yet you had decided—you had told me—it was agreed—"

"I had decided on facts as I thought they were. Other facts came before you arrived. Sir, you do me a very great compliment."

"But you loved me once," I said banally.

"I do not consider it fair to mention that now."

"I never loved that other woman. I had never seen her more than once. You do not know her."

"Ah, is that it? Perhaps I could tell you something of one Helena von Ritz. Is it not so?"

"Yes, that was the property of Helena von Ritz,"
I told her, looking her fairly in the eye

"Kind of you, indeed, to involve me, as you say,
with a lady of her precedents!"

Now her color was up full, and her words came
crisply. Had I had adequate knowledge of women,
I could have urged her on then, and brought on a
full-fledged quarrel. Strategically, that must have
been a far happier condition than mere indifference
on her part. But I did not know; and my accursed
love of fairness blinded me.

"I hardly think any one is quite just to that lady,"
said I slowly.

"Except Mr. Nicholas Trist! A beautiful and accomplished lady, I doubt not, in his mind."

"Yes, all of that, I doubt not."

"And quite kind with her little gifts."

"Elisabeth, I can not well explain all that to you.
I can not, on my honor."

"Do not!" she cried, putting out her hand as
though in alarm. "Do not invoke your honor!"

She looked at me again. I have never seen a look
like hers. She had been calm, cold, and again in-
dignant, all in a moment's time. That expression
which now showed on her face was one yet worse
for me.

Still I would not accept my dismissal, but went on
stubbornly: "But may I not see your father and have

my chance again? I *can not* let it go this way.   It is the ruin of my life."

But now she was advancing, dropping down a step at a time, and her face was turned straight ahead. The pink of her gown was matched by the pink of her cheeks.   I saw the little working of the white throat wherein some sobs seemed stifling. And so she went away and left me.

CHAPTER XXIII

SUCCESS IN SILK

As things are, I think women are generally better creatures than men.—S. T. Coleridge.

IT WAS a part of my duties, when in Washington, to assist my chief in his personal and official correspondence, which necessarily was very heavy. This work we customarily began about nine of the morning. On the following day I was on hand earlier than usual. I was done with Washington now, done with everything, eager only to be off on the far trails once more. But I almost forgot my own griefs when I saw my chief. When I found him, already astir in his office, his face was strangely wan and thin, his hands bloodless. Over him hung an air of utter weariness; yet, shame to my own despair, energy showed in all his actions. Resolution was written on his face. He greeted me with a smile which strangely lighted his grim face.

"We have good news of some kind this morning, sir?" I inquired.

In answer, he motioned me to a document which lay open upon his table. It was familiar enough to me. I glanced at the bottom. There were *two* signatures!

"Texas agrees!" I exclaimed. *"The Doña Lucrezia has won Van Zandt's signature!"*

I looked at him. His own eyes were swimming wet! This, then, was that man of whom it is only remembered that he was a pro-slavery champion.

"It will be a great country," said he at last. "This once done, I shall feel that, after all, I have not lived wholly in vain."

"But the difficulties! Suppose Van Zandt proves traitorous to us?"

"He dare not. Texas may know that he bargained with England, but he dare not traffic with Mexico and let *that* be known. He would not live a day."

"But perhaps the Doña Lucrezia herself might some time prove fickle."

"*She* dare not! She never will. She will enjoy in secret her revenge on perfidious Albion, which is to say, perfidious Pakenham. Her nature is absolutely different from that of the Baroness von Ritz. The Doña Lucrezia dreams of the torch of love, not the torch of principle!"

"The public might not approve, Mr. Calhoun; but at least there *were* advantages in this sort of aids!"

"We are obliged to find such help as we can. The public is not always able to tell which was plot and which counterplot in the accomplishment of some intricate things. The result excuses all. It was written that Texas should come to this country. Now for Oregon! It grows, this idea of democracy!"

"At least, sir, you will have done your part. Only now—"

"Only what, then?"

"We are certain to encounter opposition. The Senate may not ratify this Texas treaty."

"The Senate will *not* ratify," said he. "I am perfectly well advised of how the vote will be when this treaty comes before it for ratification. We will be beaten, two to one!"

"Then, does that not end it?"

"End it? No! There are always other ways. If the people of this country wish Texas to belong to our flag, she will so belong. It is as good as done to-day. Never look at the obstacles; look at the goal! It was this intrigue of Van Zandt's which stood in our way. By playing one intrigue against another, we have won thus far. We must go on winning!"

He paced up and down the room, one hand smiting the other. "Let England whistle now!" he exclaimed exultantly. "We shall annex Texas, in full view, indeed, of all possible consequences. There can be no consequences, for England has no excuse left for war over Texas. I only wish the situation were as clear for Oregon."

"There'll be bad news for our friend Señor Yturrio when he gets back to his own legation!" I ventured.

"Let him then face that day when Mexico shall see fit to look to *us* for aid and counsel. We will build a mighty country *here,* on *this* continent!"

"Mr. Pakenham is accredited to have certain influence in our Senate."

"Yes. We have his influence exactly weighed. Yet I rejoice in at least one thing—one of his best allies is not here."

"You mean Señor Yturrio?"

"I mean the Baroness von Ritz. And now comes on that next nominating convention, at Baltimore."

"What will it do?" I hesitated.

"God knows. For me, I have no party. I am alone! I have but few friends in all the world"—he smiled now—"you, my boy, as I said, and Doctor Ward and a few women, all of whom hate each other."

I remained silent at this shot, which came home to me; but he smiled, still grimly, shaking his head. "Rustle of silk, my boy, rustle of silk—it is over all our maps. But we shall make these maps! Time shall bear me witness."

"Then I may start soon for Oregon?" I demanded.

"You shall start to-morrow," he answered.

CHAPTER XXIV

THE WHOA-HAW TRAIL

There are no pleasures where women are not.
—*Marie de Rom....*

HOW shall I tell of those stirring times in
such way that readers who live in later and
different days may catch in full their flavor? How shall I write now so that at a later time
men may read of the way America was taken, may
see what America then was and now is, and what yet,
please God! it may be? How shall be set down that
keen zest of a nation's youth, full of ambition and
daring, full of contempt for obstacles, full of a vast
and splendid hope? How shall be made plain also
that other and stronger thing which so many of
those days have mentioned to me, half in reticence—
that feeling that, after all, this fever of the blood,
this imperious insistence upon new lands, had under
it something more than human selfishness?

I say I wish that some tongue or brush or pen
might tell the story of our people at that time. Once
I saw it in part told in color and line, in a painting
done by a master hand, almost one fit to record the

241

spirit of that day, although it wrought in this instance with another and yet earlier time. In this
old canvas, depicting an early Teutonic tribal wandering, appeared some scores of human figures, men
and women half savage in their look, clad in skins,
with fillets of hide for head covering; men whose
beards were strong and large, whose limbs, wrapped
loose in hides, were strong and large; women, strong
and large, who bore burdens on their backs. Yet in
the faces of all these there shone, not savagery alone,
but intelligence and resolution. With them were
flocks and herds and beasts of burden and carts of
rude build; and beside these traveled children.
There were young and old men and women, and
some were gaunt and weary, but most were bold and
strong. There were weapons for all, and rude implements, as well, of industry. In the faces of all
there was visible the spirit of their yellow-bearded
leader, who made the center of the picture's fore-
ground.

I saw the soul of that canvas—a splendid resolution—a look forward, a purpose, an aim to be attained at no counting of cost. I say, as I gazed at
that canvas, I saw in it the columns of my own people moving westward across the land, fierce-eyed,
fearless, doubting nothing, fearing nothing. That
was the genius of America when I myself was
young. I believe it still to be the spirit of a tri-

umphant democracy, knowing its own, taking its own, holding its own. They travel yet, the dauntless figures of that earlier day. Let them not despair. No imaginary line will ever hold them back, no mandate of any monarch ever can restrain them.

In our own caravans, now pressing on for the general movement west of the Missouri, there was material for a hundred canvases like yonder one, and yet more vast. The world of our great western country was then still before us. A stern and warlike people was resolved to hold it and increase it. Of these west-bound I now was one. I felt the joy of that thought. I was going West!

At this time, the new railroad from Baltimore extended no farther westward than Cumberland, yet it served to carry one well toward the Ohio River at Pittsburg; whence, down the Ohio and up the Missouri to Leavenworth, my journey was to be made by steamboats. In this prosaic travel, the days passed monotonously; but at length I found myself upon that frontier which then marked the western edge of our accepted domain, and the eastern extremity of the Oregon Trail.

If I can not bring to the mind of one living to-day the full picture of those days when this country was not yet all ours, and can not restore to the comprehension of those who never were concerned with that life the picture of that great highway, greatest path

244 FIFTY-FOUR FORTY OR FIGHT

of all the world, which led across our unsettled countries, that ancient trail at least may be a memory. It
is not even yet wiped from the surface of the earth.
It still remains in part, marked now no longer by
the rotting head-boards of its graves, by the bones of
the perished ones which once traveled it; but now by
its ribands cut through the turf, and lined by nod-
ding prairie flowers.

The old trail to Oregon was laid out by no government, arranged by no engineer, planned by no
surveyor, supported by no appropriation. It sprang,
a road already created, from the earth itself, covering two thousand miles of our country. Why? Because there was need for that country to be covered
by such a trail at such a time. Because we needed
Oregon. Because a stalwart and clear-eyed democracy needs America and will have it. That was the
trail over which our people outran their leaders.
If our leaders trifle again, once again we shall outrun them.

There were at this date but four places of human
residence in all the two thousand miles of this trail,
yet recent as had been the first hoofs and wheels to
mark it, it was even then a distinct and unmistakable
path. The earth has never had nor again can have
its like. If it was a path of destiny, if it was a road
of hope and confidence, so was it a road of misery
and suffering and sacrifice; for thus has the democ-

racy always gained its difficult and lasting victories. I think that it was there, somewhere, on the old road to Oregon, sometime in the silent watches of the prairie or the mountain night, that there was fought out the battle of the Old World and the New, the battle between oppressors and those who declared they no longer would be oppressed.

Providentially for us, an ignorance equal to that of our leaders existed in Great Britain. For us who waited on the banks of the Missouri, all this ignorance was matter of indifference. Our men got their beliefs from no leaders, political or editorial, at home or abroad. They waited only for the grass to come.

Now at last the grass did begin to grow upon the eastern edge of the great Plains; and so I saw begin that vast and splendid movement across our continent which in comparison dwarfs all the great people movements of the earth. Xenophon's March of the Ten Thousand pales beside this of ten thousand thousands. The movements of the Goths and Huns, the Vandals, the Cimri—in a way, they had a like significance with this, but in results those migrations did far less in the history of the world; did less to prove the purpose of the world.

I watched the forming of our caravan, and I saw again that canvas which I have mentioned, that picture of the savages who traveled a thousand years before Christ was born. Our picture was the vaster, the more splendid, the more enduring. Here were savages born of gentle folk in part, who never yet had known repulse. They marched with flocks and herds and implements of husbandry. In their faces shone a light not less fierce than that which animated the dwellers of the old Teutonic forests, but a light clearer and more intelligent. Here was the determined spirit of progress, here was the agreed insistence upon an *equal opportunity!* Ah! it was a great and splendid canvas which might have been painted there on our Plains—the caravans westbound with the greening grass of spring—that hegira of Americans whose unheard command was but the voice of democracy itself.

We carried with us all the elements of society, as has the Anglo-Saxon ever. Did any man offend against the unwritten creed of fair play, did he shirk duty when that meant danger to the common good, then he was brought before a council of our leaders, men of wisdom and fairness, chosen by the vote of all; and so he was judged and he was punished. At that time there was not west of the Missouri River any one who could administer an oath, who could execute a legal document, or perpetuate any legal testimony; yet with us the law marched *pari passu* across the land. We had leaders chosen because they were fit to lead, and leaders who felt full sense of responsibility to those who chose them. We had with us great wealth in flocks and herds—five thousand head of cattle went West with our caravan, hundreds of horses; yet each knew his own and asked not that of his neighbor. With us there were women and little children and the gray-haired elders bent with years. Along our road we left graves here and there, for death went with us. In our train also were many births, life coming to renew the cycle. At times, too, there were rejoicings of the newly wed in our train. Our young couples found society awheel valid as that abiding under permanent roof.

At the head of our column, we bore the flag of our Republic. On our flanks were skirmishers, like those guarding the flanks of an army. It *was* an army— an army of our people. With us marched women. With us marched home. *That* was the difference between our cavalcade and that slower and more selfish one, made up of men alone, which that same year was faring westward along the upper reaches of the Canadian Plains. That was why we won. It was because women and plows were with us.

Our great column, made up of more than one hundred wagons, was divided into platoons of four, each platoon leading for a day, then falling behind to take the bitter dust of those in advance. At noon we parted our wagons in platoons, and at night we drew them invariably into a great barricade, circular in form, the leading wagon marking out the circle, the others dropping in behind, the tongue of each against the tail-gate of the wagon ahead, and the last wagon closing up the gap. Our circle completed, the animals were unyoked and the tongues were chained fast to the wagons next ahead; so that each night we had a sturdy barricade, incapable of being stampeded by savages, whom more than once we fought and defeated. Each night we set out a guard, our men taking turns, and the night watches in turn rotating, so that each man got his share of the entire night during the progress of his journey. Each morn we rose to the notes of a bugle, and each day we marched in order, under command, under a certain schedule. Loosely connected, independent, individual, none the less already we were establishing a government. We took the American Republic with us across the Plains!

This manner of travel offered much monotony, yet it had its little pleasures. For my own part, my early experience in Western matters placed me in charge of our band of hunters, whose duty it was to ride at the flanks of our caravan each day and to kill sufficient buffalo for meat. This work of the chase gave us more to do than was left for those who plodded along or rode bent over upon the wagon seats; yet even for these there was some relaxation. At night we met in little social circles around the camp-fires. Young folk made love; old folk made plans here as they had at home. A church marched with us as well as the law and courts; and, what was more, the schools went also; for by the faint flicker of the firelight many parents taught their children each day as they moved westward to their new homes. History shows these children were well taught. There were persons of education and culture with us.

Music we had, and of a night time, even while the coyotes were calling and the wind whispering in the short grasses of the Plains, violin and flute would sometimes blend their voices, and I have thus heard songs which I would not exchange in memory for others which I have heard in surroundings far more ambitious. Sometimes dances were held on the greensward of our camps. Regularly the Sabbath day was observed by at least the most part of our pilgrims. Upon all our party there seemed to sit an air of content and certitude. Of all our wagons, I presume one was of greatest value. It was filled with earth to the brim, and in it were fruit trees planted, and shrubs; and its owner carried seeds of garden plants. Without doubt, it was our mission and our intent to take with us such civilization as we had left behind.

So we marched, mingled, and, as some might have said, motley in our personnel—sons of some of the best families in the South, men from the Carolinas and Virginia, Georgia and Louisiana, men from Pennsylvania and Ohio; Roundhead and Cavalier, Easterner and Westerner, Germans, Yankees, Scotch-Irish—all Americans. We marched, I say, under a form of government; yet each took his original marching orders from his own soul. We marched across an America not yet won. Below us lay the Spanish civilization—Mexico, possibly soon to be led by Britain, as some thought. North of us was Canada, now fully alarmed and surely led by Britain. West of us, all around us, lay the Indian tribes. Behind, never again to be seen by most of us who marched, lay the homes of an earlier generation. But we marched, each obeying the orders of his own soul. Some day the song of this may be sung; some day, perhaps, its canvas may be painted.

CHAPTER XXV

OREGON

The spell and the light of each path we pursue—
If woman be there, there is happiness too.

—Moore.

TWENTY miles a day, week in and week out, we edged westward up the Platte, in heat and dust part of the time, often plagued at night by clouds of mosquitoes. Our men endured the penalties of the journey without comment. I do not recall that I ever heard even the weakest woman complain. Thus at last we reached the South Pass of the Rockies, not yet half done our journey, and entered upon that portion of the trail west of the Rockies, which had still two mountain ranges to cross, and which was even more apt to be infested by the hostile Indians. Even when we reached the ragged trading post, Fort Hall, we had still more than six hundred miles to go.

By this time our forces had wasted as though under assault of arms. Far back on the trail, many had been forced to leave prized belongings, relics, heirlooms, implements, machinery, all conveniences.

251

The finest of mahogany blistered in the sun, abandoned and unheeded. Our trail might have been followed by discarded implements of agriculture, and by whitened bones as well. Our footsore teams, gaunt and weakened, began to faint and fall. Horses and oxen died in the harness or under the yoke, and were perforce abandoned where they fell. Each pound of superfluous weight was cast away as our motive power thus lessened. Wagons were abandoned, goods were packed on horses, oxen and cows.

We put cows into the yoke now, and used women instead of men on the drivers' seats, and boys who started riding finished afoot. Our herds were sadly lessened by theft of the Indians, by death, by strayings which our guards had not time to follow up. If a wagon lagged it was sawed shorter to lessen its weight. Sometimes the hind wheels were abandoned, and the reduced personal belongings were packed on the cart thus made, which nevertheless traveled on, painfully, slowly, yet always going ahead. In the deserts beyond Fort Hall, wagons disintegrated by the heat. Wheels would fall apart, couplings break under the straining teams. Still more here was the trail lined with boxes, vehicles, furniture, all the flotsam and jetsam of the long, long Oregon Trail.

The grass was burned to its roots, the streams were reduced to ribbons, the mirages of the desert mocked us desperately. Rain came seldom now, and the sage-brush of the desert was white with bitter dust, which in vast clouds rose sometimes in the wind to make our journey the harder. In autumn, as we approached the second range of mountains, we could see the taller peaks whitened with snow. Our leaders looked anxiously ahead, dreading the storms which must ere long overtake us. Still, gaunt now and haggard, weakened in body but not in soul, we pressed on across. That was the way to Oregon.

Gaunt and brown and savage, hungry and grim, ragged, hatless, shoeless, our cavalcade closed up and came on, and so at last came through. Ere autumn had yellowed all the foliage back east in gentler climes, we crossed the shoulders of the Blue Mountains and came into the Valley of the Walla Walla; and so passed thence down the Columbia to the Valley of the Willamette, three hundred miles yet farther, where there were then some slight centers of our civilization which had gone forward the year before.

Here were some few Americans. At Champoeg, at the little American missions, at Oregon City, and other scattered points, we met them, we hailed and were hailed by them. They were Americans. Women and plows were with them. There were churches and schools already started, and a beginning had been made in government. Faces and hands and ways

and customs and laws of our own people greeted us.
Yes. It was America.

Messengers spread abroad the news of the arrival
of our wagon train. Messengers, too, came down
from the Hudson Bay posts to scan our equipment
and estimate our numbers. There was no word ob-
tainable from these of any Canadian column of occupation to the northward which had crossed at the
head of the Peace River or the Saskatchewan, or
which lay ready at the head waters of the Fraser or
the Columbia to come down to the lower settlements
for the purpose of bringing to an issue, or making
more difficult, this question of the joint occupancy of
Oregon. As a matter of fact, ultimately we won that
transcontinental race so decidedly that there never
was admitted to have been a second.

As for our people, they knew how neither to hesitate nor to dread. They unhooked their oxen from
the wagons and put them to the plows. The fruit
trees, which had crossed three ranges of mountains
and two thousand miles of unsettled country, now
found new rooting. Streams which had borne no
fruit save that of the beaver traps now were made
to give tribute to little fields and gardens, or asked to
transport wheat instead of furs. The forests which
had blocked our way were now made into roofs and
walls and fences. Whatever the future might bring,
those who had come so far and dared so much feared

that future no more than they had feared the troubles which in detail they had overcome in their vast pilgrimage.

So we took Oregon by the only law of right. Our broken and weakened cavalcade asked renewal from the soil itself. We ruffled no drum, fluttered no flag, to take possession of the land. But the canvas covers of our wagons gave way to permanent roofs. Where we had known a hundred camp-fires, now we lighted the fires of many hundred homes.

CHAPTER XXVI

THE DEBATED COUNTRY

The world was sad, the garden was a wild!
The man, the hermit, sighed—till woman smiled!
—Campbell.

OUR army of peaceful occupation scattered along the more fertile parts of the land, principally among the valleys. Of course, it should not be forgotten that what was then called Oregon meant all of what now is embraced in Oregon, Washington and Idaho, with part of Wyoming as well. It extended south to the Mexican possessions of California. How far north it was to run, it was my errand here to learn.

To all apparent purposes, I simply was one of the new settlers in Oregon, animated by like motives, possessed of little more means, and disposed to adjust myself to existing circumstances, much as did my fellows. The physical conditions of life in a country abounding in wild game and fish, and where even careless planting would yield abundant crops, offered no very difficult task to young men accustomed to shifting for themselves; so that I looked forward to the winter with no dread.

I settled near the mouth of the Willamette River, near Oregon City, and not far from where the city of Portland later was begun; and builded for myself a little cabin of two rooms, with a connecting roof. This I furnished, as did my neighbors their similar abodes, with a table made of hewed puncheons, chairs sawed from blocks, a bed framed from poles, on which lay a rude mattress of husks and straw. My window-panes were made of oiled deer hide. Thinking that perhaps I might need to plow in the coming season, I made me a plow like those around me, which might have come from Mexico or Egypt —a forked limb bound with rawhide. Wood and hide, were, indeed, our only materials. If a wagon wheel showed signs of disintegration, we lashed it together with rawhide. When the settlers of the last year sought to carry wheat to market on the Willamette barges, they did so in sacks made of the hides of deer. Our clothing was of skins and furs.

From the Eastern States I scarcely could now hear in less than a year, for another wagon train could not start west from the Missouri until the following spring. We could only guess how events were going forward in our diplomacy. We did not know, and would not know for a year, the result of the Democratic convention at Baltimore, of the preceding spring! We could only wonder who might be the party nominees for the presidency. We had a national government, but did not know what it was, or who administered it. War might be declared, but we in Oregon would not be aware of it. Again, war might break out in Oregon, and the government at Washington could not know that fact.

The mild winter wore away, and I learned little. Spring came, and still no word of any land expedition out of Canada. We and the Hudson Bay folk still dwelt in peace. The flowers began to bloom in the wild meads, and the horses fattened on their native pastures. Wider and wider lay the areas of black overturned soil, as our busy farmers kept on at their work. Wider grew the clearings in the forest lands. Our fruit trees, which we had brought two thousand miles in the nursery wagon, began to put out tender leafage. There were eastern flowers— marigolds, hollyhocks, mignonette—planted in the front yards of our little cabins. Vines were trained over trellises here and there. Each flower was a rivet, each vine a cord, which bound Oregon to our Republic.

Summer came on. The fields began to whiten with the ripening grain. I grew uneasy, feeling myself only an idler in a land so able to fend for itself. I now was much disposed to discuss means of getting back over the long trail to the eastward, to carry the news that Oregon was ours. I had, it must be confessed, nothing new to suggest as to making it firmly and legally ours, beyond what had already been suggested in the minds of our settlers themselves. It was at this time that there occurred a startling and decisive event.

I was on my way on a canoe voyage up the wide Columbia, not far above the point where it receives its greatest lower tributary, the Willamette, when all at once I heard the sound of a cannon shot. I turned to see the cloud of blue smoke still hanging over the surface of the water. Slowly there swung into view an ocean-going vessel under steam and auxiliary canvas. She made a gallant spectacle. But whose ship was she? I examined her colors anxiously enough. I caught the import of her ensign. She flew the British Union Jack!

England had won the race by sea!

Something in the ship's outline seemed to me familiar. I knew the set of her short masts, the pitch of her smokestacks, the number of her guns. Yes, she was the *Modesté* of the English Navy—the same ship which more than a year before I had seen at anchor off Montreal!

News travels fast in wild countries, and it took us little time to learn the destination of the *Modesté*. She came to anchor above Oregon City, and well below Fort Vancouver. At once, of course, her officers made formal calls upon Doctor McLaughlin, the factor at Fort Vancouver, and accepted head of

the British element thereabouts. Two weeks passed
in rumors and counter rumors, and a vastly dangerous tension existed in all the American settlements,
because word was spread that England had sent a
ship to oust us. Then came to myself and certain
others at Oregon City messengers from peace-loving
Doctor McLaughlin, asking us to join him in a little
celebration in honor of the arrival of her Majesty's
vessel.

Here at last was news; but it was news not wholly
to my liking which I soon unearthed. The *Modesté*
was but one ship of fifteen! A fleet of fifteen vessels,
four hundred guns, then lay in Puget Sound. The
watch-dogs of Great Britain were at our doors. This
question of monarchy and the Republic was not yet
settled, after all!

I pass the story of the banquet at Fort Vancouver,
because it is unpleasant to recite the difficulties of a
kindly host who finds himself with jarring elements
at his board. Precisely this was the situation of
white-haired Doctor McLaughlin of Fort Vancouver. It was an incongruous assembly in the first
place. The officers of the British Navy attended in
the splendor of their uniforms, glittering in braid
and gold. Even Doctor McLaughlin made brave
display, as was his wont, in his regalia of dark blue
cloth and shining buttons—his noble features and
long, snow-white hair making him the most lordly

figure of them all. As for us Americans, lean and brown, with hands hardened by toil, our wardrobes scattered over a thousand miles of trail, buckskin tunics made our coats, and moccasins our boots. I have seen some noble gentlemen so clad in my day.

We Americans were forced to listen to many toasts at that little frontier banquet entirely to our disliking. We heard from Captain Parke that "the Columbia belonged to Great Britain as much as the Thames"; that Great Britain's guns "could blow all the Americans off the map"; that her fleet at Puget Sound waited but for the signal to "hoist the British flag over all the coast from Mexico to Russia." Yet Doctor McLaughlin, kindly and gentle as always, better advised than any one there on the intricacies of the situation now in hand, only smiled and protested and explained.

For myself, I passed only as plain settler. No one knew my errand in the country, and I took pains, though my blood boiled, as did that of our other Americans present at that board, to keep a silent tongue in my head. If this were joint occupancy, I for one was ready to say it was time to make an end of it. But how might that be done? At least the proceedings of the evening gave no answer.

It was, as may be supposed, late in the night when our somewhat discordant banqueting party broke up. We were all housed, as was the hospitable fashion of the country, in the scattered log buildings which nearly always hedge in a western fur-trading post. The quarters assigned me lay across the open space, or what might be called the parade ground of Fort Vancouver, flanked by Doctor McLaughlin's four little cannon.

As I made my way home, stumbling among the stumps in the dark, I passed many semi-drunken Indians and *voyageurs,* to whom special liberty had been accorded in view of the occasion, all of them now engaged in singing the praises of the "King George" men as against the "Bostons." I talked now and again with some of our own brown and silent border men, farmers from the Willamette, none of them any too happy, all of them sullen and ready for trouble in any form. We agreed among us that absolute quiet and freedom from any expression of irritation was our safest plan. "Wait till next fall's wagon trains come in!" That was the expression of our new governor, Mr. Applegate; and I fancy it found an echo in the opinions of most of the Americans. By snowfall, as we believed, the balance of power would be all upon our side, and our swift-moving rifles would outweigh all their anchored cannon.

I was almost at my cabin door at the edge of the forest frontage at the rear of the old post, when I

caught glimpse, in the dim light, of a hurrying
figure, which in some way seemed to be different
from the blanket-covered squaws who stalked here.
and there about the post grounds. At first I thought
she might be the squaw of one of the employees of
the company, who lived scattered about, some of
them now, by the advice of Doctor McLaughlin, beginning to till little fields; but, as I have said, there
was something in the stature or carriage or garb of
this woman which caused me idly to follow her, at
first with my eyes and then with my footsteps.

She passed steadily on toward a long and low log
cabin, located a short distance beyond the quarters.
which had been assigned to me. I saw her step up
to the door and heard her knock; then there came a
flood of light—more light than was usual in the
opening of the door of a frontier cabin. This displayed the figure of the night walker, showing her
tall and gaunt and a little stooped; so that, after all,
I took her to be only one of our American frontier
women, being quite sure that she was not Indian or
half-breed.

This emboldened me, on a mere chance—an act
whose mental origin I could not have traced—to
step up to the door after it had been closed, and
myself to knock thereat. If it were a party of Americans here, I wished to question them; if not, I

intended to make excuses by asking my way to my own quarters. It was my business to learn the news of Oregon.

I heard women's voices within, and as I knocked the door opened just a trifle on its chain. I saw appear at the crack the face of the woman whom I had followed.

She was, as I had believed, old and wrinkled, and her face now, seen close, was as mysterious, dark and inscrutable as that of any Indian squaw. Her hair fell heavy and gray across her forehead, and her eyes were small and dark as those of a native woman. Yet, as she stood there with the light streaming upon her, I saw something in her face which made me puzzle, ponder and start—and put my foot within the crack of the door.

When she found she could not close the door, she called out in some foreign tongue. I heard a voice answer. The blood tingled in the roots of my hair!

"Threlka," I said quietly, "tell Madam the Baroness it is I, Monsieur Trist, of Washington."

CHAPTER XXVII

IN THE CABIN OF MADAM

Woman must not belong to herself; she is bound to alien destinies.—Friedrich von Schiller.

WITH an exclamation of surprise, the old woman departed from the door. I heard the rustle of a footfall. I could have told in advance what face would now appear outlined in the candle glow—with eyes wide and startled, with lips half parted in query. It was the face of Helena, Baroness von Ritz!

"*Eh bien!* madam, why do you bar me out?" I said, as though we had parted but yesterday.

In her sheer astonishment, I presume, she let down the fastening chain, and without her invitation I stepped within. I heard her startled *"Mon Dieu!"* then her more deliberate exclamation of emotion. "My God!" she said. She stood, with her hands caught at her throat, staring at me. I laughed and held out a hand.

"Madam Baroness," I said, "how glad I am! Come, has not fate been kind to us again?"

I pushed shut the door behind me. Still without

a word, she stepped deeper into the room and stood looking at me, her hands clasped now loosely and awkwardly, as though she were a country girl surprised, and not the Baroness Helena von Ritz, toast or talk of more than one capital of the world.

Yet she was the same. She seemed slightly thinner now, yet not less beautiful. Her eyes were dark and brilliant as ever. The clear features of her face were framed in the roll of her heavy locks, as I had seen them last. Her garb, as usual, betokened luxury. She was robed as though for some fête, all in white satin, and pale blue fires of stones shone faintly at throat and wrist. Contrast enough she made to me, clad in smoke-browned tunic of buck, with the leggings and moccasins of a savage, my belt lacking but prepared for weapons.

I had not time to puzzle over the question of her errand here, why or whence she had come, or what she purposed doing. I was occupied with the sudden surprises which her surroundings offered.

"I see, Madam," said I, smiling, "that still I am only asleep and dreaming. But how exquisite a dream, here in this wild country! How unfit here am I, a savage, who introduce the one discordant note into so sweet a dream!"

I gestured to my costume, gestured about me, as I took in the details of the long room in which we stood. I swear it was the same as that in which I

had seen her at a similar hour in Montreal! It was
the same I had first seen in Washington!

Impossible? I am doubted? Ah, but do I not
know? Did I not see? Here were the pictures on
the walls, the carved Cupids, the candelabra with
their prisms, the chairs, the couches! Beyond yonder satin curtains rose the high canopy of the
embroidery-covered couch, its fringed drapery
reaching almost to the deep pile of the carpets. True,
opportunity had not yet offered for the full concealment of these rude walls; yet, as my senses convinced
me even against themselves, here were the apartments of Helena von Ritz, furnished as she had told
me they always were at each place she saw fit to
honor with her presence!

Yet not quite the same, it seemed to me. There
were some little things missing, just as there were
some little things missing from her appearance. For
instance, these draperies at the right, which formerly had cut off the Napoleon bed at its end of the
room, now were of blankets and not of silk. The
bed itself was not piled deep in down, but con-
tained, as I fancied from my hurried glance, a thin
mattress, stuffed perhaps with straw. A roll of
blankets lay across its foot. As I gazed to the
farther extremity of this side of the long suite, I saw
other evidences of change. It was indeed as though
Helena von Ritz, creature of luxury, woman of an

old, luxurious world, exotic of monarchical surroundings, had begun insensibly to slip into the ways
of the rude democracy of the far frontiers.

I saw all this; but ere I had finished my first hurried glance I had accepted her, as always one must,
just as she was; had accepted her surroundings, pre-
posterously impossible as they all were from any
logical point of view, as fitting to herself and to her
humor. It was not for me to ask how or why she
did these things. She had done them; because, here
they were; and here was she. We had found England's woman on the Columbia!

"Yes," said she at length, slowly, "yes, I now
believe it to be fate."

She had not yet smiled. I took her hand and held
it long. I felt glad to see her, and to take her hand;
it seemed pledge of friendship; and as things now
were shaping, I surely needed a friend.

At last, her face flushing slightly, she disengaged
her hand and motioned me to a seat. But still we
stood silent for a few moments. "Have you *no* curiosity?" said she at length.

"I am too happy to have curiosity, my dear
Madam."

"You will not even ask me why I am here?" she
insisted.

"I know. I have known all along. You are in the
pay of England. When I missed you at Montreal, I

knew you had sailed on the *Modesté* for Oregon. We knew all this, and planned for it. I have come across by land to meet you. I have waited. I greet you now!"

She looked me now clearly in the face. "I am not sure," said she at length, slowly.

"Not sure of what, Madam? When you travel on England's warship," I smiled, "you travel as the guest of England herself. If, then, you are not for England, in God's name, *whose friend are you?*"

"Whose friend am I?" she answered slowly. "I say to you that I do not know. Nor do I know who is my friend. A friend—what is that? I never knew one!"

"Then be mine. Let me be your friend. You know my history. You know about me and my work. I throw my secret into your hands. You will not betray me? You warned me once, at Montreal. Will you not shield me once again?"

She nodded, smiling now in an amused way. "Monsieur always takes the most extraordinary times to visit me! Monsieur asks always the most extraordinary things! Monsieur does always the most extraordinary acts! He takes me to call upon a gentleman in a night robe! He calls upon me himself, of an evening, in dinner dress of hides and beads—"

" 'Tis the best I have, Madam!" I colored, but

her eye had not criticism, though her speech had mockery.

"This is the costume of your American savages," she said. "I find it among the most beautiful I have ever seen. Only a man can wear it. You wear it like a man. I like you in it—I have never liked you so well. Betray you, Monsieur? Why should I? How could I?"

"That is true. Why should you? You are Helena von Ritz. One of her breeding does not betray men or women. Neither does she make any journeys of this sort without a purpose."

"I had a purpose, when I started. I changed it in mid-ocean. Now, I was on my way to the Orient."

"And had forgotten your report to Mr. Pakenham?" I shook my head. "Madam, you are the guest of England."

"I never denied that," she said. "I was that in Washington. I was so in Montreal. But I have never given pledge which left me other than free to go as I liked. I have studied, that is true—but I have *not* reported."

"Have we not been fair with you, Baroness? Has my chief not proved himself fair with you?"

"Yes," she nodded. "You have played the game fairly, that is true."

"Then you will play it fair with us? Come, I say

you have still that chance to win the gratitude of a people."

"I begin to understand you better, you Americans," she said irrelevantly, as was sometimes her fancy. "See my bed yonder. It is that couch of husks of which Monsieur told me! Here is the cabin of logs. There is the fireplace. Here is Helena von Ritz—even as you told me once before she sometime might be. And here on my wrists are the imprints of your fingers! What does it mean, Monsieur? Am I not an apt student? See, I made up that little bed with my own hands! I— Why, see, I can cook! What you once said to me lingered in my mind. At first, it was matter only of curiosity. Presently I began to see what was beneath your words, what fullness of life there might be even in poverty. I said to myself, 'My God! were it not, after all, enough, this, if one be loved?' So then, in spite of myself, without planning, I say, I began to understand. I have seen about me here these savages—savages who have walked thousands of miles in a pilgrimage—for what?"

"For what, Madam?" I demanded. "For what? For a cabin! For a bed of husks! Was it then for the sake of ease, for the sake of selfishness? Come, can you betray a people of whom you can say so much?"

"Ah, now you would try to tempt me from a trust which has been reposed in me!"

"Not in the least. I would not have you break your word with Mr. Pakenham; but I know you are here on the same errand as myself. You are to learn facts and report them to Mr. Pakenham—as I am to Mr. Calhoun."

"What does Monsieur suggest?" she asked me, with her little smile.

"Nothing, except that you take back all the facts —and allow them to mediate. Let them determine between the Old World and this New one—yon satin couch and this rude one you have learned to make. Tell the truth only. Choose, then, Madam!"

"Nations do not ask the truth. They want only excuses."

"Quite true. And because of that, all the more rests with you. If this situation goes on, war must come. It can not be averted, unless it be by some agency quite outside of these two governments. Here, then, Madam, is Helena von Ritz!"

"At least, there is time," she mused. "These ships are not here for any immediate active war. Great Britain will make no move until—"

"Until Madam the Baroness, special agent of England, most trusted agent, makes her report to Mr. Pakenham! Until he reports to his government, and until that government declares war!

'Twill take a year or more. Meantime, you have not reported?"

"No, I am not yet ready."

"Certainly not. You are not yet possessed of your facts. You have not yet seen this country. You do not yet know these men—the same savages who once accounted for another Pakenham at New Orleans—hardy as buffaloes, fierce as wolves. Wait and see them come pouring across the mountains into Oregon. Then make your report to this Pakenham. Ask him if England wishes to fight our backwoodsmen once more!"

"You credit me with very much ability!" she smiled.

"With all ability. What conquests you have made in the diplomacy of the Old World I do not know. You have known courts. I have known none. Yet you are learning life. You are learning the meaning of the only human idea of the world, that of a democracy of endeavor, where all are equal in their chances and in their hopes. That, Madam, is the only diplomacy which will live. If you have passed on that torch of principle of which you spoke—if I can do as much—then all will be well. We shall have served."

She dropped now into a chair near by a little table, where the light of the tall candles, guttering in their enameled sconces, fell full upon her face.

She looked at me fixedly, her eyes dark and mournful in spite of their eagerness.

"Ah, it is easy for you to speak, easy for you who have so rich and full a life—who have all! But I —my hands are empty!" She spread out her curved fingers, looking at them, dropping her hands, pathetically drooping her shoulders.

"All, Madam? What do you mean? You see me almost in rags. Beyond the rifle at my cabin, the pistol at my tent, I have scarce more in wealth than what I wear, while you have what you like."

"All but everything!" she murmured; "all but home!"

"Nor have I a home."

"All, except that my couch is empty save for myself and my memories!"

"Not more than mine, nor with sadder memories, Madam."

"Why, what do you mean?" she asked me suddenly. "What do you *mean?*" She repeated it again, as though half in horror.

"Only that we are equal and alike. That we are here on the same errand. That our view of life should be the same."

"What do you mean about home? But tell me, *were you not then married?*"

"No, I am alone, Madam. I never shall be married."

There may have been some slight motion of a hand which beckoned me to a seat at the opposite side of the table. As I sat, I saw her search my face carefully, slowly, with eyes I could not read. At last she spoke, after her frequent fashion, half to herself.

"It succeeded, then!" said she. "Yet I am not happy! Yet I have failed!"

"I pause, Madam," said I, smiling. "I await your pleasure."

"Ah, God! Ah, God!" she sighed. "What have I done?" She staggered to her feet and stood beating her hands together, as was her way when perturbed. "What have I *done!*"

"Threlka!" I heard her call, half chokingly. The old servant came hurriedly.

"Wine, tea, anything, Threlka!" She dropped down again opposite me, panting, and looking at me with wide eyes.

"Tell me, do you know what you have said?" she began.

"No, Madam. I grieve if I have caused you any pain."

"Well, then, you are noble; when look, what pain I have caused you! Yet not more than myself. No, not so much. I hope not so much!"

Truly there is thought which passes from mind to mind. Suddenly the thing in her mind sped across to mine. I looked at her suddenly, in my eyes also, perhaps, the horror which I felt.

"It was you!" I exclaimed. "It was you! Ah, now I begin to understand! How could you? You parted us! *You* parted me from Elisabeth!"

"Yes," she said regretfully, "I did it. It was my fault."

I rose and drew apart from her, unable to speak. She went on.

"But I was not then as I am now. See, I was embittered, reckless, desperate. I was only beginning to think—I only wanted time. I did not really mean to do all this. I only thought— Why, I had not yet known you a day nor her an hour. 'Twas all no more than half a jest."

"How could you do it?" I demanded. "Yet that is no more strange. How *did* you do it?"

"At the door, that first night. I was mad then over the wrong done to what little womanhood I could claim for my own. I hated Yturrio. I hated Pakenham. They had both insulted me. I hated every man. I had seen nothing but the bitter and desperate side of life—I was eager to take revenge even upon the innocent ones of this world, seeing that I had suffered so much. I had an old grudge against women, against women, I say—against *women!*"

She buried her face in her hands. I saw her eyes

no more till Threlka came and lifted her head, offering her a cup of drink, and so standing patiently
uutil again she had dismissal.

"But still it is all a puzzle to me, Madam," I began. "I do not understand."

"Well, when you stood at the door, my little shoe
in your pocket, when you kissed my hand that first
night, when you told me what you would do did you
love a woman—when I saw something new in life I
had not seen—why, then, in the devil's resolution
that no woman in the world should be happy if I
could help it, I slipped in the body of the slipper a
little line or so that I had written when you did not
see, when I was in the other room.   'Twas that took
the place of Van Zandt's message, after all!   Monsieur, it was fate.   Van Zandt's letter, without plan,
fell out on my table.   Your note, sent by plan, remained in the shoe!"

"And what did it say?   Tell me at once."

"Very little.   Yet enough for a woman who loved
and who expected.   Only this: *"In spite of that
other woman, come to me still.   Who can teach yon
love of woman as can I ?   Helena.'*   I think it was
some such words as those."

I looked at her in silence.

"You did not see that note?" she demanded.
"After all, at first I meant it only for *you*. I wanted
to see you again.   I did not want to lose you.   Ah,

God! I was so lonely, so—so—I can not say. But you did not find my message?"

I shook my head. "No," I said, "I did not look in the slipper. I do not think my friend did."

"But she—that girl, did!"

"How could she have believed?"

"Ah, grand! I reverence your faith. But she is a woman! She loved you and expected you that hour, I say. Thus comes the shock of finding you untrue, of finding you at least a common man, after all. She is a woman. 'Tis the same fight, all the centuries, after all! Well, I did that."

"You ruined the lives of two, neither of whom had ever harmed you, Madam."

"What is it to the tree which consumes another tree—the flower which devours its neighbor? Was it not life?"

"You had never seen Elisabeth."

"Not until the next morning, no. Then I thought still on what you had said. I envied her—I say, I coveted the happiness of you both. What had the world ever given me? What had I done—what had I been—what could I ever be? Your messenger came back with the slipper. The note was in the shoe untouched. Your messenger had not found it, either. See, I *did* mean it for you alone. But now some sudden thought came to me. I tucked it back and sent your drunken friend away with it for her

—where I knew it would be found! I did not know what would be the result. I was only desperate over what life had done to me. I wanted to get *out*— out into a wider and brighter world."

"Ah, Madam, and was so mean a key as this to open that world for you? Now we all three wander, outside that world."

"No, it opened no new world for me," she said. "I was not meant for that. But at least, I only acted as I have been treated all my life. I knew no better then."

"I had not thought any one capable of that," said I.

"Ah, but I repented on the instant! I repented before night came. In the twilight I got upon my knees and prayed that all my plan might go wrong —if I could call it plan. 'Now,' I said, as the hour approached, 'they are before the priest; they stand there—she in white, perhaps; he tall and grave. Their hands are clasped each in that of the other. They are saying those tremendous words which may perhaps mean so much.' Thus I ran on to myself. I say I followed you through the hour of that ceremony. I swore with her vows, I pledged with her pledge, promised with her promise. Yes, yes—yes, though I prayed that, after all, I might lose, that I might pay back; that I might some time have opportunity to atone for my own wickedness! Ah! I was only a woman. The strongest of women are weak sometimes.

"Well, then, my friend, I have paid. I thank God that I failed then to make another wretched as myself. It was only I who again was wretched. Ah! is there no little pity in your heart for me, after all? —who succeeded only to fail so miserably?"

But again I could only turn away to ponder.

"See," she went on; "for myself, this is irremediable, but it is not so for you, nor for her. It is not too ill to be made right again. There in Montreal, I thought that I had failed in my plan, that you indeed were married. You held yourself well in hand; like a man, Monsieur. But as to that, you *were* married, for your love for her remained; your pledge held. And did not I, repenting, marry you to her—did not I, on my knees, marry you to her that night? Oh, do not blame me too much!"

"She should not have doubted," said I. "I shall not go back and ask her again. The weakest of men are strong sometimes!"

"Ah, now you are but a man! Being such, you can not understand how terribly much the faith of man means for a woman. It was her *need* for you that spoke, not her *doubt* of you. Forgive her. She was not to blame. Blame me! Do what you like to punish me! Now, I shall make amends. Tell me

what I best may do. Shall I go to her, shall I tell
her?"

"Not as my messenger. Not for me."

"No? Well, then, for myself? That is my right.
I shall tell her how priestly faithful a man you
were."

I walked to her, took her arms in my hands and
raised her to my level, looking into her eyes.

"Madam," I said, "God knows, I am no priest. I
deserve no credit. It was chance that cast Elisabeth
and me together before ever I saw you. I told you
one fire was lit in my heart and had left room for no
other. I meet youth and life with all that there is
in youth and life. I am no priest, and ask you not
to confess with me. We both should confess to our
own souls."

"It is as I said," she went on; "you were married!"

"Well, then, call it so—married after my fashion
of marriage; the fashion of which I told you, of a
cabin and a bed of husks. As to what you have said,
I forget it, I have not heard it. Your sort could
have no heart beat for one like me. 'Tis men like
myself are slaves to women such as you. You could
never have cared for me, and never did. What you
loved, Madam, was only what you had *lost,* was only
what you saw in this country—was only what this

country means! Your past life, of course, I do not know."

"Sometime," she murmured, "I will tell you."

"Whatever it was, Madam, you have been a brilliant woman, a power in affairs. Yes, and an enigma, and to none more than to yourself. You show that now. You only loved what Elisabeth loved. As woman, then, you were born for the first time, touched by that throb of her heart, not your own. 'Twas mere accident I was there to feel that throb, as sweet as it was innocent. You were not woman yet, you were but a child. You had not then chosen. You have yet to choose. It was Love that you loved! Perhaps, after all, it was America you loved. You began to see, as you say, a wider and a sweeter world than you had known."

She nodded now, endeavoring to smile.

"*Gentilhomme!*" I heard her murmur.

"So then I go on, Madam, and say we are the same. I am the agent of one idea, you of another. I ask you once more to choose. I know how you will choose."

She went on, musing to herself. "Yes, there is a gulf between male and female, after all. As though what he said could be true! Listen!" She spoke up more sharply. "If results came as you liked, what difference would the motives make?"

"How do you mean?"

"Only this, Monsieur, that I am not so lofty as you think. I might do something. If so, 'twould need to be through some motive wholly sufficient to *myself.*"

"Search, then, your own conscience."

"I have one, after all! It might say something to me, yes."

"Once you said to me that the noblest thing in life was to pass on the torch of a great principle."

"I lied! I lied!" she cried, beating her hands together. "I am a woman! Look at me!"

She threw back her shoulders, standing straight and fearless. God wot, she was a woman. Curves and flame! Yes, she was a woman. White flesh and slumbering hair! Yes, she was a woman. Round flesh and the red-flecked purple scent arising! Yes, she was a woman. Torture of joy to hold in a man's arms! Yes, she was a woman!

"How, then, could I believe"—she laid a hand upon her bosom—"how, then, could I believe that principle was more than life? It is for you, a *man,* to believe that. Yet even you will not. You leave it to me, and I answer that I will not! What I did I did, and I bargain with none over that now. I pay my wagers. I make my own reasons, too. If I do anything for the sake of this country, it will not be through altruism, not through love of principle! 'Twill be because I am a woman. Yes, once I was a girl. Once I was born. Once, even, I had a mother, and was loved!"

I could make no answer; but presently she changed again, swift as the sky when some cloud is swept away in a strong gust of wind.

"Come," she said, "I will bargain with you, after all!"

"Any bargain you like, Madam."

"And I will keep my bargain. You know that I will."

"Yes, I know that."

"Very well, then. I am going back to Washington."

"How do you mean?"

"By land, across the country; the way you came."

"You do not know what you say, Madam. The journey you suggest is incredible, impossible."

"That matters nothing. I am going. And I am going alone— No, you can not come with me. Do you think I would risk more than I have risked? I go alone. I am England's spy; yes, that is true. I am to report to England; yes, that is true. Therefore, the more I see, the more I shall have to report. Besides, I have something else to do."

"But would Mr. Pakenham listen to your report, after all?"

Now she hesitated for a moment. "I can induce him to listen," she said. "That is part of my errand.

First, before I see Mr. Pakenham I am going to see
Miss Elisabeth Churchill.   I shall report also to her.
Then I shall have done my duty.   Is it not so?"

"You could do no more," said I.   "But what bargain—"

"Listen.   If she uses me ill and will not believe
either you or me—then, being a woman, I shall hate
her; and in that case I shall go to Sir Richard for
my own revenge.   I shall tell him to bring on this
war.   In that case, Oregon will be lost to you, or at
least bought dear by blood and treasure."

"We can attend to that, Madam," said I grimly,
and I smiled at her, although a sudden fear caught
at my heart.   I knew what damage she was in position to accomplish if she liked.   My heart stood still.
I felt the faint sweat again on my forehead.

"If I do not find her worthy of you, then she can
not have you," went on Helena von Ritz.

"But Madam, you forget one thing.   She *is* worthy of me, or of any other man!"

"I shall be judge of that.   If she is what you
think, you shall have her—and Oregon!"

"But as to myself, Madam?   The bargain?"

"I arrive, Monsieur!   If she fails you, then I ask
only time.   I have said to you I am a woman!"

"Madam," I said to her once more, "who are you
and what are you?"

In answer, she looked me once more straight in

the face. "Some day, back there, after I have made
my journey, I shall tell you."

"Tell me now."

"I shall tell you nothing. I am not a little girl.
There is a bargain which I offer, and the only one I
shall offer. It is a gamble. I have gambled all my
life. If you will not accord me so remote a chance
as this, why, then, I shall take it in any case."

"I begin to see, Madam," said I, "how large these
stakes may run."

"In case I lose, be sure at least I shall pay. I shall
make my atonement," she said.

"I doubt not that, Madam, with all your heart
and mind and soul."

"And *body!*" she whispered. The old horror
came again upon her face. She shuddered, I did
not know why. She stood now as one in devotions
for a time, and I would no more have spoken than
had she been at her prayers, as, indeed, I think she
was. At last she made some faint movement of her
hands. I do not know whether it was the sign of
the cross.

She rose now, tall, white-clad, shimmering, a
vision of beauty such as that part of the world certainly could not then offer. Her hair was loosened
now in its masses and drooped more widely over her
temples, above her brow. Her eyes were very large
and dark, and I saw the faint blue shadows coming

"I want—" said she. "I wish—I wish——" Page 287

again beneath them. Her hands were clasped, her chin raised just a trifle, and her gaze was rapt as that of some longing soul. I could not guess of these things, being but a man, and, I fear, clumsy alike of body and wit.

"There is one thing, Madam, which we have omitted," said I at last. "What are *my* stakes? How may I pay?"

She swayed a little on her feet, as though she were weak. "I want," said she, "I wish—I wish—"

The old childlike look of pathos came again. I have never seen so sad a face. She was a lady, white and delicately clad; I, a rude frontiersman in camp-grimed leather. But I stepped to her now and took her in my arms and held her close, and pushed back the damp waves of her hair. And because a man's tears were in my eyes, I have no doubt of absolution when I say I had been a cad and a coward had I not kissed her own tears away. I no longer made pretense of ignorance, but ah! how I wished that I were ignorant of what it was not my right to know. . . .

I led her to the edge of the little bed of husks and found her kerchief. Ah, she was of breeding and courage! Presently, her voice rose steady and clear as ever. "Threlka!" she called. "Please!"

When Threlka came, she looked closely at her lady's face, and what she read seemed, after all, to content her.

"Threlka," said my lady in French, "I want the little one."

I turned to her with query in my eyes.

"*Tiens!*" she said. "Wait. I have a little surprise."

"You have nothing at any time save surprises, Madam."

"Two things I have," said she, sighing: "a little dog from China, Chow by name. He sleeps now, and I must not disturb him, else I would show you how lovely a dog is Chow. Also here I have found a little Indian child running about the post. Doctor McLaughlin was rejoiced when I adopted her."

"Well, then, Madam, what next!"

—"Yes, with the promise to him that I would care for that little child. I want something for my own. See now. Come, Natoka!"

The old servant paused at the door. There slid across the floor with the silent feet of the savage the tiny figure of a little child, perhaps four years of age, with coal-black hair and beady eyes, clad in all the bequilled finery that a trading-post could furnish—a little orphan child, as I learned later, whose parents had both been lost in a canoe accident at the Dalles. She was an infant, wild, untrained, unloved, unable to speak a word of the language that she heard. She stood now hesitating, but that was only by reason of her sight of me. As I stepped aside, the little one

walked steadily but with quickening steps to my
satin-clad lady on her couch of husks. She took up
the child in her arms. . . . Now, there must be
some speech between woman and child. I do not
know, except that the Baroness von Ritz spoke and
that the child put out a hand to her cheek. Then, as
I stood awkward as a clown myself and not knowing
what to do, I saw tears rain again from the eyes of
Helena von Ritz, so that I turned away, even as I
saw her cheek laid to that of the child while she
clasped it tight.

"Monsieur!" I heard her say at last.

I did not answer. I was learning a bit of life myself this night. I was years older than when I had
come through that door.

"Monsieur!" I heard her call yet again.

"*Eh bien,* Madam?" I replied, lightly as I could,
and so turned, giving her all possible time. I saw
her holding the Indian child out in front of her in
her strong young arms, lightly as though the weight
were nothing.

"See, then," she said; "here is my companion
across the mountains."

Again I began to expostulate, but now she tapped
her foot impatiently in her old way. "You have
heard me say it. Very well. Follow if you like.
Listen also if you like. In a day or so, Doctor Mc-
Laughlin plans a party for us all far up the Colum-

bia to the missions at Wailatpu. That is in the valley of the Walla Walla, they tell me, just at this
edge of the Blue Mountains, where the wagon trains
come down into this part of Oregon."

"They may not see the wagon trains so soon," I
ventured. "They would scarcely arrive before October, and now it is but summer."

"At least, these British officers would see a part of
this country, do you not comprehend? We start
within three days at least. I wish only to say that
perhaps—"

"Ah, I will be there surely, Madam!"

"If you come independently. I have heard, however, that one of the missionary women wishes to go
back to the States. I have thought that perhaps it
might be better did we go together. Also Natoka.
Also Chow."

"Does Doctor McLaughlin know of your plans?"

"I am not under his orders, Monsieur. I only
thought that, since you were used to this western
travel, you could, perhaps, be of aid in getting me
proper guides and vehicles. I should rely upon your
judgment very much, Monsieur."

"You are asking me to aid you in your own folly,"
said I discontentedly, "but I will be there; and be
sure also you can not prevent me from following—if
you persist in this absolute folly. A woman—to
cross the Rockies!"

I rose now, and she was gracious enough to follow me part way toward the door. We hesitated there, awkwardly enough. But once more our hands met in some sort of fellowship.

"Forget!" I heard her whisper. And I could think of no reply better than that same word.

I turned as the door swung for me to pass out into the night. I saw her outlined against the lights within, tall and white, in her arms the Indian child, whose cheek was pressed to her own. I do not concern myself with what others may say of conduct or of constancy. To me it seemed that, had I not made my homage, my reverence, to one after all so brave as she, I would not be worthy the cover of that flag which to-day floats both on the Columbia and the Rio Grande.

CHAPTER XXVIII

WHEN A WOMAN WOULD

The two pleasantest days of a woman are her marriage day and the day of her funeral.—Hipponax.

M Y garden at the Willamette might languish if it liked, and my little cabin might stand in uncut wheat. For me, there were other matters of more importance now. I took leave of hospitable Doctor McLaughlin at Fort Vancouver with proper expressions of the obligation due for his hospitality; but I said nothing to him, of course, of having met the mysterious baroness, nor did I mention definitely that I intended to meet them both again at no distant date. None the less, I prepared to set out at once up the Columbia River trail.

From Fort Vancouver to the missions at Wailatpu was a distance by trail of more than two hundred miles. This I covered horseback, rapidly, and arrived two or three days in advance of the English. Nothing disturbed the quiet until, before noon of one day, we heard the gun fire and the shoutings which in that country customarily made announcement of the arrival of a party of travelers. Being on the lookout for these, I soon discovered them to be my late friends of the Hudson Bay Post.

One old brown woman, unhappily astride a native pony, I took to be Threlka, my lady's servant, but she rode with her class, at the rear. I looked again, until I found the baroness, clad in buckskins and blue cloth, brave as any in finery of the frontier. Doctor McLaughlin saw fit to present us formally, or rather carelessly, it not seeming to him that two so different would meet often in the future; and of course there being no dream even in his shrewd mind that we had ever met in the past. This supposition fitted our plans, even though it kept us apart. I was but a common emigrant farmer, camping like my kind. She, being of distinction, dwelt with the Hudson Bay party in the mission buildings.

We lived on here for a week, visiting back and forth in amity, as I must say. I grew to like well enough those blunt young fellows of the Navy. With young Lieutenant Peel especially I struck up something of a friendship. If he remained hopelessly British, at least I presume I remained quite as hopelessly American; so that we came to set aside the topic of conversation on which we could not agree.

"There is something about which you don't know," he said to me, one evening. "I am wholly unacquainted with the interior of your country. What would you say, for instance, regarding its safety for a lady traveling across—a small party, you know, of her own? I presume of course you know whom I mean?"

I nodded. "You must mean the Baroness von Ritz."

"Yes. She has been traveling abroad. Of course we took such care of her on shipboard as we could, although a lady has no place on board a warship. She had with her complete furnishings for a suite of apartments, and these were delivered ashore at Fort Vancouver. Doctor McLaughlin gave her quarters. Of course you do not know anything of this?"

I allowed him to proceed.

"Well, she has told us calmly that she plans crossing this country from here to the Eastern States!"

"That could not possibly be!" I declared.

"Quite so. The old trappers tell me that the mountains are impassable even in the fall. They say that unless she met some west-bound train and came back with it, the chance would be that she would never be heard of again."

"You have personal interest in this?" I interrupted.

He nodded, flushing a little. "Awfully so," said he.

"I would have the right to guess you were hit pretty hard?"

"To the extent of asking her to become my wife!" said he firmly, although his fair face flushed again.

"You do not in the least know her," he went on. "In my case, I have done my turn at living, and have seen my share of women, but never her like in any part of the world! So when she proposed to make this absurd journey, I offered to go with her. It meant of course my desertion from the Navy, and so I told her. She would not listen to it. She gives me no footing which leaves it possible for me to accompany her or to follow her. Frankly, I do not know what to do."

"It seems to me, Lieutenant Peel," I ventured, "that the most sensible thing in the world for us to do is to get together an expedition to follow her."

He caught me by the hand. "You do not tell me *you* would do that?"

"It seems a duty."

"But could you yourself get through?"

"As to that, no one can tell. I did so coming west."

He sat silent for a time. "It will be the last I shall ever see of her in any case," said he, at length. "We don't know how long it will be before we leave the mouth of the Columbia, and then I could not count on finding her. You do not think me a fool for telling you what I have?"

"No," said I. "I do not blame you for being a fool. All men who are men are fools over women, one time or other."

"Good luck to you, then! Now, what shall we do?"

"In the first place," said I, "if she insists upon going, let us give her every possible chance for success."

"It looks an awfully slender chance," he sighed. "You will follow as close on their heels as you can?"

"Of that you may rest assured."

"What is the distance, do you think?"

"Two thousand miles at least, before she could be safe. She could not hope to cover more than twenty-five miles a day, many days not so much as that. To be sure, there might be such a thing as her meeting wagons coming out; and, as you say, she might return."

"You do not know her!" said he. "She will not turn back."

I had full reason to agree with him.

CHAPTER XXIX

IN EXCHANGE

Great women belong to history and to self-sacrifice.
—Leigh Hunt.

FOR sufficient reasons of my own, which have been explained, I did not care to mingle more than was necessary with the party of the Hudson Bay folk who made their quarters with the missionary families. I kept close to my own camp when not busy with my inquiries in the neighborhood, where I now began to see what could be done in the preparation of a proper outfit for the baroness. Herself I did not see for the next two days; but one evening I met her on the narrow log gallery of one of the mission houses. Without much speech we sat and looked over the pleasant prospect of the wide flats, the fringe of willow trees, the loom of the mountains off toward the east.

"Continually you surprise me, Madam," I began, at last. "Can we not persuade you to abandon this foolish plan of your going east?"

"I see no reason for abandoning it," said she. "There are some thousands of your people, men, women and children, who have crossed that trail. Why should not I?"

"But they come in large parties; they come well prepared. Each helps his neighbor."

"The distance is the same, and the method is the 'same."

I ceased to argue, seeing that she would not be persuaded. "At least, Madam," said I, "I have done what little I could in securing you a party. You are to have eight mules, two carts, six horses, and two men, beside old Joe Meek, the best guide now in Oregon. He would not go to save his life. He goes to save yours."

"You are always efficient," said she. "But why is it that we always have some unpleasant argument? Come, let us have tea!"

"Many teas together, Madam, if you would listen to me. Many a pot brewed deep and black by scores of camp-fires."

"Fie! Monsieur proposes a scandal."

"No, Monsieur proposes only a journey to Washington—with you, or close after you."

"Of course I can not prevent your following," she said.

"Leave it so. But as to pledges—at least I want to keep my little slipper. Is Madam's wardrobe with her? Could she humor a peevish friend so much as that? Come, now, I will make fair exchange. I will trade you again my blanket clasp for that one little shoe!"

I felt in the pocket of my coat, and held out in my hand the remnants of the same little Indian ornament which had figured between us the first night we had met. She grasped at it eagerly, turning it over in her hand.

"But see," she said, "one of the clasps is gone."

"Yes, I parted with it. But come, do I have my little slipper?"

"Wait!" said she, and left me for a moment. Presently she returned, laughing, with the little white satin foot covering in her hand.

"I warrant it is the only thing of the sort ever was seen in these buildings," she went on. "Alas! I fear I must leave most of my possessions here! I have already disposed of the furnishings of my apartment to Mr. James Douglas at Fort Vancouver. I hear he is to replace this good Doctor McLaughlin. Well, his half-breed wife will at least have good setting up for her household. Tell me, now," she concluded, "what became of the other shell from this clasp?"

"I gave it to an old man in Montreal," I answered. I went on to show her the nature of the device, as it had been explained to me by old Doctor von Rittenhofen.

"How curious!" she mused, as it became more

plain to her. "Life, love, eternity! The beginning and the end of all this turmoil about passing on the torch of life. It is old, old, is it not? Tell me, who was the wise man who described all this to you?"

"Not a stranger to this very country, I imagine," was my answer. "He spent some years here in Oregon with the missionaries, engaged, as he informed me, in classifying the butterflies of this new region. A German scientist, I think, and seemingly a man of breeding."

"If I were left to guess," she broke out suddenly, "I would say it must have been this same old man who told you about the plans of the Canadian land expedition to this country."

"Continually, Madam, we find much in common. At least we both know that the Canadian expedition started west. Tell me, when will it arrive on the Columbia?"

"It will never arrive. It will never cross the Rockies. Word has gone up the Columbia now that for these men to appear in this country would bring on immediate war. That does not suit the book of England more than it does that of America."

"Then the matter will wait until you see Mr. Pakenham?"

She nodded. "I suppose so."

"You will find facts enough. Should you persist in your mad journey and get far enough to the east, you will see two thousand, three thousand men coming out to Oregon this fall. It is but the beginning. But you and I, sitting here, three thousand miles and more away from Washington, can determine this question. Madam, perhaps yet you may win your right to some humble home, with a couch of husks or straw. Sleep, then, by our camp-fires across America, and let our skies cover you at night. Our men will watch over you faithfully. Be our guest—our friend!"

"You are a good special pleader," said she; "but you do not shake me in my purpose, and I hold to my terms. It does not rest with you and me, but with another. As I have told you—as we have both agreed—"

"Then let us not speak her name," said I.

Again her eyes looked into mine, straight, large and dark. Again the spell of her beauty rose all around me, enveloped me as I had felt it do before. "You can not have Oregon, except through me," she said at last. "You can not have—her—except through me!"

"It is the truth," I answered. "In God's name, then, play the game fair."

CHAPTER XXX

COUNTER CURRENTS

Woman is like the reed that bends to every breeze, but breaks not in the tempest.—Bishop Richard Whately.

THE Oregon immigration for 1845 numbered, according to some accounts, not less than three thousand souls. Our people still rolled westward in a mighty wave. The history of that great west-bound movement is well known. The story of a yet more decisive journey of that same year never has been written—that of Helena von Ritz, from Oregon to the east. The price of that journey was an empire; its cost—ah, let me not yet speak of that.

Although Meek and I agreed that he should push east at the best possible speed, it was well enough understood that I should give him no more than a day or so start. I did not purpose to allow so risky a journey as this to be undertaken by any woman in so small a party, and made no doubt that I would overtake them at least at Fort Hall, perhaps five hundred miles east of the Missions, or at farthest at

Fort Bridger, some seven hundred miles from the starting point in Oregon.

The young wife of one of the missionaries was glad enough to take passage thus for the East; and there was the silent Threlka. Those two could offer company, even did not the little Indian maid, adopted by the baroness, serve to interest her. Their equipment and supplies were as good as any purchasable. What could be done, we now had done.

Yet after all Helena von Ritz had her own way. I did not see her again after we parted that evening at the Mission. I was absent for a couple of days with a hunting party, and on my return discovered that she was gone, with no more than brief farewell to those left behind! Meek was anxious as herself to be off; but he left word for me to follow on at once.

Gloom now fell upon us all. Doctor Whitman, the only white man ever to make the east-bound journey from Oregon, encouraged us as best he could; but young Lieutenant Peel was the picture of despair, nor did he indeed fail in the prophecy he made to me; for never again did he set eyes on the face of Helena von Ritz, and never again did I meet him. I heard, years later, that he died of fever on the China coast.

It may be supposed that I myself now hurried in my plans. I was able to make up a small party of four men, about half the number Meek took with him; and I threw together such equipment as I could find remaining, not wholly to my liking, but good enough, I fancied, to overtake a party headed by a woman. But one thing after another cost us time, and we did not average twenty miles a day. I felt half desperate, as I reflected on what this might mean. As early fall was approaching, I could expect, in view of my own lost time, to encounter the annual wagon train two or three hundred miles farther westward than the object of my pursuit naturally would have done. As a matter of fact, my party met the wagons at a point well to the west of Fort Hall.

It was early in the morning we met them coming west,—that long, weary, dust-covered, creeping caravan, a mile long, slow serpent, crawling westward across the desert. In time I came up to the head of the tremendous wagon train of 1845, and its leader and myself threw up our hands in the salutation of the wilderness.

The leader's command to halt was passed back from one wagon to another, over more than a mile of trail. As we dismounted, there came hurrying up about us men and women, sunburned, lean, ragged, abandoning their wagons and crowding to hear the news from Oregon. I recall the picture well enough to-day—the sun-blistered sands all about, the short and scraggly sage-brush, the long line of white-topped wagons dwindling in the distance, the thin-faced figures which crowded about.

The captain stood at the head of the front team, his hand resting on the yoke as he leaned against the bowed neck of one of the oxen. The men and women were thin almost as the beasts which dragged the wagons. These latter stood with lolling tongues even thus early in the day, for water hereabout was scarce and bitter to the taste. So, at first almost in silence, we made the salutations of the desert. So, presently, we exchanged the news of East and West. So, I saw again my canvas of the fierce west-bound.

There is to-day no news of the quality which we then communicated. These knew nothing of Oregon. I knew nothing of the East. A national election had been held, regarding which I knew not even the names of the candidates of either party, not to mention the results. All I could do was to guess and to point to the inscription on the white top of the foremost wagon: *"Fifty-four Forty or Fight!"*

"Is Polk elected?" I asked the captain of the train.

He nodded. "He shore is," said he. "We're comin' out to take Oregon. What's the news?"

My own grim news was that Oregon was ours and must be ours. I shook hands with a hundred men on that, our hands clasped in stern and silent grip.

Then, after a time, I urged other questions foremost in my own mind. Had they seen a small party east-bound?

Yes, I had answer. They had passed this light outfit east of Bridger's post. There was one chance in a hundred they might get over the South Pass that fall, for they were traveling light and fast, with good animals, and old Joe Meek was sure he would make it through. The women? Well, one was a preacher's wife, another an old Gipsy, and another the most beautiful woman ever seen on the trail or anywhere else. Why was she going east instead of west, away from Oregon instead of to Oregon? Did I know any of them? I was following them? Then I must hurry, for soon the snow would come in the Rockies. They had seen no Indians. Well, if I was following them, there would be a race, and they wished me well! But why go East, instead of West?

Then they began to question me regarding Oregon. How was the land? Would it raise wheat and corn and hogs? How was the weather? Was there much game? Would it take much labor to clear a farm? Was there any likelihood of trouble with the Indians or with the Britishers? Could a man really get a mile square of good farm land without trouble? And so on, and so on, as we sat in the blinding sun in the sage-brush desert until midday.

Of course it came to politics. Yes, Texas had

been annexed, somehow, not by regular vote of the
Senate. There was some hitch about that. My leader
reckoned there was no regular treaty. It had just
been done by joint resolution of the House—done by
Tyler and Calhoun, just in time to take the feather
out of old Polk's cap! The treaty of annexation—
why, yes, it was ratified by Congress, and everything
signed up March third, just one day before Polk's
inaugural! Polk was on the warpath, according to
my gaunt leader. There was going to be war as sure
as shooting, unless we got all of Oregon. We had
offered Great Britain a fair show, and in return she
had claimed everything south to the Columbia, so
now we had withdrawn all soft talk. It looked like
war with Mexico and England both. Never mind,
in that case we would whip them both!

"Do you see that writin' on my wagon top?" asked
the captain. *"Fifty-four Forty or Fight.* That's
us!"

And so they went on to tell us how this cry was
spreading, South and West, and over the North as
well; although the Whigs did not dare cry it quite
so loudly.

"They want the *land,* just the same," said the captain. "We *all* want it, an', by God! we're goin' to
git it!"

And so at last we parted, each the better for the
information gained, each to resume what would to-

day seem practically an endless journey. Our fare-
wells were as careless, as confident, as had been our
greetings. Thousands of miles of unsettled country
lay east and west of us, and all around us, our empire, not then won.

History tells how that wagon train went through,
and how its settlers scattered all along the Willamette and the Columbia and the Walla Walla, and
helped us to hold Oregon. For myself, the chapter
of accidents continued. I was detained at Fort Hall,
and again east of there. I met straggling immi-
grants coming on across the South Pass to winter at
Bridger's post; but finally I lost all word of Meek's
party, and could only suppose that they had got over
the mountains.

I made the journey across the South Pass, the
snow being now beaten down on the trails more than
usual by the west-bound animals and vehicles. Of
all these now coming on, none would get farther
west than Fort Hall that year. Our own party, although over the Rockies, had yet the Plains to cross.
I was glad enough when we staggered into old Fort
Laramie in the midst of a blinding snow-storm.
Winter had caught us fair and full. I had lost the
race!

Here, then, I must winter. Yet I learned that Joe
Meek had outfitted at Laramie almost a month ear-

lier, with new animals; had bought a little grain,
and, under escort of a cavalry troop which had come
west with the wagon train, had started east in time,
perhaps, to make it through to the Missouri. In a
race of one thousand miles, the baroness had already
beaten me almost by a month! Further word was, of
course, now unobtainable, for no trains or wagons
would come west so late, and there were then no
stages carrying mail across the great Plains. There
was nothing for me to do except to wait and eat out
my heart at old Fort Laramie, in the society of Indians and trappers, half-breeds and traders. The winter seemed years in length, so gladly I make its story
brief.

It was now the spring of 1846, and I was in my
second year away from Washington. Glad enough
I was when in the first sunshine of spring I started
east, taking my chances of getting over the Plains.
At last, to make the long journey also brief, I did
reach Fort Leavenworth, by this time a five months'
loser in the transcontinental race. It was a new annual wagon train which I now met rolling westward.
Such were times and travel not so long ago.

Little enough had come of my two years' journey
out to Oregon. Like to the army of the French
king, I had marched up the hill and then marched
down again. As much might have been said of the

United States; and the same was yet more true of Great Britain, whose army of occupation had not even marched wholly up the hill. So much as this latter fact I now could tell my own government; and I could say that while Great Britain's fleet held the sea entry, the vast and splendid interior of an unknown realm was open on the east to our marching armies of settlers. Now I could describe that realm, even though the plot of events advanced but slowly regarding it. It was a plot of the stars, whose work is done in no haste.

Oregon still was held in that oft renewed and wholly absurd joint occupancy, so odious and so dangerous to both nations. Two years were taken from my life in learning that—and in learning that this question of Oregon's final ownership was to be decided not on the Pacific, not on the shoulders of the Blues or the Cascades, but in the east, there at Washington, after all. The actual issue was in the hands of the God of Battles, who sometimes uses strange instruments for His ends. It was not I, it was not Mr. Calhoun, not any of the officers of our government, who could get Oregon for us. It was the God of Battles, whose instrument was a woman, Helena von Ritz. After all, this was the chief fruit of my long journey.

As to the baroness, she had long since left Fort

Leavenworth for the East.   I followed still with
what speed I could employ. I could not reach Washington now until long after the first buds would be
out and the creepers growing green on the gallery of
Mr. Calhoun's residence.   Yes, green also on all the
lattices of Elmhurst Mansion.   What had happened
there for me?

CHAPTER XXXI

THE PAYMENT

What man seeks in love is woman; what woman seeks in man is love.—Houssaye.

WHEN I reached Washington it was indeed spring, warm, sweet spring. In the wide avenues the straggling trees were doing their best to dignify the city, and flowers were blooming everywhere. Wonderful enough did all this seem to me after thousands of miles of rude scenery of bare valleys and rocky hills, wild landscapes, seen often through cold and blinding storms amid peaks and gorges, or on the drear, forbidding Plains.

Used more, of late, to these wilder scenes, I felt awkward and still half savage. I did not at once seek out my own friends. My first wish was to get in touch with Mr. Calhoun, for I knew that so I would most quickly arrive at the heart of events.

He was away when I called at his residence on Georgetown Heights, but at last I heard the wheels of his old omnibus, and presently he entered with his usual companion, Doctor Samuel Ward. When they saw me there, then indeed I received a greeting which repaid me for many things! This over, we all three broke out in laughter at my uncouth appearance. I was clad still in such clothing as I could pick up in western towns as I hurried on from the Missouri eastward; and I had as yet found no time for barbers.

"We have had no word from you, Nicholas," said Mr. Calhoun presently, "since that from Laramie, in the fall of eighteen forty-four. This is in the spring of eighteen forty-six! Meantime, we might all have been dead and buried and none of us the wiser. What a country! 'Tis more enormous than the mind of any of us can grasp."

"You should travel across it to learn that," I grinned.

"Many things have happened since you left. You know that I am back in the Senate once more?"

I nodded. "And about Texas?" I began.

"Texas is ours,". said he, smiling grimly. "You have heard how? It was a hard fight enough—a bitter, selfish, sectional fight among politicians. But there is going to be war. Our troops crossed the Sabine more than a year ago. They will cross the Rio Grande before this year is done. The Mexican minister has asked for his passports. The administration has ordered General Taylor to advance. Mr. Polk is carrying out annexation with a vengeance.

Seeing a chance for more territory, now that Texas is safe from England, he plans war on helpless and deserted Mexico! We may hear of a battle now at any time. But this war with Mexico may yet mean war with England. That, of course, endangers our chance to gain all or any of that great Oregon country. Tell me, what have you learned?"

I hurried on now with my own news, briefly as I might. I told them of the ships of England's Navy waiting in Oregon waters; of the growing suspicion of the Hudson Bay people; of the changes in the management at Fort Vancouver; of the change also from a conciliatory policy to one of half hostility. I told them of our wagon trains going west, and of the strength of our frontiersmen; but offset this, justly as I might, by giving facts also regarding the opposition these might meet.

"Precisely," said Calhoun, walking up and down, his head bent. "England is prepared for war! How much are we prepared? It would cost us the revenues of a quarter of a century to go to war with her to-day. It would cost us fifty thousand lives. We would need an army of two hundred and fifty thousand men. Where is all that to come from? Can we transport our army there in time? But had all this bluster ceased, then we could have deferred this war with Mexico; could have bought with coin what now will cost us blood; and we could also have bought Oregon without the cost of either coin or blood. *Delay* was what we needed! *All* of Oregon should have been ours!"

"But, surely, this is not all news to you?" I began. "Have you not seen the Baroness von Ritz? Has she not made her report?"

"The baroness?" queried Calhoun. "That stormy petrel—that advance agent of events! Did she indeed sail with the British ships from Montreal? *Did* you find her there—in Oregon?"

"Yes, and lost her there! She started east last summer, and beat me fairly in the race. Has she not made known her presence here? She told me she was going to Washington."

He shook his head in surprise. "Trouble now, I fear! Pakenham has back his best ally, our worst antagonist."

"That certainly is strange," said I. "She had five months the start of me, and in that time there is no telling what she has done or undone. Surely, she is somewhere here, in Washington! She held Texas in her shoes. I tell you she holds Oregon in her gloves to-day!"

I started up, my story half untold.

"Where are you going?" asked Mr. Calhoun of me. Doctor Ward looked at me, smiling. "He does not inquire of a certain young lady—"

"I am going to find the Baroness von Ritz!" said

I. I flushed red under my tan, I doubt not; but I would not ask a word regarding Elisabeth.

Doctor Ward came and laid a hand on my shoulder. "Republics forget," said he, "but men from South Carolina do not. Neither do girls from Maryland. Do you think so?"

"That is what I am going to find out."

"How then? Are you going to Elmhurst as you look now?"

"No. I shall find out many things by first finding the Baroness von Ritz." And before they could make further protests, I was out and away.

I hurried now to a certain side street, of which I have made mention, and knocked confidently at a door I knew. The neighborhood was asleep in the warm sun. I knocked a second time, and began to doubt, but at last heard slow footsteps.

There appeared at the crack of the door the wrinkled visage of the old serving-woman, Threlka. I knew that she would be there in precisely this way, because there was every reason in the world why it should not have been. She paused, scanning me closely, then quickly opened the door and allowed me to step inside, vanishing as was her wont. I heard another step in a half-hidden hallway beyond, but this was not the step which I awaited; it was that of a man, slow, feeble, hesitating. I started forward as a face appeared at the parted curtains.

A glad cry welcomed me in turn. A tall, bent form approached me, and an arm was thrown about my shoulder. It was my whilom friend, our ancient scientist, Von Rittenhofen! I did not pause to ask how he happened to be there. It was quite natural, since it was wholly impossible. I made no wonder at the Chinese dog Chow, or the little Indian maid, who both came, stared, and silently vanished. Seeing these, I knew that their strange protector must also have won through safe.

"*Ach, Gott! Gesegneter Gott!* I see you again, my friend!" Thus the old Doctor.

"But tell me," I interrupted, "where is the mistress of this house, the Baroness von Ritz?"

He looked at me in his mild way. "You mean my daughter Helena?"

Now at last I smiled. His daughter! This at least was too incredible! He turned and reached behind him to a little table. He held up before my eyes my little blanket clasp of shell. Then I knew that this last and most impossible thing also was true, and that in some way these two had found each other! But *why?* What could he now mean?

"Listen now," he began, "and I shall tell you. I wass in the street one day. When I walk alone, I do not much notice. But now, as I walk, before my eyes on the street, I see what? This—this, the Tah Gook! At first, I see nothing but it. Then I look up. Before me iss a woman, young and beautiful. Ach! what should I do but take her in my arms!"

"It was she; it was—"

"My daughter! Yess, my daughter. It iss *Helena!* I haf not seen her for many years, long, cruel years. I suppose her dead. But now there we were, standing, looking in each other's eyes! We see there— *Ach, Gott!* what do we not see? Yet in spite of all, it wass Helena! But she shall tell you." He tottered from the room.

I heard his footsteps pass down the hall. Then softly, almost silently, Helena von Ritz again stood before me. The light from a side window fell upon her face. Yes, it was she! Her face was thinner now, browner even than was its wont. Her hair was still faintly sunburned at its extremities by the western winds. Yet hers was still imperishable youth and beauty.

I held out my hands to her. "Ah," I cried, "you played me false! You ran away! By what miracle did you come through? I confess my defeat. You beat me by almost half a year."

"But now you have come," said she simply.

"Yes, to remind you that you have friends. You have been here in secret all the winter. Mr. Calhoun did not know you had come. Why did you not go to him?"

"I was waiting for you to come. Do you not remember our bargain? Each day I expected you. In some way, I scarce knew how, the weeks wore on."

"And now I find you both here—you and your father—where I would expect to find neither. Continually you violate all law of likelihood. But now, you have seen Elisabeth?"

"Yes, I have seen her," she said, still simply.

I could think of no word suited to that moment. I stood only looking at her. She would have spoken, but on the instant raised a hand as though to demand my silence. I heard a loud knock at the door, peremptory, commanding, as though the owner came.

"You must go into another room," said Helena von Ritz to me hurriedly.

"Who is it? Who is it at the door?" I asked.

She looked at me calmly. "It is Sir Richard Pakenham," said she. "This is his usual hour. I will send him away. Go now—quick!"

I rapidly passed behind the screening curtains into the hall, even as I heard a heavy foot stumbling at the threshold and a somewhat husky voice offer some sort of salutation.

CHAPTER XXXII

PAKENHAM'S PRICE

The happiest women, like nations, have no history.
              —George Eliot.

THE apartment into which I hurriedly stepped
I found to be a long and narrow hall, heavily draped. A door or so made off on the
right-hand side, and a closed door also appeared at
the farther end; but none invited me to enter, and I
did not care to intrude. This situation did not
please me, because I must perforce hear all that went
on in the rooms which I had just left. I heard the
thick voice of a man, apparently none the better for
wine.

"My dear," it began, "I—" Some gesture must
have warned him.

"God bless my soul!" he began again. "Who is
here, then? What is wrong?"

"My father is here to-day," I heard her clear
voice answer, "and, as you suggest, it might perhaps
be better—"

"God bless my soul!" he repeated. "But, my

dear, then I must go! *To-night,* then! Where is that other key? It would never do, you know—"

"No, Sir Richard, it would never do. Go, then!" spoke a low and icy voice, hers, yet not hers. "Hasten!" I heard her half whisper. "I think perhaps my father—"

But it was my own footsteps they heard. This was something to which I could not be party. Yet, rapidly as I walked, her visitor was before me. I caught sight only of his portly back, as the street door closed behind him. She stood, her back against the door, her hand spread out against the wall, as though to keep me from passing.

I paused and looked at her, held by the horror in her eyes. She made no concealment, offered no apologies, and showed no shame. I repeat that it was only horror and sadness mingled which I saw upon her face.

"Madam," I began. And again, "Madam!" and then I turned away.

"You see," she said, sighing.

"Yes, I fear I see; but I wish I did not. Can I not—may I not be mistaken?"

"No, it is true. There is no mistake."

"What have you done? Why? *Why?*"

"Did you not always credit me with being the good friend of Mr. Pakenham years ago—did not all the city? Well, then I was *not;* but I *am,* now!

I was England's agent only—*until last night.* Monsieur, you have come too soon, too late, too late. Ah, my God! my God! Last night I gave at last that consent. He comes now to claim, to exact, to take— possession—of me . . . Ah, my God!"

"I can not, of course, understand you, Madam. *What* is it? Tell me!"

"For three years England's minister besought me to be his, not England's, property. It was not true, what the town thought. It was not true in the case either of Yturrio. Intrigue—yes—I loved it. I intrigued with England and Mexico both, because it was in my nature; but no more than that. No matter what I once was in Europe, I was not here—not, as I said, until last night. Ah, Monsieur! Ah, Monsieur!" Now her hands were beating together.

"But *why* then? Why *then?* What do you mean?" I demanded.

"Because no other way sufficed. All this winter, here, alone, I have planned and thought about other means. Nothing would do. There was but the one way. Now you see why I did not go to Mr. Calhoun, why I kept my presence here secret."

"But you saw Elisabeth?"

"Yes, long ago. My friend, you have won! You both have won, and I have lost. She loves you, and is worthy of you. You are worthy of each other, yes. I saw I had lost; and I told you I would pay my wager. I told you I would give you her—and Oregon! Well, then, that last was—hard." She choked. "That was—hard to do." She almost sobbed. "But I have—paid! Heart and soul . . . and *body* . . . I have . . . *paid!* Now, he comes . . . for . . . the *price!*"

"But then—but then!" I expostulated. "What does this mean, that I see here? There was no need for this. Had you no friends among us? Why, though it meant war, I myself to-night would choke that beast Pakenham with my own hands!"

"No, you will not."

"But did I not hear him say there was a key—*his* key—to-night?"

"Yes, England once owned that key. Now, *he* does. Yes, it is true. Since yesterday. Now, he comes . . ."

"But, Madam—ah, how could you so disappoint my belief in you?"

"Because"—she smiled bitterly—"in all great causes there are sacrifices."

"But no cause could warrant this."

"I was judge of that," was her response. "I saw her—Elisabeth—that girl. Then I saw what the future years meant for me. I tell you, I vowed with her, that night when I thought you two were wedded. I did more. I vowed myself to a new and wider world that night. Now, I have lost it. After all, seeing I could not now be a woman and be happy, I—Monsieur—I pass on to others, after this, not that torture of life, but that torturing *principle* of which we so often spoke. Yes, I, even as I am; because by this—this act—this sacrifice—I can win you for her. And I can win that wider America which you have coveted; which I covet for you— which I covet *with* you!"

I could do no more than remain silent, and allow her to explain what was not in the least apparent to me. After a time she went on.

"Now—now, I say—Pakenham the minister is sunk in Pakenham the man. He does as I demand —because he is a man. He signs what I demand because I am a woman. I say, to-night—but, see!"

She hastened now to a little desk, and caught up a folded document which lay there. This she handed to me, unfolded, and I ran it over with a hasty glance. It was a matter of tremendous importance which lay in those few closely written lines.

England's minister offered, over the signature of England, a compromise of the whole Oregon debate, provided this country would accept the line of the forty-ninth degree! That, then, was Pakenham's price for this key that lay here.

"This—this is all I have been able to do with him thus far," she faltered. "It is not enough. But I did it for you!"

"Madam, this is more than all America has been able to do before! This has not been made public?"

"No, no! It is not enough. But to-night I shall make him surrender all—all north, to the very ice, for America, for the democracy! See, now, I was born to be devoted, immolated, after all, as my mother was before me. That is fate! But I shall make fate pay! Ah, Monsieur! Ah, Monsieur!"

She flung herself to her feet. "I can get it all for you, you and yours!" she reiterated, holding out her hands, the little pink fingers upturned, as was often her gesture. "You shall go to your chief and tell him that Mr. Polk was right—that you yourself, who taught Helena von Ritz what life is, taught her that after all she was a woman—are able, because she was a woman, to bring in your own hands all that country, yes, to fifty-four forty, or even farther. I do not know what all can be done. I only know that a fool will part with everything for the sake of his body."

I stood now looking at her, silent, trying to fathom the vastness of what she said, trying to understand at all their worth the motives which impelled her. The largeness of her plan, yes, that could be seen. The largeness of her heart and brain, yes, that also. Then, slowly, I saw yet more. At last I understood. What I saw was a horror to my soul.

"Madam," said I to her, at last, "did you indeed

think me so cheap as that? Come here!" I led her to the central apartment, and motioned her to a seat.

"Now, then, Madam, much has been done here, as you say. It is all that ever can be done. You shall not see Pakenham to-night, nor ever again!"

"But think what that will cost you!" she broke out. "This is only part. It should *all* be yours."

I flung the document from me. "This has already cost too much," I said. "We do not buy states thus."

"But it will cost you your future! Polk is your enemy, now, as he is Calhoun's. He will not strike you now; but so soon as he dares, he will. Now, if you could do this—if you could take this to Mr. Calhoun, to America, it would mean for you personally all that America could give you in honors."

"Honors without honor, Madam, I do not covet," I replied. Then I would have bit my tongue through when I saw the great pallor cross her face at the cruelty of my speech.

"And *myself?*" she said, spreading out her hands again. "But no! I know you would not taunt me. I know, in spite of what you say, there must be a sacrifice. Well, then, I have made it. I have made my atonement. I say I can give you now, even thus, at least a part of Oregon. I can perhaps give you *all* of Oregon—to-morrow! The Pakenhams have always dared much to gain their ends. This one will dare even treachery to his country. To-morrow—if

I do not kill him—if I do not die—I can perhaps
give you all of Oregon—bought—bought and . . .
paid!" Her voice trailed off into a whisper which
seemed loud as a bugle call to me.

"No, you can not give us Oregon," I answered.
"We are men, not panders. We fight; we do not
traffic thus. But you have given me Elisabeth!"

"My rival!" She smiled at me in spite of all.
"But no, not my rival. Yes, I have already given
you her and given you to her. To do that—to atone,
as I said, for my attempt to part you—well, I will
give Mr. Pakenham the key that Sir Richard Pakenham of England lately held. I told you a woman
pays, *body* and soul! In what coin fate gave me, I
will pay it. You think my morals mixed. No, I tell
you I am clean! I have only bought my own peace
with my own conscience! Now, at last, Helena von
Ritz knows why she was born, to what end! I have
a work to do, and, yes, I see it now—my journey to
America after all was part of the plan of fate. I
have learned much—through you, Monsieur."

Hurriedly she turned and left me, passing through
the heavy draperies which cut off the room where
stood the great satin couch. I saw her cast herself
there, her arms outflung. Slow, deep and silent
sobs shook all her body.

"Madam! Madam!" I cried to her. "Do not!
Do not! What you have done here is worth a hun-

dred millions of dollars, a hundred thousand of lives, perhaps. Yes, that is true. It means most of Oregon, with honor, and without war. That is true, and it is much. But the price paid—it is more than all this continent is worth, if it cost so much as that. Nor shall it!"

Black, with a million pin-points of red, the world swam around me. Millions of dead souls or souls unborn seemed to gaze at me and my unhesitating rage. I caught up the scroll which bore England's signature, and with one clutch cast it in two pieces on the floor. As it lay, we gazed at it in silence. Slowly, I saw a great, soft radiance come upon her face. The red pin-points cleared away from my own vision.

CHAPTER XXXIII

THE STORY OF HELENA VON RITZ

There is in every true woman's heart a spark of heavenly fire, which beams and blazes in the dark hours of adversity.—Washington Irving.

"But Madam; but Madam—" I tried to begin. At last, after moments which seemed to me ages long, I broke out: "But once, at least, you promised to tell me who and what you are. Will you do that now?"

"Yes! yes!" she said. "Now I shall finish the clearing of my soul. You, after all, shall be my confessor."

We heard again a faltering footfall in the hallway. I raised an eyebrow in query.

"It is my father. Yes, but let him come. He also must hear. He is indeed the author of my story, such as it is.

"Father," she added, "come, sit you here. I have something to say to Mr. Trist."

She seated herself now on one of the low couches, her hands clasped across its arm, her eyes looking far away out of the little window, beyond which could be seen the hills across the wide Potomac.

"We are foreigners," she went on, "as you can tell. I speak your language better than my father does, because I was younger when I learned. It is quite true he is my father. He is an Austrian nobleman, of one of the old families. He was educated in Germany, and of late has lived there."

"I could have told most of that of you both," I said.

She bowed and resumed:

"My father was always a student. As a young man in the university, he was devoted to certain theories of his own. *N' est-ce pas vrai, mon drôle?*" she asked, turning to put her arm on her father's shoulder as he dropped weakly on the couch beside her.

He nodded. "Yes, I wass student," he said. "I wass not content with the ways of my people."

"So, my father, you will see," said she, smiling at him, "being much determined on anything which he attempted, decided, with five others, to make a certain experiment. It was the strangest experiment, I presume, ever made in the interest of what is called science. It was wholly the most curious and the most cruel thing ever done."

She hesitated now. All I could do was to look from one to the other, wonderingly.

"This dear old dreamer, my father, then, and five others—"

"I name them!" he interrupted. "There were Karl von Goertz, Albrecht Hardman, Adolph zu Sternbern, Karl von Starnack, and Rudolph von Wardberg. We were all friends—"

"Yes," she said softly, "all friends, and all fools. Sometimes I think of my mother."

"My dear, your mother!"

"But I must tell this as it was! Then, sir, these six, all Heidelberg men, all well born, men of fortune, all men devoted to science, and interested in the study of the hopelessness of the average human being in Central Europe—these fools, or heroes, I say not which—they decided to do something in the interest of science. They were of the belief that human beings were becoming poor in type. So they determined to marry—"

"Naturally," said I, seeking to relieve a delicate situation—"they scorned the marriage of convenience—they came to our American way of thinking, that they would marry for love."

"You do them too much credit!" said she slowly. "That would have meant no sacrifice on either side. They married in the interest of *science!* They married with the deliberate intention of improving individuals of the human species! Father, is it not so?"

Some speech stumbled on his tongue; but she raised her hand. "Listen to me. I will be fair to you, fairer than you were either to yourself or to my mother.

"Yes, these six concluded to improve the grade of human animals! They resolved to marry *among the peasantry*—because thus they could select finer specimens of womankind, younger, stronger, more fit to bring children into the world. Is not that the truth, my father?"

"It wass the way we thought," he whispered. "It wass the way we thought wass wise."

"And perhaps it was wise. It was selection. So now they selected. Two of them married German working girls, and those two are dead, but there is no child of them alive. Two married in Austria, and of these one died, and the other is in a mad house. One married a young Galician girl, and so fond of her did he become that she took him down from his station to hers, and he was lost. The other—"

"Yes; it was my father," she said, at length. "There he sits, my father. Yes, I love him. I would forfeit my life for him now—I would lay it down gladly for him. Better had I done so. But in my time I have hated him.

"He, the last one, searched long for this fitting animal to lead to the altar. He was tall and young and handsome and rich, do you see? He could have chosen among his own people any woman he liked.

Instead, he searched among the Galicians, the lower Austrians, the Prussians. He examined Bavaria and Saxony. Many he found, but still none to suit his scientific ideas. He bethought him then of searching among the Hungarians, where, it is said, the most beautiful women of the world are found. So, at last he found her, that peasant, *my mother!*"

The silence in the room was broken at last by her low, even, hopeless voice as she went on.

"Now the Hungarians are slaves to Austria. They do as they are bid, those who live on the great estates. They have no hope. If they rebel, they are cut down. They are not a people. They belong to no one, not even to themselves."

"My God!" said I, a sigh breaking from me in spite of myself. I raised my hand as though to beseech her not to go on. But she persisted.

"Yes, we, too, called upon *our* gods! So, now, my father came among that people and found there a young girl, one much younger than himself. She was the most beautiful, so they say, of all those people, many of whom are very beautiful."

"Yes—proof of that!" said I. She knew I meant no idle flattery.

"Yes, she was beautiful. But at first she did not fancy to marry this Austrian student nobleman. She said no to him, even when she found who he was and what was his station—even when she found that he meant her no dishonor. But our ruler heard of it, and, being displeased at this mockery of the traditions of the court, and wishing in his sardonic mind to teach these fanatical young nobles to rue well their bargain, he sent word to the girl that she *must* marry this man—my father. It was made an imperial order!

"And so now, at last, since he was half crazed by her beauty, as men are sometimes by the beauty of women, and since at last this had its effect with her, as sometimes it does with women, and since it was perhaps death or some severe punishment if she did not obey, she married him—my father."

"And loved me all her life!" the old man broke out. "Nefer had man love like hers, I will haf it said. I will haf it said that she loved me, always and always; and I loved *her* always, with all my heart!"

"Yes," said Helena von Ritz, "they two loved each other, even as they were. So here am I, born of that love."

Now we all sat silent for a time. "That birth was at my father's estates," resumed the same even, merciless voice. "After some short time of travels, they returned to the estates; and, yes, there I was born, half noble, half peasant; and then there began the most cruel thing the world has ever known.

"The nobles of the court and of the country all

around began to make existence hideous for my
mother. The aristocracy, insulted by the republican-
ism of these young noblemen, made life a hell for the
most gentle woman of Hungary. Ah, they found
new ways to make her suffer. They allowed her
to share in my father's estate, allowed her to appear
with him when he could prevail upon her to do so.
Then they twitted and taunted her and mocked her
in all the devilish ways of their class. She was more
beautiful than any court beauty of them all, and they
hated her for that. She had a good mind, and they
hated her for that. She had a faithful, loyal heart,
and they hated her for that. And in ways more
cruel than any man will ever know, women and men
made her feel that hate, plainly and publicly, made
her admit that she was chosen as breeding stock and
nothing better. Ah, it was the jest of Europe, for a
time. They insulted my mother, and that became the
jest of the court, of all Vienna. She dared not go
alone from the castle. She dared not travel alone."

"But your father resented this?"

She nodded. "Duel after duel he fought, man
after man he killed, thanks to his love for her and
his manhood. He would not release what he loved.
He would not allow his class to separate him from
his choice. But the *women!* Ah, he could not fight
them! So I have hated women, and made war on
them all my life. My father could not placate his

Emperor. So, in short, that scientific experiment ended in misery—and me!"

The room had grown dimmer. The sun was sinking as she talked. There was silence, I know, for a long time before she spoke again.

"In time, then, my father left his estates and went out to a small place in the country; but my mother—her heart was broken. Malice pursued her. Those who were called her superiors would not let her alone. See, he weeps, my father, as he thinks of these things.

"There was cause, then, to weep. For two years, they tell me, my mother wept. Then she died. She gave me, a baby, to her friend, a woman of her village—Threlka Mazoff. You have seen her. She has been my mother ever since. She has been the sole guardian I have known all my life. She has not been able to do with me as she would have liked."

"You did not live at your own home with your father?" I asked.

"For a time. I grew up. But my father, I think, was permanently shocked by the loss of the woman he had loved and whom he had brought into all this cruelty. She had been so lovable, so beautiful—she was so beautiful, my mother! So they sent me away to France, to the schools. I grew up, I presume, proof in part of the excellence of my father's theory. They told me that I was a beautiful animal!"

The contempt, the scorn, the pathos—the whole tragedy of her voice and bearing—were such as I can not set down on paper, and such as I scarce could endure to hear. Never in my life before have I felt such pity for a human being, never so much desire to do what I might in sheer compassion.

But now, how clear it all became to me! I could understand many strange things about the character of this singular woman, her whims, her unaccountable moods, her seeming carelessness, yet, withal, her dignity and sweetness and air of breeding—above all her mysteriousness. Let others judge her for themselves. There was only longing in my heart that I might find some word of comfort. What could comfort her? Was not life, indeed, for her to remain a perpetual tragedy?

"But, Madam," said I, at length, "you must not wrong your father and your mother and yourself. These two loved each other devotedly. Well, what more? You are the result of a happy marriage. You are beautiful, you are splendid, by that reason."

"Perhaps. Even when I was sixteen, I was beautiful," she mused. "I have heard rumors of that. But I say to you that then I was only a beautiful animal. Also, I was a vicious animal. I had in my heart all the malice which my mother never spoke. I felt in my soul the wish to injure women, to punish men, to torment them, to make them pay! To set even

those balances of torture!— ah, that was my ambition! I had not forgotten that, when I first met you,
when I first heard of—her, the woman whom you
love, whom already in your savage strong way you
have wedded—the woman whose vows I spoke with
her—I—I, Helena von Ritz, with history such as
mine!

"Father, father,"— she turned to him swiftly;
"rise—go! I can not now speak before you. Leave
us alone until I call!"

Obedient as though he had been the child and she
the parent, the old man rose and tottered feebly from
the room.

"There are things a woman can not say in the
presence of a parent," she said, turning to me. Her
face twitched. "It takes all my bravery to talk to
you."

"Why should you? There is not need. Do not!"

"Ah, I must, because it is fair," said she. "I have
lost, lost! I told you I would pay my wager."

After a time she turned her face straight toward
mine and went on with her old splendid bravery.

"So, now, you see, when I was young and beautiful I had rank and money. I had brains. I had
hatred of men. I had contempt for the aristocracy.
My heart was peasant after all. My principles were
those of the republican. Revolution was in my soul,
I say. Thwarted, distorted, wretched, unscrupulous,

I did what I could to make hell for those who had
made hell for us. I have set dozens of men by the
ears. I have been promised in marriage to I know
not how many. A dozen men have fought to the
death in duels over me. For each such death I had
not even a thought. The more troubles I made, the
happier I was. Oh, yes, in time I became known—I
had a reputation; there is no doubt of that.

"But still the organized aristocracy had its revenge—it had its will of me, after all. There came
to me, as there had to my mother, an imperial order.
In punishment for my fancies and vagaries, I was
condemned to marry a certain nobleman. That was
the whim of the new emperor, Ferdinand, the degenerate. He took the throne when I was but sixteen years of age. He chose for me a degenerate
mate from his own sort." She choked, now.

"You did marry him?"

She nodded. "Yes. Debauché, rake, monster,
degenerate, product of that aristocracy which had
oppressed us, I was obliged to marry him, a man
three times my age! I pleaded. I begged. I was
taken away by night. I was—I was— They say I
was married to him. For myself, I did not know
where I was or what happened. But after that they
said that I was the wife of this man, a sot, a monster,
the memory only of manhood. Now, indeed, the revenge of the aristocracy was complete!"

She went on at last in a voice icy cold. "I fled one night, back to Hungary. For a month they could not find me. I was still young. I saw my people then as I had not before. I saw also the monarchies of Europe. Ah, now I knew what oppression meant! Now I knew what class distinction and special privileges meant! I saw what ruin it was spelling for our country—what it will spell for your country, if they ever come to rule here. Ah, then that dream came to me which had come to my father, that beautiful dream which justified me in everything I did. My friend, can it—can it in part justify me—now?

"For the first time, then, I resolved to live! I have loved my father ever since that time. I pledged myself to continue that work which he had undertaken! I pledged myself to better the condition of humanity if I might.

"There was no hope for me. I was condemned and ruined as it was. My life was gone. Such as I had left, that I resolved to give to—what shall we call it?—the *idée démocratique*.

"Now, may God rest my mother's soul, and mine also, so that some time I may see her in another world—I pray I may be good enough for that some time. I have not been sweet and sinless as was my mother. Fate laid a heavier burden upon me. But what remained with me throughout was the idea which my father had bequeathed me—"

"Ah, but also that beauty and sweetness and loyalty which came to you from your mother," I insisted.

She shook her head. "Wait!" she said. "Now they pursued me as though I had been a criminal, and they took me back—horsemen about me who did as they liked. I was, I say, a sacrifice. News of this came to that man who was my husband. They shamed him into fighting. He had not the courage of the nobles left. But he heard of one nobleman against whom he had a special grudge; and him one night, foully and unfairly, he murdered.

"News of that came to the Emperor. My husband was tried, and, the case being well known to the public, it was necessary to convict him for the sake of example. Then, on the day set for his beheading, the Emperor reprieved him. The hour for the execution passed, and, being now free for the time, he fled the country. He went to Africa, and there he so disgraced the state that bore him that of late times I hear he has been sent for to come back to Austria. Even yet the Emperor may suspend the reprieve and send him to the block for his ancient crime. If he had a thousand heads, he could not atone for the worse crimes he has done!

"But of him, and of his end, I know nothing. So, now, you see, I was and am wed, and yet am not wed, and never was. I do not know what I am, nor who I am. After all, I can not tell you who I am, or what I am, because I myself do not know.

"It was now no longer safe for me in my own country. They would not let me go to my father any more. As for him, he went on with his studies, some part of his mind being bright and clear. They did not wish him about the court now. All these matters were to be hushed up. The court of England began to take cognizance of these things. Our government was scandalized. They sent my father, on pretext of scientific errands, into one country and another—to Sweden, to England, to Africa, at last to America. Thus it happened that you met him. You must both have been very near to meeting me in Montreal. It was fate, as we of Hungary would say.

"As for me, I was no mere hare-brained radical. I did not go to Russia, did not join the revolutionary circles of Paris, did not yet seek out Prussia. That is folly. My father was right. It must be the years, it must be the good heritage, it must be the good environment, it must be even opportunity for all, which alone can produce good human beings! In short, believe me, a victim, *the hope of the world is in a real democracy*. Slowly, gradually, I was coming to believe that."

She paused a moment. "Then, one time, Monsieur,—I met you, here in this very room! God pity me! You were the first man I had ever seen. God

pity me!—I believe I—loved you—that night, that
very first night! We are friends. We are brave.
You are man and gentleman, so I may say that, now.
I am no longer woman. I am but sacrifice. '

"Opportunity must exist, open and free for all
the world," she went on, not looking at me more
than I could now at her. "I have set my life to
prove this thing. When I came here to this America
—out of pique, out of a love of adventure, out of
sheer daring and exultation in imposture—*then* I
saw why I was born, for what purpose! It was to do
such work as I might to prove the theory of my
father, and to justify the life of my mother. For that
thing I was born. For that thing I have been damned
on this earth; I may be damned in the life to come,
unless I can make some great atonement. For these
I suffer and shall always suffer. But what of that?
There must always be a sacrifice."

The unspeakable tragedy of her voice cut to my
soul. "But listen!" I broke out. "You are young.
You are free. All the world is before you. You can
have anything you like—"

"Ah, do not talk to me of that," she exclaimed
imperiously. "Do not tempt me to attempt the de-
ceit of myself! I made myself as I am, long ago.
I did not love. I did not know it. As to marriage, I
did not need it. I had abundant means without. I
was in the upper ranks of society. I was there; I was

classified; I lived with them. But always I had my purposes, my plans. F r them I paid, paid, paid, as a woman 1 .ust, with—what a woman has.

"But now, I am far ahead of my story. Let me bring it on. I went to Paris. I have sown some seeds of venom, some seeds of revolution, in one place or another in Europe in my time. Ah, it works; it will go! Here and there I have cost a human life. Here and there work was to be done which I disliked; but I did it. Misguided, uncared for, mishandled as I had been—well, as I said, I went to Paris.

"Ah, sir, will you not, too, leave the room, and let me tell on this story to myself, to my own soul? It is fitter for my confessor than for you."

"Let me, then, l? your confessor!" said I. "Forget! Forget! You have not been this which you say. Do I not know?"

"No, you do not know. Well, let be. Let me go on! I say I went to Paris. I was close to the throne of France. That little Duke of Orleans, son of Louis Philippe, was a puppet in my hands. Oh, I do not doubt I did mischief in that court, or at least if I failed it was through no lack of effort! I was called there 'America Vespucci.' They thought me Italian! At last they came to know who I was. They dared not make open rupture in the face of the courts of Europe. Certain of their high officials came to me and my young Duke of Orleans. They asked me to leave Paris. They did not command it—the Duke of Orleans cared for that part of it. But they requested me outside—not in his presence. They offered me a price, a bribe—such an offering as would, I fancied, leave me free to pursue my own ideas in my own fashion and in any corner of the world. You have perhaps seen some of my little fancies. I imagined that love and happiness were never for me—only ambition and unrest. With these goes luxury, sometimes. At least this sort of personal liberty was offered me—the price of leaving Paris, and leaving the son of Louis Philippe to his own devices. I did so."

"And so, then you came to Washington? That must have been some years ago."

"Yes; some five years ago. I still was young. I told you that you must have known me, and so, no doubt, you did. Did *you* ever hear of 'America Vespucci'?"

A smile came to my face at the suggestion of that celebrated adventuress and mysterious impostress who had figured in the annals of Washington—a fair Italian, so the rumor ran, who had come to this country to set up a claim, upon our credulity at least, as to being the descendant of none less than Amerigo Vespucci himself! This supposititious Italian had indeed gone so far as to secure the introduction of a bill in Congress granting to her certain lands. The fate of that bill even then hung in the balance. I had no reason to put anything beyond the audacity of this woman with whom I spoke! My smile was simply that which marked the eventual voting down of this once celebrated measure, as merry and as bold a jest as ever was offered the credulity of a nation—one conceivable only in the mad and bitter wit of Helena von Ritz!

"Yes, Madam," I said, "I have heard of 'America Vespucci.' I presume that you are now about to repeat that you are she!"

She nodded, the mischievous enjoyment of her colossal jest showing in her eyes, in spite of all. "Yes," said she, "among other things, I have been 'America Vespucci'! There seemed little to do here in intrigue, and that was my first endeavor to amuse myself. Then I found other employment. England needed a skilful secret agent. Why should I be faithful to England? At least, why should I not also enjoy intrigue with yonder government of Mexico at the same time? There came also Mr. Van Zandt of this Republic of Texas. Yes, it is true, I have seen some sport here in Washington! But all the time as I played in my own little game—with no one to enjoy it save myself—I saw myself begin to lose. This country—this great splendid country of savages—

began to take me by the hands, began to look me in the eyes, and to ask me, '*Helena von Ritz, what are you? What might you have been?*'

"So now," she concluded, "you asked me, asked me what I was, and I have told you. I ask you myself, what am I, what am I to be; and I say, I am unclean. But, being as I am, I have done what I have done. It was for a principle—or it was—for you! I do not know."

"There are those who can be nothing else but clean," I broke out. "I shall not endure to hear you speak thus of yourself. You—you, what have you not done for us? Was not your mother clean in her heart? Sins such as you mention were never those of scarlet. If you have sinned, your sins are white as snow. I at least am confessor enough to tell you that."

"Ah, my confessor!" She reached out her hands to me, her eyes swimming wet. Then she pushed me back suddenly, beating with her little hands upon my breast as though I were an enemy. "Do not!" she said. "Go!"

My eye caught sight of the great key, *Pakenham's key,* lying there on the table. Maddened, I caught it up, and, with a quick wrench of my naked hands, broke it in two, and threw the halves on the floor to join the torn scroll of England's pledge.

I divided Oregon at the forty-ninth parallel, and not at fifty-four forty, when I broke Pakenham's key. But you shall see why I have never regretted that.

"Ask Sir Richard Pakenham if he wants his key *now!*" I said.

CHAPTER XXXIV

THE VICTORY

She will not stay the siege of loving terms,
Nor bide the encounter of assailing eyes,
Nor ope her lap to soul-seducing gold . . .
For she is wise, if I can judge of her;
And fair she is, if that mine eyes be true;
And true she is, as she hath proved herself.
—*Shakespeare.*

"WHAT have you done?" she exclaimed. "Are you mad? He may be here at any moment now. Go, at once!"

"I shall not go!"

"My house is my own! I am my own!"

"You know it is not true, Madam!"

I saw the slow shudder that crossed her form, the the fringe of wet which sprang to her eyelashes. Again the pleading gesture of her half-open fingers.

"Ah, what matter?" she said. "It is only one woman more, against so much. What is past, is past, Monsieur. Once down, a woman does not rise."

"You forget history,—you forget the thief upon the cross!"

349

"The thief on the cross was not a woman. No, I am guilty beyond hope!"

"Rather, you are only mad beyond reason, Madam. I shall not go so long as you feel thus,— although God knows I am no confessor."

"I confessed to you,—told you my story, so there could be no bridge across the gulf between us. My happiness ended then."

"It is of no consequence that we be happy, Madam. I give you back your own words about yon torch of principles."

For a time she sat and looked at me steadily. There was, I say, some sort of radiance on her face, though I, dull of wit, could neither understand nor describe it. I only knew that she seemed to ponder for a long time, seemed to resolve at last. Slowly she rose and left me, parting the satin draperies which screened her boudoir from the outer room. There was silence for some time. Perhaps she prayed,—I do not know.

Now other events took this situation in hand. I heard a footfall on the walk, a cautious knocking on the great front door. So, my lord Pakenham was prompt. Now I could not escape even if I liked.

Pale and calm, she reappeared at the parted draperies. I lifted the butts of my two derringers into view at my side pockets, and at a glance from her, hurriedly stepped into the opposite room. After a time I heard her open the door in response to a second knock.

I could not see her from my station, but the very silence gave me a picture of her standing, pale, forbidding, rebuking the first rude exclamation of his ardor.

"Come now, is he gone? Is the place safe at last?" he demanded.

"Enter, my lord," she said simply.

"This is the hour you said," he began; and she answered:

"My lord, it is the hour."

"But come, what's the matter, then? You act solemn, as though this were a funeral, and not— just a kiss," I heard him add.

He must have advanced toward her. Continually I was upon the point of stepping out from my concealment, but as continually she left that not quite possible by some word or look or gesture of her own with him.

"Oh, hang it!" I heard him grumble, at length; "how can one tell what a woman'll do? Damn it, Helen!"

" 'Madam,' you mean!"

"Well, then, Madam, why all this hoighty-toighty? Haven't I stood flouts and indignities enough from you? Didn't you make a show of me before that ass, Tyler, when I was at the very point of my greatest coup? You denied knowledge that I knew you had. But did I discard you for that? I have found you since then playing with Mexico, Texas, United States all at once? Have I punished you for *that?* No, I have only shown you the more regard."

"My lord, you punish me most when you most show me your regard."

"Well, God bless my soul, listen at that! Listen at that—here, now, when I've—Madam, you shock me, you grieve me. I—could I have a glass of wine?"

I heard her ring for Threlka, heard her fasten the door behind her as she left, heard him gulp over his glass. For myself, although I did not yet disclose myself, I felt no doubt that I should kill Pakenham in these rooms. I even pondered whether I should shoot him through the temple and cut off his consciousness, or through the chest and so let him know why he died.

After a time he seemed to look about the room, his eye falling upon the littered floor.

"My key!" he exclaimed; "broken! Who did that? I can't use it now!"

"You will not need to use it, my lord."

"But I bought it, yesterday! Had I given you all of the Oregon country it would not have been worth twenty thousand pounds. What I'll have to-night—what I'll take—will be worth twice that. But I bought that key, and what I buy I keep."

I heard a struggle, but she repulsed him once more in some way. Still my time had not come. He seemed now to stoop, grunting, to pick up something from the floor.

"How now? My memorandum of treaty, and torn in two! Oh, I see—I see," he mused. "You wish to give it back to me—to be wholly free! It means only that you wish to love me for myself, for what I am! You minx!"

"You mistake, my lord," said her calm, cold voice.

"At least, 'twas no mistake that I offered you this damned country at risk of my own head. Are you then with England and Sir Richard Pakenham? Will you give my family a chance for revenge on these accursed heathen—these Americans? Come, do that, and I leave this place with you, and quit diplomacy for good. We'll travel the continent, we'll go the world over, you and I. I'll quit my estates, my family for you. Come, now, why do you delay?"

"Still you misunderstand, my lord."

"Tell me then what you do mean."

"Our old bargain over this is broken, my lord. We must make another."

His anger rose. "What? You want more?

You're trying to lead me on with your damned cour-
tezan tricks!"

I heard her voice rise high and shrill, even as I
started forward.

"Monsieur," she cried, "back with you!"

Pakenham, angered as he was, seemed half to
hear my footsteps, seemed half to know the swinging of the draperies, even as I stepped back in
obedience to her gesture. Her wit was quick as
ever.

"My lord," she said, "pray close yonder window.
The draft is bad, and, moreover, we should have
secrecy." He obeyed her, and she led him still further from the thought of investigating his surroundings.

"Now, my lord," she said, *"take back* what you
have just said!"

"Under penalty?" he sneered.

"Of your life, yes."

"So!" he grunted admiringly; "well, now, I like
fire in a woman, even a deceiving light-o'-love like
you!"

"Monsieur!" her voice cried again; and once
more it restrained me in my hiding.

"You devil!" he resumed, sneering now in all his
ugliness of wine and rage and disappointment.
"What were *you?* Mistress of the prince of France!
Toy of a score of nobles! Slave of that infamous

rake, your husband! Much you've got in your life to make you uppish now with me!"

"My lord," she said evenly, "retract that. If you do not, you shall not leave this place alive."

In some way she mastered him, even in his ugly mood.

"Well, well," he growled, "I admit we don't get on very well in our little love affair; but I swear you drive me out of my mind. I'll never find another woman in the world like you. It's Sir Richard Pakenham asks you to begin a new future with himself."

"We begin no future, my lord."

"What do you mean? Have you lied to me? Do you mean to break your word—your promise?"

"It is within the hour that I have learned what the truth is."

"God damn my soul!" I heard him curse, growling.

"Yes, my lord," she answered, "God will damn your soul in so far as it is that of a brute and not that of a gentleman or a statesman."

I heard him drop into a chair. "This from one of your sort!" he half whimpered.

"Stop, now!" she cried. "Not one word more of that! I say within the hour I have learned what is the truth. I am Helena von Ritz, thief on the cross, and at last clean!"

"God A'might, Madam! How pious!" he sneered. "Something's behind all this. I know your record. What woman of the court of Austria or France comes out with *morals?* We used you here because you had none. And now, when it comes to the settlement between you and me, you talk like a nun. As though a trifle from virtue such as yours would be missed!"

"Ah, my God!" I heard her murmur. Then again she called to me, as he thought to himself; so that all was as it had been, for the time.

A silence fell before she went on.

"Sir Richard," she said at length, "we do not meet again. I await now your full apology for these things you have said. Such secrets as I have learned of England's, you know will remain safe with me. Also your own secret will be safe. Retract, then, what you have said, of my personal life!"

"Oh, well, then," he grumbled, "I admit I've had a bit of wine to-day. I don't mean much of anything by it. But here now, I have come, and by your own invitation—your own agreement. Being here, I find this treaty regarding Oregon torn in two and you gone nun all a-sudden."

"Yes, my lord, it is torn in two. The consideration moving to it was not valid. But now I wish you to amend that treaty once more, and for a con-

sideration valid in every way. My lord, I promised
that which was not mine to give—myself! Did you
lay hand on me now, I should die. If you kissed me,
I should kill you and myself! As you say, I took
yonder price, the devil's shilling. Did I go on, I
would be enlisting for the damnation of my soul;
but I will not go on. I recant!"

"But, good God! woman, what are you asking
now? Do you want me to let you have this paper
anyhow, to show old John Calhoun? I'm no such
ass as that. I apologize for what I've said about
you. I'll be your friend, because I can't let you go.
But as to this paper here, I'll put it in my pocket."

"My lord, you will do nothing of the kind. Before you leave this room there shall be two miracles
done. You shall admit that one has gone on in me;
I shall see that you yourself have done another."

"What guessing game do you propose, Madam?"
he sneered. He seemed to toss the torn paper on
the table, none the less. "The condition is forfeited," he began.

"No, it is not forfeited except by your own word,
my lord," rejoined the same even, icy voice. "You
shall see now the first miracle!"

"Under duress?" he sneered again.

"*Yes,* then! Under duress of what has not often
come to surface in you, Sir Richard. I ask you to
do truth, and not treason, my lord! She who was

Helena von Ritz is dead—has passed away. There can be no question of forfeit between you and her. Look, my lord!"

I heard a half sob from him. I heard a faint rustling of silks and laces. Still her even, icy voice went on.

"Rise, now, Sir Richard," she said. "Unfasten my girdle, if you like! Undo my clasps, if you can. You say you know my past. Tell me, do you see me now? Ungird me, Sir Richard! Look at me! Covet me! Take me!"

Apparently he half rose, shuffled towards her, and stopped with a stifled sound, half a sob, half a growl.

I dared not picture to myself what he must have seen as she stood fronting him, her hands, as I imagined, at her bosom, tearing back her robes.

Again I heard her voice go on, challenging him. "Strip me now, Sir Richard, if you can! Take now what you bought, if you find it here. You can not? You do not? Ah, then tell me that miracle has been done! She who was Helena von Ritz, as you knew her, or as you thought you knew her, *is not here!*"

Now fell long silence. I could hear the breathing of them both, where I stood in the farther corner of my room. I had dropped both the derringers back in my pockets now, because I knew there would be no need for them. Her voice was softer as she went on.

"Tell me, Sir Richard, has not that miracle been done?" she demanded. "Might not in great stress that thief upon the cross have been a woman? Tell me, Sir Richard, am I not clean?"

He flung his body into a seat, his arm across the table. I heard his groan.

"God! Woman! What are you?" he exclaimed. "Clean? By God, yes, as a lily! I wish I were half as white myself."

"Sir Richard, did you ever love a woman?"

"One other, beside yourself, long ago."

"May not we two ask that other miracle of yourself?"

"How do you mean? You have beaten me already."

"Why, then, this! If I could keep my promise, I would. If I could give you myself, I would. Failing that, I may give you gratitude. Sir Richard, I would give you gratitude, did you restore this treaty as it was, for that new consideration. Come, now, these savages here are the same savages who once took that little island for you yonder. Twice they have defeated you. Do you wish a third war? You say England wishes slavery abolished. As you know, Texas is wholly lost to England. The armies of America have swept Texas from your reach for ever, even at this hour. But if you give a new state in the north to these same savages, you go so far against oppression, against slavery—you do *that* much for the doctrine of England, and her altruism in the world. Sir Richard, never did I believe in hard bargains, and never did any great soul believe in such. I own to you that when I asked you here this afternoon I intended to wheedle from you all of Oregon north to fifty-four degrees, forty minutes. I find in you done some such miracle as in myself. Neither of us is so bad as the world has thought, as we ourselves have thought. Do then, that other miracle for me. Let us compose our quarrel, and so part friends."

"How do you mean, Madam?"

"Let us divide our dispute, and stand on this treaty as you wrote it yesterday. Sir Richard, you are minister with extraordinary powers. Your government ratifies your acts without question. Your signature is binding—and there it is, writ already on this scroll. See, there are wafers there on the table before you. Take them. Patch together this treaty for me. That will be *your* miracle, Sir Richard, and 'twill be the mending of our quarrel. Sir, I offered you my body and you would not take it. I offer you my hand. Will you have *that,* my lord? I ask this of a gentleman of England."

It was not my right to hear the sounds of a man's

shame and humiliation; or of his rising resolve, of his reformed manhood; but I did hear it all. I think that he took her hand and kissed it. Presently I heard some sort of shufflings and crinkling of paper on the table. I heard him sigh, as though he stood and looked at his work. His heavy footfalls crossed the room as though he sought hat and stick. Her lighter feet, as I heard, followed him, as though she held out both her hands to him. There was a pause, and yet another; and so, with a growling half sob, at last he passed out the door; and she closed it softly after him.

When I entered, she was standing, her arms spread out across the door, her face pale, her eyes large and dark, her attire still disarrayed. On the table, as I saw, lay a parchment, mended with wafers.

Slowly she came, and put her two arms across my shoulders. "Monsieur!" she said, "Monsieur!"

CHAPTER XXXV

THE PROXY OF PAKENHAM

A man can not possess anything that is better than a good woman, nor anything that is worse than a bad one.—Simonides.

WHEN I reached the central part of the city, I did not hasten thence to Elm-hurst Mansion. Instead, I returned to my hotel. I did not now care to see any of my friends or even to take up matters of business with my chief. It is not for me to tell what feelings came to me when I left Helena von Ritz.

Sleep such as I could gain, reflections such as were inevitable, occupied me for all that night. It was mid-morning of the following day when finally I once more sought out Mr. Calhoun.

He had not expected me, but received me gladly. It seemed that he had gone on about his own plans and with his own methods. "The Señora Yturrio is doing me the honor of an early morning call," he began. "She is with my daughter in another part of the house. As there is matter of some importance to come up, I shall ask you to attend."

He despatched a servant, and presently the lady mentioned joined us. She was a pleasing picture enough in her robe of black laces and sulphur-colored silks, but her face was none too happy, and her eyes, it seemed to me, bore traces either of unrest or tears. Mr. Calhoun handed her to a chair, where she began to use her languid but effective fan.

"Now, it gives us the greatest regret, my dear Señora," began Mr. Calhoun, "to have General Almonte and your husband return to their own country. We have valued their presence here very much, and I regret the disruption of the friendly relations between our countries."

She made any sort of gesture with her fan, and he went on: "It is the regret also of all, my dear lady, that your husband seems so shamelessly to have abandoned you. I am quite aware, if you will allow me to be so frank, that you need some financial assistance."

"My country is ruined," said she. "Also, Señor, I am ruined. As you say, I have no means of life. I have not even money to secure my passage home. That Señor Van Zandt—"

"Yes, Van Zandt did much for us, through your agency, Señora. We have benefited by that, and I therefore regret he proved faithless to you personally. I am sorry to tell you that he has signified his wish to join our army against your country. I hear also that your late friend, Mr. Polk, has forgotten most of his promises to you."

"Him I hate also!" she broke out. "He broke his promise to Señor Van Zandt, to my husband, to me!"

Calhoun smiled in his grim fashion. "I am not surprised to hear all that, my dear lady, for you but point out a known characteristic of that gentleman. He has made me many promises which he has forgotten, and offered me even of late distinguished honors which he never meant me to accept. But, since I have been personally responsible for many of these things which have gone forward, I wish to make what personal amends I can; and ever I shall thank you for the good which you have done to this country. Believe me, Madam, you served your own country also in no ill manner. This situation could not have been prevented, and it is not your fault. I beg you to believe that. Had you and I been left alone there would have been no war."

"But I am poor, I have nothing!" she rejoined.

There was indeed much in her situation to excite sympathy. It had been through her own act that negotiations between England and Texas were broken off. All chance of Mexico to regain property in Texas was lost through her influence with Van Zandt. Now, when all was done, here she was, deserted even by those who had been her allies in this work.

"My dear Señora," said John Calhoun, becoming

less formal and more kindly, "you shall have funds
sufficient to make you comfortable at least for a time
after your return to Mexico. I am not authorized
to draw upon our exchequer, and you, of course,
must prefer all secrecy in these matters. I regret
that my personal fortune is not so large as it might
be, but, in such measure as I may, I shall assist you,
because I know you need assistance. In return, you
must leave this country. The flag is down which
once floated over the house of Mexico here."

She hid her face behind her fan, and Calhoun
turned aside.

"Señora, have you ever seen this slipper?" he
asked, suddenly placing upon the table the little shoe
which for a purpose I had brought with me and
meantime thrown upon the table.

She flashed a dark look, and did not speak.

"One night, some time ago, your husband pursued
a lady across this town to get possession of that very
slipper and its contents! There was in the toe of that
little shoe a message. As you know, we got from it
certain information, and therefore devised certain
plans, which you have helped us to carry out. Now,
as perhaps you have had some personal animus
against the other lady in these same complicated affairs, I have taken the liberty of sending a special
messenger to ask her presence here this morning. I
should like you two to meet, and, if that be possible,

to part with such friendship as may exist in the premises."

I looked suddenly at Mr. Calhoun. It seemed he was planning without my aid.

"Yes," he said to me, smiling, "I have neglected to mention to you that the Baroness von Ritz also is here, in another apartment of this place. If you please, I shall now send for her also."

He signaled to his old negro attendant. Presently the latter opened the door, and with a deep bow announced the Baroness von Ritz, who entered, followed closely by Mr. Calhoun's inseparable friend, old Doctor Ward.

The difference in breeding between these two women was to be seen at a glance. The Doña Lucrezia was beautiful in a way, but lacked the thoroughbred quality which comes in the highest types of womanhood. Afflicted by nothing but a somewhat mercenary or personal grief, she showed her lack of gameness in adversity. On the other hand, Helena von Ritz, who had lived tragedy all her life, and now was in the climax of such tragedy, was smiling and debonaire as though she had never been anything but wholly content with life! She was robed now in some light filmy green material, caught up here and there on the shoulders and secured with silken knots. Her white neck showed, her arms were partly bare with the short sleeves of the time. She stood, composed and easy, a figure fit for any company or any court, and somewhat shaming our little assembly, which never was a court at all, only a private meeting in the office of a discredited and disowned leader in a republican government. Her costume and her bearing were Helena von Ritz's answer to a woman's fate! A deep color flamed in her cheeks. She stood with head erect and lips smiling brilliantly. Her curtsey was grace itself. Our dingy little office was glorified.

"I interrupt you, gentlemen," she began.

"On the contrary, I am sure, my dear lady," said Doctor Ward, "Senator Calhoun told me he wished you to meet Señora Yturrio."

"Yes," resumed Calhoun, "I was just speaking with this lady over some matters concerned with this little slipper." He smiled as he held it up gingerly between thumb and finger. "Do you recognize it, Madam Baroness?"

"Ah, my little shoe!" she exclaimed. "But see, it has not been well cared for."

"It traveled in my war bag from Oregon to Washington," said I. "Perhaps bullet molds and powder flasks may have damaged it."

"It still would serve as a little post-office, perhaps," laughed the baroness. "But I think its days are done on such errands."

"I will explain something of these errands to the

Señora Yturrio," said Calhoun. "I wish you personally to say to that lady, if you will, that Señor Yturrio regarded this little receptacle rather as official than personal post."

For one moment these two women looked at each other, with that on their faces which would be hard to describe. At last the baroness spoke:

"It is not wholly my fault, Señora Yturrio, if your husband gave you cause to think there was more than diplomacy between us. At least, I can say to you that it was the sport of it alone, the intrigue, if you please, which interested me. I trust you will not accuse me beyond this."

A stifled exclamation came from the Doña Lucrezia. I have never seen more sadness nor yet more hatred on a human face than hers displayed. I have said that she was not thoroughbred. She arose now, proud as ever, it is true, but vicious. She declined Helena von Ritz's outstretched hand, and swept us a curtsey. *"Adios!"* said she. "I go!"

Mr. Calhoun gravely offered her an arm; and so with a rustle of her silks there passed from our lives one unhappy lady who helped make our map for us.

The baroness herself turned. "I ought not to remain," she hesitated.

"Madam," said Mr. Calhoun, "we can not spare you yet."

She flashed upon him a keen look. "It is a young

country," said she, "but it raises statesmen. You foolish, dear Americans! One could have loved you all."

"Eh, what?" said Doctor Ward, turning to her. "My dear lady, two of us are too old for that; and as for the other—"

He did not know how hard this chance remark might smite, but as usual Helena von Ritz was brave and smiling.

"You are men," said she, "such as we do not have in our courts of Europe. Men and women—that is what this country produces."

"Madam," said Calhoun, "I myself am a very poor sort of man. I am old, and I fail from month to month. I can not live long, at best. What you see in me is simply a purpose—a purpose to accomplish something for my country—a purpose which my country itself does not desire to see fulfilled. Republics do not reward us. What *you* say shall be our chief reward. I have asked you here also to accept the thanks of all of us who know the intricacies of the events which have gone forward. Madam, we owe you Texas! 'Twas not yonder lady, but yourself, who first advised of the danger that threatened us. Hers was, after all, a simpler task than yours, because she only matched faiths with Van Zandt, representative of Texas, who had faith in neither men, women nor nations. Had all gone well, we might perhaps have owed you yet more, for Oregon."

"Would you like Oregon?" she asked, looking at him with the full glance of her dark eyes.

"More than my life! More than the life of myself and all my friends and family! More than all my fortune!" His voice rang clear and keen as that of youth.

"All of Oregon?" she asked.

"All? We do not own all! Perhaps we do not deserve it. Surely we could not expect it. Why, if we got one-half of what that fellow Polk is claiming, we should do well enough—that is more than we deserve or could expect. With our army already at war on the Southwest, England, as we all know, is planning to take advantage of our helplessness in Oregon."

Without further answer, she held out to him a document whose appearance I, at least, recognized.

"I am but a woman," she said, "but it chances that I have been able to do this country perhaps something of a favor. Your assistant, Mr. Trist, has done me in his turn a favor. This much I will ask permission to do for him."

Calhoun's long and trembling fingers were nervously opening the document. He turned to her with eyes blazing with eagerness. *"It is Oregon!"* He dropped back into his chair.

"Yes," said Helena von Ritz slowly. "It is Ore-gon. It is bought and paid for. It is yours!"

So now they all went over that document, signed by none less than Pakenham himself, minister pleni-potentiary for Great Britain. That document exists to-day somewhere in our archives, but I do not feel empowered to make known its full text. I would I had never need to set down, as I have, the cost of it. These others never knew that cost; and now they never can know, for long years since both Calhoun and Doctor Ward have been dead and gone. I turned aside as they examined the document which within the next few weeks was to become public property. The red wafers which mended it—and which she smilingly explained at Calhoun's demand—were, as I knew, not less than red drops of blood.

In brief I may say that this paper stated that, in case the United States felt disposed to reopen dis-cussions which Mr. Polk peremptorily had closed, Great Britain might be able to listen to a compro-mise on the line of the forty-ninth parallel. This compromise had three times been offered her by diplomacy of United States under earlier adminis-trations. Great Britain stated that in view of her deep and abiding love of peace and her deep and abiding admiration for America, she would resign her claim of all of Oregon down to the Columbia; and more, she would accept the forty-ninth parallel;

provided she might have free navigation rights upon
the Columbia. In fact, this was precisely the memorandum of agreement which eventually established
the lines of the treaty as to Oregon between Great
Britain and the United States.

Mr. Calhoun is commonly credited with having
brought about this treaty, and with having been author of its terms. So he was, but only in the singular
way which in these foregoing pages I have related.
States have their price. Texas was bought by blood.
Oregon—ah, we who own it ought to prize it. None
of our territory is half so full of romance, none of it
is half so clean, as our great and bodeful far Northwest, still young in its days of destiny.

"We should in time have had *all* of Oregon, perhaps," said Mr. Calhoun; "at least, that is the talk
of these fierce politicians."

"But for this fresh outbreak on the Southwest
there would have been a better chance," said Helena von Ritz; "but I think, as matters are to-day,
you would be wise to accept this compromise. I have
seen your men marching, thousands of them, the
grandest sight of this century or any other. They
give full base for this compromise. Given another
year, and your rifles and your plows would make
your claims still better. But this is to-day—"

"Believe me, Mr. Calhoun," I broke in, "your signature must go on this."

"How now? Why so anxious, my son?"

"Because it is right!"

Calhoun turned to Helena von Ritz. "Has this been presented to Mr. Buchanan, our secretary of state?" he asked.

"Certainly not. It has been shown to no one. I have been here in Washington working—well, working in secret to secure this document for you. I do this—well, I will be frank with you—I do it for Mr. Trist. He is my friend. I wish to say to you that he has been—a faithful—"

I saw her face whiten and her lips shut tight. She swayed a little as she stood. Doctor Ward was at her side and assisted her to a couch. For the first time the splendid courage of Helena von Ritz seemed to fail her. She sank back, white, unconscious.

"It's these damned stays, John!" began Doctor Ward fiercely. "She has fainted. Here, put her down, so. We'll bring her around in a minute. Great Jove! I want her to *hear* us thank her. It's splendid work she has done for us. But *why?*"

When, presently, under the ministrations of the old physician, Helena von Ritz recovered her consciousness, she arose, fighting desperately to pull herself together and get back her splendid courage.

"Would you retire now, Madam?" asked Mr. Calhoun. "I have sent for my daughter."

"No, no. It is nothing!" she said. "Forgive me, it is only an old habit of mine. See, I am quite well!"

Indeed, in a few moments she had regained something of that magnificent energy which was her heritage. As though nothing had happened, she arose and walked swiftly across the room. Her eyes were fixed upon the great map which hung upon the walls—a strange map it would seem to us to-day. Across this she swept a white hand.

"I saw your men cross this," she said, pointing along the course of the great Oregon Trail—whose detailed path was then unknown to our geographers. "I saw them go west along that road of destiny. I told myself that by virtue of their courage they had won this war. Sometime there will come the great war between your people and those who rule them. The people still will win."

She spread out her two hands top and bottom of the map. "All, all, ought to be yours,—from the Isthmus to the ice, for the sake of the people of the world. The people—but in time they will have their own!"

We listened to her silently, crediting her enthusiasm to her sex, her race; but what she said has remained in one mind at least from that day to this. Well might part of her speech remain in the minds to-day of people and rulers alike. Are we worth the price paid for the country that we gained? And when we shall be worth that price, what numerals shall mark our territorial lines?

"May I carry this document to Mr. Pakenham?" asked John Calhoun, at last, touching the paper on the table.

"Please, no. Do not. Only be sure that this proposition of compromise will meet with his acceptance."

"I do not quite understand why you do not go to Mr. Buchanan, our secretary of state."

"Because I pay my debts," she said simply. "I told you that Mr. Trist and I were comrades. I conceived it might be some credit for him in his work to have been the means of doing this much."

"He shall have that credit, Madam, be sure of that," said John Calhoun. He held out to her his long, thin, bloodless hand.

"Madam," he said, "I have been mistaken in many things. My life will be written down as failure. I have been misjudged. But at least it shall not be said of me that I failed to reverence a woman such as you. All that I thought of you, that first night I met you, was more than true. And did I not tell you you would one day, one way, find your reward?"

He did not know what he said; but I knew, and I spoke with him in the silence of my own heart, knowing that his speech would be the same were his knowledge even with mine.

"To-morrow," went on Calhoun, "to-morrow evening there is to be what we call a ball of our diplomacy at the White House. Our administration, knowing that war is soon to be announced in the country, seeks to make a little festival here at the capital. We whistle to keep up our courage. We listen to music to make us forget our consciences. To-morrow night we dance. All Washington will be there. Baroness von Ritz, a card will come to you."

She swept him a curtsey, and gave him a smile.

"Now, as for me," he continued, "I am an old man, and long ago danced my last dance in public. To-morrow night all of us will be at the White House—Mr. Trist will be there, and Doctor Ward, and a certain lady, a Miss Elisabeth Churchill, Madam, whom I shall be glad to have you meet. You must not fail us, dear lady, because I am going to ask of you one favor."

He bowed with a courtesy which might have come from generations of an old aristocracy. "If you please, Madam, I ask you to honor me with your hand for my first dance in years—my last dance in all my life."

Impulsively she held out both her hands, bowing her head as she did so to hide her face. Two old gray men, one younger man, took her hands and kissed them.

Now our flag floats on the Columbia and on the

Rio Grande. I am older now, but when I think of that scene, I wish that flag might float yet freer; and though the price were war itself, that it might float over a cleaner and a nobler people, over cleaner and nobler rulers, more sensible of the splendor of that heritage of principle which should be ours.

CHAPTER XXXVI

THE PALO ALTO BALL

A beautiful woman pleases the eye, a good woman pleases the heart; one is a jewel, the other a treasure.—Napoleon I.

ON THE evening of that following day in May, the sun hung red and round over a distant unknown land along the Rio Grande. In that country, no iron trails as yet had come. The magic of the wire, so recently applied to the service of man, was as yet there unknown. Word traveled slowly by horses and mules and carts. There came small news from that far-off country, half tropic, covered with palms and crooked dwarfed growth of mesquite and chaparral. The long-horned cattle lived in these dense thickets, the spotted jaguar, the wolf, the ocelot, the javelina, many smaller creatures not known in our northern lands. In the loam along the stream the deer left their tracks, mingled with those of the wild turkeys and of countless water fowl. It was a far-off, unknown, unvalued land. Our flag, long past the Sabine, had halted at the Nueces. Now it was to advance across this wild region to the Rio Grande. Thus did smug James Polk keep his promises!

Among these tangled mesquite thickets ran sometimes long bayous, made from the overflow of the greater rivers—*resacas,* as the natives call them. Tall palms sometimes grew along the bayous, for the country is half tropic. Again, on the drier ridges, there might be taller detached trees, heavier forests —*palo alto,* the natives call them. In some such place as this, where the trees were tall, there was fired the first gun of our war in the Southwest. There were strange noises heard here in the wilderness, followed by lesser noises, and by human groans. Some faces that night were upturned to the moon—the same moon which swam so gloriously over Washington. Taylor camped closer to the Rio Grande. The fight was next to begin by the lagoon called the Resaca de la Palma. But that night at the capital that same moon told us nothing of all this. We did not hear the guns. It was far from Palo Alto to our ports of Galveston or New Orleans. Our cockaded army made its own history in its own unreported way.

We at the White House ball that night also made history in our own unrecorded way. As our army was adding to our confines on the Southwest, so there were other, though secret, forces which added to our territory in the far Northwest. As to this and as to the means by which it came about, I have already been somewhat plain.

It was a goodly company that assembled for the

grand ball, the first one in the second season of Mr. Polk's somewhat confused and discordant adminis- tration. Social matters had started off dour enough. Mrs. Polk was herself of strict religious practice, and I imagine it had taken somewhat of finesse to get her consent to these festivities. It was called sometimes the diplomats' ball. At least there was diplomacy back of it. It was mere accident which set this cele- bration upon the very evening of the battle of Palo Alto, May eighth, 1846.

By ten o'clock there were many in the great room which had been made ready for the dancing, and rather a brave company it might have been called. We had at least the splendor of the foreign diplomats' uniforms for our background, and to this we added the bravest of our attire, each one in his own indi- vidual fashion, I fear. Thus my friend Jack Dan- dridge was wholly resplendent in a new waistcoat of his own devising, and an evening coat which almost swept the floor as he executed the evolutions of his western style of dancing. Other gentlemen were, perhaps, more grave and staid. We had with us at least one man, old in government service, who dared the silk stockings and knee breeches of an earlier generation. Yet another wore the white powdered queue, which might have been more suited for his grandfather. The younger men of the day wore their hair long, in fashion quite different, yet this did not detract from the distinction of some of the faces which one might have seen among them—some of them to sleep all too soon upturned to the moon in another and yet more bitter war, aftermath of this with Mexico. The tall stock was still in evidence at that time, and the ruffled shirts gave something of a formal and old-fashioned touch to the assembly. Such as they were, in their somewhat varied but not uninteresting attire, the best of Washington were present. Invitation was wholly by card. Some said that Mrs. Polk wrote these invitations in her own hand, though this we may be permitted to doubt.

Whatever might have been said as to the democratic appearance of our gentlemen in Washington, our women were always our great reliance, and these at least never failed to meet the approval of the most sneering of our foreign visitors. Thus we had present that night, as I remember, two young girls both later to become famous in Washington society; tall and slender young Térèse Chalfant, later to become Mrs. Pugh of Ohio, and to receive at the hands of Denmark's minister, who knelt before her at a later public ball, that jeweled clasp which his wife had bade him present to the most beautiful woman he found in America. Here also was Miss Harriet Williams of Georgetown, later to become the second wife of that Baron Bodisco of Russia who had represented his government with us since the year 1838

—a tall, robust, blonde lady she later grew to be. Brown's Hotel, home of many of our statesmen and their ladies, turned out a full complement. Mr. Clay was there, smiling, though I fear none too happy. Mr. Edward Everett, as it chanced, was with us at that time. We had Sam Houston of Texas, who would not, until he appeared upon the floor, relinquish the striped blanket which distinguished him— though a splendid figure of a man he appeared when he paced forth in evening dress, a part of which was a waistcoat embroidered in such fancy as might have delighted the eye of his erstwhile Indian wife had she been there to see it. Here and there, scattered about the floor, there might have been seen many of the public figures of America at that time, men from North and South and East and West, and from many other nations beside our own.

Under Mrs. Polk's social administration, we did not waltz, but our ball began with a stately march, really a grand procession, in its way distinctly interesting, in scarlet and gold and blue and silks, and all the flowered circumstance of brocades and laces of our ladies. And after our march we had our own polite Virginia reel, merry as any dance, yet stately too.

I was late in arriving that night, for it must be remembered that this was but my second day in town, and I had had small chance to take my chief's advice, and to make myself presentable for an occasion such as this. I was fresh from my tailor, and very new-made when I entered the room. I came just in time to see what I was glad to see; that is to say, the keeping of John Calhoun's promise to Helena von Ritz.

It was not to be denied that there had been talk regarding this lady, and that Calhoun knew it, though not from me. Much of it was idle talk, based largely upon her mysterious life. Beyond that, a woman beautiful as she has many enemies among her sex. There were dark glances for her that night, I do not deny, before Mr. Calhoun changed them. For, however John Calhoun was rated by his enemies, the worst of these knew well his austerely spotless private life, and his scrupulous concern for decorum.

Beautiful she surely was. Her ball gown was of light golden stuff, and there was a coral wreath upon her hair, and her dancing slippers were of coral hue. There was no more striking figure upon the floor than she. Jewels blazed at her throat and caught here and there the filmy folds of her gown. She was radiant, beautiful, apparently happy. She came mysteriously enough; but I knew that Mr. Calhoun's carriage had been sent for her. I learned also that he had waited for her arrival.

As I first saw Helena von Ritz, there stood by her

side Doctor Samuel Ward, his square and stocky figure not undignified in his dancing dress, the stiff gray mane of his hair waggling after its custom as he spoke emphatically over something with her. A gruff man, Doctor Ward, but under his gray mane there was a clear brain, and in his broad breast there beat a large and kindly heart.

Even as I began to edge my way towards these two, I saw Mr. Calhoun himself approach, tall, gray and thin.

He was very pale that night; and I knew well enough what effort it cost him to attend any of these functions. Yet he bowed with the grace of a younger man and offered the baroness an arm. Then, methinks, all Washington gasped a bit. Not all Washington knew what had gone forward between these two. Not all Washington knew what that couple meant as they marched in the grand procession that night—what they meant for America. Of all those who saw, I alone understood.

So they danced; he with the dignity of his years, she with the grace which was the perfection of dancing, the perfection of courtesy and of dignity also, as though she knew and valued to the full what was offered to her now by John Calhoun. Grave, sweet and sad Helena von Ritz seemed to me that night. She was wholly unconscious of those who looked and whispered. Her face was pale and rapt as that of some devotee.

Mr. Polk himself stood apart, and plainly enough saw this little matter go forward. When Mr. Calhoun approached with the Baroness von Ritz upon his arm, Mr. Polk was too much politician to hesitate or to inquire. He knew that it was safe to follow where John Calhoun led! These two conversed for a few moments. Thus, I fancy, Helena von Ritz had her first and last acquaintance with one of our politicians to whom fate gave far more than his deserts. It was the fortune of Mr. Polk to gain for this country Texas, California and Oregon—not one of them by desert of his own! My heart has often been bitter when I have recalled that little scene. Politics so unscrupulous can not always have a John Calhoun, a Helena von Ritz, to correct, guard and guide.

After this the card of Helena von Ritz might well enough indeed been full had she cared further to dance. She excused herself gracefully, saying that after the honor which had been done her she could not ask more. Still, Washington buzzed; somewhat of Europe as well. That might have been called the triumph of Helena von Ritz. She felt it not. But I could see that she gloried in some other thing.

I approached her as soon as possible. "I am about to go," she said. "Say good-by to me, now, here!

We shall not meet again. Say good-by to me, now, quickly! My father and I are going to leave. The treaty for Oregon is prepared. Now I am done. Yes. Tell me good-by."

"I will not say it," said I. "I can not."

She smiled at me. Others might see her lips, her smile. I saw what was in her eyes. "We must not be selfish," said she. "Come, I must go."

"Do not go," I insisted. "Wait."

She caught my meaning. "Surely," she said, "I will stay a little longer for that one thing. Yes, I wish to see her again, Miss Elisabeth Churchill. I hated her. I wish that I might love her now, do you know? Would—would she let me—if she knew?"

"They say that love is not possible between women," said I. "For my own part, I wish with you."

She interrupted with a light tap of her fan upon my arm. "Look, is not that she?"

I turned. A little circle of people were bowing before Mr. Polk, who held a sort of levee at one side of the hall. I saw the tall young girl who at the moment swept a graceful curtsey to the president. My heart sprang to my mouth. Yes, it was Elisabeth! Ah, yes, there flamed up on the altar of my heart the one fire, lit long ago for her. So we came now to meet, silently, with small show, in such way as to thrill none but our two selves. She, too, had served, and that largely. And my constant altar fire had

done its part also, strangely, in all this long coil of
large events.   Love—ah, true love wins and rules.
It makes our maps.   It makes our world.

Among all these distinguished men, these beautiful women, she had her own tribute of admiration.
I felt rather than saw that she was in some pale,
filmy green, some crêpe of China, with skirts and
sleeves looped up with pearls.   In her hair were
green leaves, simple and sweet and cool.   To me she
seemed graver, sweeter, than when I last had seen
her.   I say, my heart came up into my throat.   All I
could think was that I wanted to take her into my
arms.   All I did was to stand and stare.

My companion was more expert in social maneu-
vers.   She waited until the crowd had somewhat
thinned about the young lady and her escort.   I
saw now with certain qualms that this latter was
none other than my whilom friend Jack Dandridge.
For a wonder, he was most unduly sober, and he
made, as I have said, no bad figure in his finery.   He
was very merry and just a trifle loud of speech, but,
being very intimate in Mr. Polk's household, he was
warmly welcomed by that gentleman and by all
around him.

"She is beautiful!" I heard the lady at my arm
whisper.

"Is she beautiful to you?" I asked.

"Very beautiful!"   I heard her catch her breath.

"She is good. I wish I could love her. I wish, I wish—"

I saw her hands beat together as they did when she was agitated. I turned then to look at her, and what I saw left me silent. "Come," said I at last, "let us go to her." We edged across the floor.

When Elisabeth saw me she straightened, a pallor came across her face. It was not her way to betray much of her emotions. If her head was a trifle more erect, if indeed she paled, she too lacked not in quiet self-possession. She waited, with wide straight eyes fixed upon me. I found myself unable to make much intelligent speech. I turned to see Helena von Ritz gazing with wistful eyes at Elisabeth, and I saw the eyes of Elisabeth make some answer. So they spoke some language which I suppose men never will understand—the language of one woman to another.

I have known few happier moments in my life than that. Perhaps, after all, I caught something of the speech between their eyes. Perhaps not all cheap and cynical maxims are true, at least when applied to noble women.

Elisabeth regained her wonted color and more.

"I was very wrong in many ways," I heard her whisper. For almost the first time I saw her perturbed. Helena von Ritz stepped close to her. Amid the crash of the reeds and brasses, amid all the broken conversation which swept around us, I knew what she said. Low down in the flounces of the wide embroidered silks, I saw their two hands meet, silently, and cling. This made me happy.

Of course it was Jack Dandridge who broke in between us. "Ah!" said he, "you jealous beggar, could you not leave me to be happy for one minute? Here you come back, a mere heathen, and proceed to monopolize all our ladies. I have been making the most of my time, you see. I have proposed half a dozen times more to Miss Elisabeth, have I not?"

"Has she given you any answer?" I asked him, smiling.

"The same answer!"

"Jack," said I, "I ought to call you out."

"Don't," said he. "I don't want to be called out. I am getting found out. That's worse. Well—Miss Elisabeth, may I be the first to congratulate?"

"I am glad," said I, with just a slight trace of severity, "that you have managed again to get into the good graces of Elmhurst. When I last saw you, I was not sure that either of us would ever be invited there again."

"Been there every Sunday regularly since you went away," said Jack. "I am not one of the family in one way, and in another way I am. Honestly, I have tried my best to cut you out. Not that you have not played your game well enough, but there never was a game played so well that some other fellow could not win by coppering it. So I coppered everything you did—played it for just the reverse. No go—lost even that way. And I thought *you* were the most perennial fool of your age and generation."

I checked as gently as I could a joviality which I thought unsuited to the time. "Mr. Dandridge," said I to him, "you know the Baroness von Ritz?"

"Certainly! The *particeps criminis* of our bungled wedding—of course I know her!"

"I only want to say," I remarked, "that the Baroness von Ritz has that little shell clasp now all for her own, and that I have her slipper again, all for my own. So now, we three—no, four—at last understand one another, do we not? Jack, will you do two things for me?"

"All of them but two."

"When the Baroness von Ritz insists on her intention of leaving us—just at the height of all our happiness—I want you to hand her to her carriage. In the second place, I may need you again—"

"Well, what would any one think of that!" said Jack Dandridge.

I never knew when these two left us in the crowd. I never said good-by to Helena von Ritz. I did not catch that last look of her eye. I remember her as she stood there that night, grave, sweet and sad.

I turned to Elisabeth. There in the crash of the

reeds and brasses, the rise and fall of the sweet and bitter conversation all around us, was the comedy and the tragedy of life.

"Elisabeth," I said to her, "are you not ashamed?"

She looked me full in the eye. "No!" she said, and smiled.

I have never seen a smile like Elisabeth's.

THE END

EPILOGUE

" 'Tis the Star Spangled Banner; O, long may it wave,
O'er the land of the free, and the home of the brave!"
—*Francis Scott Key*.

ON the night that Miss Elisabeth Churchill
gave me her hand and her heart for ever—
for which I have not yet ceased to thank
God—there began the guns of Palo Alto. Later,
there came the fields of Monterey, Buena Vista,
Cerro Gordo, Contreras, Cherubusco, Molino del
Rey—at last the guns sounded at the gate of the old
City of Mexico itself. Some of that fighting I myself saw; but much of the time I was employed in
that manner of special work which had engaged me
for the last few years. It was through Mr. Calhoun's agency that I reached a certain importance
in these matters; and so I was chosen as the commis-
sioner to negotiate a peace with Mexico.

This honor later proved to be a dangerous and
questionable one. General Scott wanted no interference of this kind, especially since he knew Mr.
Calhoun's influence in my choice. He thwarted all
my attempts to reach the headquarters of the enemy,
and did everything he could to secure a peace of his

own, at the mouth of the cannon. I could offer no
terms better than Mr. Buchanan, then our secretary
of state, had prepared for me, and these were re-
jected by the Mexican government at last. I was
ordered by Mr. Polk to state that we had no better
terms to offer; and as for myself, I was told to return
to Washington. At that time I could not make my
way out through the lines, nor, in truth, did I much
care to do so.

A certain event not written in history influenced
me to remain for a time at the little village of Guadalupe Hidalgo. Here, in short, I received word
from a lady whom I had formerly known, none less
than Señora Yturrio, once a member of the Mexican legation at Washington. True to her record,
she had again reached influential position in her
country, using methods of her own. She told me
now to pay no attention to what had been reported
by Mexico. In fact, I was approached again by
the Mexican commissioners, introduced by her!
What was done then is history. We signed then and
there the peace of Guadalupe Hidalgo, in accordance with the terms originally given me by our
secretary of state. So, after all, Calhoun's kindness
to a woman in distress was not lost; and so, after all,
he unwittingly helped in the ending of the war he
never wished begun.

Meantime, I had been recalled to Washington, but

did not know the nature of that recall. When at last I arrived there I found myself disgraced and discredited. My actions were repudiated by the administration. I myself was dismissed from the service without pay—sad enough blow for a young man who had been married less than a year.

Mr. Polk's jealousy of John Calhoun was not the only cause of this. Calhoun's prophecy was right. Polk did not forget his revenge on me. Yet, none the less, after his usual fashion, he was not averse to receiving such credit as he could. He put the responsibility of the treaty upon the Senate! It was debated hotly there for some weeks, and at last, much to his surprise and my gratification, it was ratified!

The North, which had opposed this Mexican War —that same war which later led inevitably to the War of the Rebellion—now found itself unable to say much against the great additions to our domain which the treaty had secured. We paid fifteen millions, in addition to our territorial indemnity claim, and we got a realm whose wealth could not be computed. So much, it must be owned, did fortune do for that singular favorite, Mr. Polk. And, curiously enough, the smoke had hardly cleared from Palo Alto field before Abraham Lincoln, a young member in the House of Congress, was introducing a resolution which asked the marking of "the spot where that outrage was committed." Perhaps it was an outrage. Many still hold it so. But let us reflect what would have been Lincoln's life had matters not gone just as they did.

With the cessions from Mexico came the great domain of California. Now, look how strangely history sometimes works out itself. Had there been any suspicion of the discovery of gold in California, neither Mexico nor our republic ever would have owned it! England surely would have taken it. The very year that my treaty eventually was ratified was that in which gold was discovered in California! But it was too late then for England to interfere; too late then, also, for Mexico to claim it. We got untold millions of treasure there. Most of those millions went to the Northern States, into manufactures, into commerce. The North owned that gold; and it was that gold which gave the North the power to crush that rebellion which was born of the Mexican War—that same rebellion by which England, too late, would gladly have seen this Union disrupted, so that she might have yet another chance at these lands she now had lost for ever.

Fate seemed still to be with us, after all, as I have so often had occasion to believe may be a possible thing. That war of conquest which Mr. Calhoun opposed, that same war which grew out of the slavery tenets which he himself held—the great error of his otherwise splendid public life—found its own correction in the Civil War. It was the gold of California which put down slavery. Thenceforth slavery has existed legally only *north* of the Mason and Dixon line!

We have our problems yet. Perhaps some other war may come to settle them. Fortunate for us if there could be another California, another Texas, another Oregon, to help us pay for them!

I, who was intimately connected with many of these less known matters, claim for my master a reputation wholly different from that given to him in any garbled "history" of his life. I lay claim in his name for foresight beyond that of any man of his time. He made mistakes, but he made them bravely, grandly, and consistently. Where his convictions were enlisted, he had no reservations, and he used every means, every available weapon, as I have shown. But he was never self-seeking, never cheap, never insincere. A detester of all machine politicians, he was a statesman worthy to be called the William Pitt of the United States. The consistency of his career was a marvelous thing; because, though he changed in his beliefs, he was first to recognize the changing conditions of our country. He failed, and he is execrated. He won, and he is forgot.

My chief, Mr. Calhoun, did not die until some

six years after that first evening when Doctor Ward
and I had our talk with him. He was said to have
died of a disease of the lungs, yet here again history,
is curiously mistaken. Mr. Calhoun slept himself·
away. I sometimes think with a shudder that perhaps this was the revenge which Nemesis took of
him for his mistakes. His last days were dreamlike
in their passing. His last speech in the Senate was
read by one of his friends, as Doctor Ward had advised him. Some said afterwards that his illness
was that accursed "sleeping sickness" imported from
Africa with these same slaves. It were a strange
thing had John Calhoun indeed died of his error!
At least he slept away. At least, too, he made his
atonement. The South, following his doctrines,
itself was long accursed of this same sleeping sickness; but in the providence of God it was not lost
to us, and is ours for a long and splendid history.

It was through John Calhoun, a grave and somber
figure of our history, that we got the vast land of
Texas. It was through him also—and not through
Clay nor Jackson, nor any of the northern statesmen, who never could see a future for the West—
that we got all of our vast Northwest realm. Within
a few days after the Palo Alto ball, a memorandum
of agreement was signed between Minister Pakenham and Mr. Buchanan, our secretary of state.
This was done at the instance and by the aid of John

Calhoun. It was he—he and Helena von Ritz—who brought about that treaty which, on June fifteenth, of the same year, was signed, and gladly signed, by the minister from Great Britain. The latter had been fully enough impressed (such was the story) by the reports of the columns of our west-bound farmers, with rifles leaning at their wagon seats and plows lashed to the tail-gates. Calhoun himself never ceased to regret that we could not delay a year or two years longer. In this he was thwarted by the impetuous war with the republic on the south, although, had that never been fought, we had lost California—lost also the South, and lost the Union!

Under one form or other, one name of government or another, the flag of democracy eventually must float over all this continent. Not a part, but all of this country must be ours, must be the people's. It may cost more blood and treasure now. Some time we shall see the wisdom of John Calhoun; but some time, too, I think, we shall see come true that prophecy of a strange and brilliant mentality, which in Calhoun's presence and in mine said that all of these northern lands and all Mexico as well must one day be ours—which is to say, the people's—for the sake of human opportunity, of human hope and happiness. Our battles are but partly fought. But at least they are not, then, lost.

For myself, the close of the Mexican War found

me somewhat worn by travel and illy equipped in financial matters. I had been discredited, I say, by my own government. My pay was withheld. Elisabeth, by that time my wife, was a girl reared in all the luxury that our country then could offer. Shall I say whether or not I prized her more when gladly she gave up all this and joined me for one more long and final journey out across that great trail which I had seen—the trail of democracy, of America, of the world?

At last we reached Oregon. It holds the grave of one of ours; it is the home of others. We were happy; we asked favor of no man; fear of no one did we feel. Elisabeth has in her time slept on a bed of husks. She has cooked at a sooty fireplace of her own; and at her cabin door I myself have been the guard. We made our way by ourselves and for ourselves, as did those who conquered America for our flag. "The citizen standing in the doorway of his home, shall save the Republic." So wrote a later pen.

It was not until long after the discovery of gold in California had set us all to thinking that I was reminded of the strange story of the old German, Von Rittenhofen, of finding some pieces of gold while on one of his hunts for butterflies. I followed out his vague directions as best I might. We found gold enough to make us rich without our land. That claim is staked legally. Half of it awaits an owner who perhaps will never come.

There are those who will accept always the solemn asseverations of politicians, who by word of mouth or pen assert that this or that *party* made our country, wrote its history. Such as they might smile if told that not even men, much less politicians, have written all our story as a nation; yet any who smile at woman's influence in American history do so in ignorance of the truth. Mr. Webster and Lord Ashburton have credit for determining our boundary on the northeast—England called it Ashburton's capitulation to the Yankee. Did you never hear the other gossip? England laid all that to Ashburton's American wife! Look at that poor, hot-tempered devil, Yrujo, minister from Spain with us, who saw his king's holdings on this continent juggled from hand to hand between us all. His wife was daughter of Governor McKean in Pennsylvania yonder. If she had no influence with her husband, so much the worse for her. In important times a generation ago M. Genêt, of France, as all know, was the husband of the daughter of Governor Clinton of New York. Did that hurt our chances with France? My Lord Oswald, of Great Britain, who negotiated our treaty of peace in 1782—was not his worldly fortune made by virtue of his American wife? All of us should remember that Marbois, Napoleon's minister,

who signed the great treaty for him with us, married his wife while he was a mere *chargé* here in
Washington; and she, too, was an American.   Ers-
kine, of England, when times were strained in 1808,
and later—and our friend for the most part—was
not he also husband of an American?   It was as
John Calhoun said—our history, like that of England and France, like that of Rome and Troy, was
made in large part by women.

Of that strange woman, Helena, Baroness von
Ritz, I have never definitely heard since then.   But
all of us have heard of that great uplift of Central
Europe, that ferment of revolution, most noticeable
in Germany, in 1848.   Out of that revolutionary
spirit there came to us thousands and thousands of
our best population, the sturdiest and the most lib-
erty-loving citizens this country ever had.   They
gave us scores of generals in our late war, and gave
us at least one cabinet officer.   But whence came
that spirit of revolution in Europe?   *Why* does it
live, grow, increase, even now?   *Why* does it sound
now, close to the oldest thrones?   *Where* originated
that germ of liberty which did its work so well?   I
am at least one who believes that I could guess something of its source.

The revolution in Hungary failed for the time.
Kossuth came to see us with pleas that we might aid
Hungary.   But republics forget.   We gave no aid to

Hungary. I was far away and did not meet Kossuth. I should have been glad to question him. I did not forget Helena von Ritz, nor doubt that she worked out in full that strange destiny for which, indeed, she was born and prepared, to which she devoted herself, made clean by sacrifice. She was not one to leave her work undone. She, I know, passed on her torch of principle.

Elisabeth and I speak often of Helena von Ritz. I remember her still—brilliant, beautiful, fascinating, compelling, pathetic, tragic. If it was asked of her, I know that she still paid it gladly—all that sacrifice through which alone there can be worked out the progress of humanity, under that idea which blindly we attempted to express in our Declaration; that idea which at times we may forget, but which eventually must triumph for the good of all the world. She helped us make our map. Shall not that for which she stood help us hold it?

At least, let me say, I have thought this little story might be set down; and, though some to-day may smile at flags and principles, I should like, if I may be allowed, to close with the words of yet another man of those earlier times: "The old flag of the Union was my protector in infancy and the pride and glory of my riper years; and, by the grace of God, under its shadow I shall die!"   N. T.

FINIS